To Jeanne

I hope you enjoy the story

And remember the [...] you free

Keith [...]

If there's a Beatles' song that makes you happy, then you have something in common with a serial killer...

Maldonado gulped some coffee and pointed toward the envelope. "Before I show you what's in here," he said, "I'm going to tell you something about Ms. Franklin's murderer that we've known from the beginning." Rolling his tongue around the inside of his mouth, he looked away for a moment before returning his attention to Sean. "Do you recall the writing on the two pieces of paper above the headboard?"

"One paper had 'hello' written on it," Sean answered. "The other one, 'goodbye.'"

"You're a rock 'n roll guy," Maldonado said. "Do those two words sound familiar?"

"Only if you're talking about The Beatles' song," he answered.

Maldonado nodded. "That's exactly what I'm talking about, Sean. The same man who murdered Ms. Franklin has done the identical thing seven other times, dating back six years. He's a serial killer the press has dubbed, 'The Beatles' Song Murderer.' He's left pieces of paper with the name of a different Beatles' song every time."

KUDOS for *You Say Goodbye*

In *You Say Goodbye* by Keith Steinbaum, Sean Hightower, an aging, "one-hit," rock star, returns home from work one night to find his girlfriend murdered. Sean doesn't take it well, spiraling down into depression and even contemplating suicide. But a chance encounter with a neighbor girl suffering from cancer changes Sean's perspective and makes him determined to help the detective find his girlfriend's killer, the only clue to his identity being the words to a Beatles' song left on the wall above the bed where she was murdered. As Sean begins investigating the men close to his girlfriend, he unwittingly places his own life in danger. With wonderful characters, plenty of tension and suspense, and a number of twists and turns, Steinbaum has crafted a worthy addition to the mystery genre. A great read. ~ *Taylor Jones, The Review Team of Taylor Jones & Regan Murphy*

You Say Goodbye by Keith Steinbaum is the story of Sean Hightower, an aging musician whose one claim to fame is "Looking Glass," the one big hit of his career. Now fifty, Sean works at his father's auto dealership, plays his guitar part time at a bar, and dreams of once again writing a hit song. Sean's main source of comfort and strength in his life is his girlfriend Merissa. But when Sean returns home from the bar one evening, he finds Merissa's naked body on the bed with a bullet in her head. Devastated, Sean eventually contemplates suicide, but two things happen to return his will to live. He meets the cancer-stricken neighbor girl, Kayleigh, and the detective investigating Merissa's murder asks for Sean's help. Kayleigh's strength and determination to fight her disease impacts Sean deeply, making him realize how much he has to be thankful for. And the detective convinces him that together they can find the killer and get justice for Merissa. But as Sean digs for the truth, he is unprepared for all the dark secrets he uncovers—or the target he has painted on his own back. *You Say Goodbye* combines marvelous character development with an intriguing mystery and spine-tingling suspense, creating a moving and poignant tale that will keep you on the edge of your seat all the way through. ~ *Regan Murphy, The Review Team of Taylor Jones & Regan Murphy*

ACKNOWLEDGMENTS

My story is in honor of three people: two of whom are quite familiar to me, and a third who made her acquaintance from the obituary section of the Los Angeles Times. For my parents, Bunny and Jerry Steinbaum, and their sterling example of humanitarian efforts that provided aid and comfort for those less fortunate, I will always remember the example you set for what it means to be charitable and compassionate.

And for Alexandra Scott, a heroic little girl who died of cancer at the age of eight, the story of your short but impactful life gripped me with the hand of perspective, guiding me toward the inspiration for creating a character whose everyday battles served as a lesson for a deeper appreciation of my own life and further admiration for the international movement you generated.

You Say Goodbye

KEITH STEINBAUM

A Black Opal Books Publication

GENRE: MYSTERY-DETECTIVE/SUSPENSE

YOU SAY GOODBYE
Copyright © 2019 by Keith Steinbaum
Cover Design by Jim Avery
All cover art copyright © 2019
All Rights Reserved
Print ISBN: 9781644371992

First Publication: FEBRUARY 2019

Published by Black Opal Books **http://www.blackopalbooks.com**

Can we ever trust our point of view
When what seemed real is far from true?

~ from "Looking Glass" by The Sean Hightower Band

Chapter 1

April 11, 2008, 9:35 p.m.:

Your time has come, Merissa," he told her, his words uncoiling snakelike in venomous intention. "I have no further use for you."

"No!" she screamed, her desperate plea rendered to a garbled wail from the cheekbone-to-cheekbone gray duct tape covering her mouth. "*No!*"

Looking at him standing in the doorway, gun in his hand, the juxtaposition of events culminating in this moment ripped through her consciousness with the unrelenting speed of an assault rifle…

ഐഐഐ

He'd called from his car, explaining that he wanted to give her a gift "to show his appreciation for what she did for him."

"I just bought it," he told her, "and I think you're really going to like it."

With her makeup already off and lounging in Sean's sweats and her slippers, Merissa's plan centered around a glass of wine and finishing her book, but the thoughtfulness of his gift softened her resistance.

"You didn't have to do that."

"I wanted to," he said.

"How far away are you?"

"Twenty minutes, max."

"All right, but it's Friday night, and it's been a crazy week at work, so no shop talk, okay?"

"I promise. The only thing I'll say is I'm sorry you got upset with me. You were right and I learned a lesson."

"It's over with," she replied. "I'll see you soon."

"Hey, one more thing. If you don't mind, I want to show you a magic trick I just learned. It's a good one."

"Bring it on," she said, laughing.

"Is Sean there?" he asked. "I want him to see it, too."

"No," she answered. "He performs at a club on Friday nights."

"That's right, I forgot. You told me that before."

When she opened the door, his first comment pertained to her new hairstyle.

"Wow, look at you," he said. "You've got short hair now."

She had no reason to be anything but unsuspecting when he walked in carrying the wrapped, box-shaped gift. Reaching into the inside pocket of his jacket, he removed a deck of cards.

"First the trick, then the gift," he told her.

Directing her to sit at the table in the front room, he asked her to examine the cards before shuffling them several times.

"Take any card you wish, but don't let me see it."

Selecting the Jack of Hearts, she followed his request to insert the card back into the deck wherever she desired. "Now," he said, "shuffle them as often as you want."

She did as instructed before returning the cards to him. Placing the deck face up on the table, he spread them around to allow the visibility of every card except for one, which remained face down.

"Is that your card?" he asked.

Merissa squinted and shook her head in disbelief after turning over the Jack of Hearts. "That's a good one," she told him.

"I've got one more to show you," he said, placing the cards on the table, "but I'll need two sheets of blank paper and something to write with. In the meantime, may I use your bathroom?"

Merissa entered the kitchen but dashed back to the table when she heard the bathroom door close.

"This will be my little disappearing trick," she said, chuckling to herself. "To reappear as you leave."

Grasping the Jack of Hearts from the top, she placed it in her pocket before hurrying into the kitchen to retrieve the requested items. When he returned, she watched as he printed the word *hello* on one of the sheets of paper.

"Now on this one," he said, handing her the other sheet, "write the word *goodbye* in your regular handwriting."

The instant she finished, before she even had the chance to look up, the violent motion of a clamping hand slammed over her mouth in the simultaneous placement of the gun against her cheekbone.

"If you scream, I'll kill you." His voice was a muted shout. "Do you understand me?"

Merissa couldn't think at first, too shocked and terrified to respond.

"Answer me!"

Eyes shut tight, she nodded her head.

"Now lead me to your bedroom."

With one arm wrapped around her neck, he placed the metal gun tip inside her ear, nudging Merissa forward until they stood at the edge of the bed.

"Lie face down and keep your mouth shut."

"Is this really *you*?" she hissed. "How could you do this?"

She winced as he placed his mouth near the same ear as the gun. "Don't waste my time," he whispered, his hot breath icing her blood.

Doing as he commanded, she felt his immediate weight drop on top of her.

"Lift your head."

"*No!*"

Grabbing her hair, he made her cry out in pain.

"Do it!"

After feeling the entire gun placed down between her shoulder blades, a sticky, ripping sound preceded the sight of the duct tape, the same kind found in hundreds of thousands of kitchen drawers and garage shelves. Sliding a long strip across her field of vision on the way toward her mouth, he jerked back hard, like on the reins of a runaway horse, as he secured the ends of the tape firmly on the back of each cheekbone. Maintaining the force of his weight, he pushed his hand on the back of her head, forcing it back down. Unable to see anything, she felt the end of the gun barrel again.

"I'm only going to say this once," he told her. "We're going to stand up now, and you're going to do exactly what I tell you to do. If you don't..." He tapped the gun along the back of her head. "But we don't need to think about that, do we?"

Rising from the bed, her eyes yo-yo'd between his and the gun in his hand.

"Take off your sweatshirt."

The tears blurred Merissa's vision as she stared, helpless, still struggling to comprehend her cluelessness and the horrifying string of events. Bending forward to avoid his vile gaze, her hands shook as she fumbled with the zipper. Removing the sweatshirt, she dropped it to the floor while maintaining a hunched position.

"Straighten up!"

Unsure whether to oblige him at first, she did as he asked, leaving her arms pressed against her breasts.

"No bra? How typical," he said, his tone seemingly scornful. "Now everything else."

Standing naked before him, Merissa's attempt to maintain her composure collapsed under an avalanche of ice-cold fear as his eyes spider-crawled her body. At first, the words emanating from his mouth didn't register and she couldn't move.

"We're wasting time!" he spat. "I said, 'face down on the bed!'"

Within moments of following his order, he pounced, straddling her back as he clutched her left wrist. He attempted to grasp her right one, but Merissa tore away from his grip twice before a painful upward jerk of her arm forced her to relent. The clicking sound of the locking handcuffs signaled and sealed her fate, and when he turned her over, he glared, as if incensed over something she'd done wrong.

"You're just another whore like all the others, Merissa," he whispered, his voice robotic in its cold inhumanity. "And now you're going to get what you always wanted."

Merissa kicked at him, but he caught her by the ankle, extending her leg out and squeezing in a vice-like grip.

"Don't make me hurt you," he told her. "That'll ruin all the fun."

Turning her eyes away as he leered at her naked body, she couldn't prevent herself from hearing his voice.

"You were meant to be mine from the first time we met, Merissa. But you knew that, didn't you? Oh, yes, of course you knew."

She slammed her teary eyes shut as he undressed, keeping them closed when he fell upon her. A spate of hateful cussing spewed from his mouth as he proceeded to penetrate her with a painful, merciless aggression. She couldn't bear to listen to him, didn't dare glimpse the face of someone so evil. She tried to think him away, to envision herself in a loving embrace with Sean, but the physical reality overwhelmed any attempt to escape inside her mind.

Merissa didn't know how long her ordeal lasted, but after he lifted his body off, she retained hope the worst was over. He continued focusing his attention on her as he dressed, presenting an expression she couldn't decipher while straightening his collar and slipping on his jacket. Retrieving the thick roll of tape from the floor, he secured her ankles together, preventing any chance at movement.

"Can't have you kicking the door closed while I'm gone," he said, removing a glove from his pocket.

He walked out, leaving Merissa praying for his immediate departure. She listened for the opening of the front door but instead heard the sound of the sliding door leading to her balcony, followed by a jangling of keys.

"*Go away!*" she wailed.

Devastation shrouded her senses as he reappeared in the doorway with his gun in one hand and, in the other, the two pieces of paper with the words *hello* and *goodbye.*

"Your time has come, Merissa. I have no further use for you."

"No! *No!*"

"I have no choice, do I?" he told her, closing the door. "After all, now that I've had you, you're no good to me anymore."

He placed the sheet that said *hello* above one side of the headboard, using another strip of the tape. He attached the one that read *goodbye* on the other side. Merissa screamed in raw, stifled helplessness, begging with her eyes for mercy. He took a deep breath and gazed at her with an expression that seemed almost waxen.

"Don't you see, Merissa? Now that I've had you, no other man ever can. Not like my spread-legged *mother.*"

As his gun hovered above her head, the cold-blooded, detached tone of his voice sent her mind reeling toward the realization of experiencing her final moments. A sudden, overpowering calm blanketed her senses as the unmistakable vision of her mother appeared—maybe in her mind, maybe in the room…she couldn't tell…smiling at her daughter and beckoning her.

"I'll make this quick and painless, Merissa," he whispered, "but no one must hear."

He rolled her over, sat on the side of her body, and leaned forward to place a pillow over her head with his hand remaining on top. The ringing of her telephone didn't register under the weighted blackness, nor did the end of his gun nudged under the pillow against the right side of her forehead, as his concluding words crooned the chorus of the familiar Beatles' refrain, signified by the title of those two indicative words on the wall.

Chapter 2

April 11, 2008, 8:43 p.m. ~ 52 minutes earlier:

Sean Hightower, whiskers-graying, hair-thinning candidate for a "Whatever Happened To?" television feature, peered out from behind his microphone and memories to make an announcement.

"I wrote a new song," he said, "and I'd like to sing it for you now."

A booming voice bellowed from the back of the room. "'Looking Glass,' Sean! Let's hear it!" A smattering of people from other tables responded with applause. Somebody whistled. That same voice hollered again. "'Looking Glass'!"

Sean lowered his head and took a slow, deep breath. A hard cough followed before he rolled the tip of his tongue along the inside of his upper lip, downward stroked his goatee, and addressed the request.

"I'll sing it soon," he said, raising his hand in acknowledgment. "But like I was saying, this is a song I just wrote. A little autobiographical, I guess. It's called 'Rearview Years.'"

Staring for several moments at his left hand poised and ready on the guitar neck, he felt transfixed in a momentary sense of elation at debuting what he perceived to be his latest, and greatest, song— a musical masterpiece serving as an announcement that Sean Hightower still has what it takes. Strumming the opening chords, he started to sing.

> "Like many before he sang a dreamer's words
> Of hope and peace and trust and change
> A determined soul with songs to be heard

A beating heart for the home on the range."

Sean couldn't help but notice the number of people talking among themselves or texting on their cell phones. His excitement over the unveiling of a song he'd completed that morning vanished like the numerous puffs of cigarette smoke he exhaled each day.

"Now the voice in his head seems to echo defeat
And the man he was has disappeared
His unfinished story they say is complete
A consequence…"

Two men and a woman rose from different tables and headed for the bar.

"of his…"

Irritated, the unmistakable scent of garlic from a passing server drifted toward him as he struggled to finish the line.

"rearview…years."

At the song's completion, Sean stared into the darkened depths of his guitar hole, wounded and weakened by the sting of indifference from the crowd. His exasperation worsened as tepid, glad-that's-over-with handclapping followed. Fighting back the urge to smash his guitar on the ground in a reenactment of an old Who concert, he sprang from his chair.

"I'm outta here," he grumbled.

"Come on, Sean," someone shouted, sounding like the same voice from before. "Play 'Looking Glass'!"

'*Looking Glass,*' Sean thought to himself, reflecting on his 1985 hit. *A blessing then, a fucking curse now.*

"'Looking Glass,' man!"

"That same fucking guy again," he muttered. "Enough!"

Sean turned toward the man.

"Shut up, asshole! I ain't singin' it."

Dropping his guitar, Sean hurried from the stage by means of the slightly arthritic gait he now dealt with and headed toward Rocco's office.

"Hey, fuck you, Sean!" the man yelled back. "Who do you think you are, Springsteen or somethin'? You're a fucking has-been, man!"

Sean tried disregarding the painful stab of those shard-of-glass remarks but couldn't ignore the jabbing to the nerve endings of his pride. He entered Rocco's office, slammed the door, and stood staring misty-eyed at the fuzzy gray carpet under his feet, waiting out the storm of frustration. After another few moments, he grabbed a cup from the water cooler, crumpled into the desk chair, and reached into his jacket pocket for the pack of cigarettes. Fumbling at first for one of the last three remaining smokes, he found his hands shaking as he attempted to light it, not as much because of what had transpired on stage, but because of the truth in the man's comments. Nobody cared about Sean Hightower anymore.

The long, painful descent from that magical year in 1985 as Tom Petty's opening act saw him performing twenty-three years later as nothing more than a dustbin memory at gigs like Rocco's Bar and Grill.

A third of his cigarette later, Rocco shouldered his way through the door carrying Sean's guitar in one hand and the case in the other.

Throwing the case on the floor, he backhanded the door closed before lifting the guitar high in the air, staring wild-eyed at his ex-bandmate. "I ought to break this fucking thing over your goddamn head," he growled. "Calling one of my customers an *asshole*? Are you kidding me? Not only did I have to comp his dinner and drinks because of you, but his wife and two friends, dammit!" His jaw tightening, he glared at Sean. "What the hell were you thinking?"

"The guy was an obnoxious prick," he said, firing off a quick puff. "Didn't you hear him? He kept shouting at me to play 'Looking Glass.'"

Rocco rubbed a hand across his mouth and stared at Sean, his eyes opening wide. "That's because people like him come to hear songs they already know, you stupid ass! The Eagles, Credence Clearwater, Bob Seger, Paul Simon, Bob Dylan—*those* guys, get it? And whether you like it or not, they also want to hear you sing our hit."

Sean remained silent, exhaling his smoke with the same force as if he were blowing out candles.

"I don't get it," Rocco said, his voice quieting. "You played 'Looking Glass' every damn time you performed here before. Why should tonight be any different?"

"Because tonight…" Sean paused, nibbling on his lip. "Tonight wasn't just going to be the debut of my new song, it was going to be the debut of the new me. All I'm asking is for a chance to show everyone I'm not a one-hit wonder, but all they fucking care about is 'Looking Glass.' It's like those TV actors who play one character for so long they aren't given an opportunity to try something new." His eyes narrowed. "I'm trapped, Rocco, and it's eating me up inside."

"I understand what you're saying," Rocco said, "but you still need to embrace that song as a special part of you. Don't you think Paul Simon's burned out from playing 'The Sound of Silence'? Or The Eagles, when they play 'Hotel California'? Sean Hightower should do what they do. Put a new spin on it. Change the chording and the rhythm. Keep it fresh."

Sean couldn't help but ease into a smile, his bright green eyes still boyish even through the extended crinkles spreading like branching rivers. "I love you, Rocco," he said. "That's the first time I've ever heard my name mentioned in the same breath as Paul Simon and The Eagles."

Rocco's brown eyes narrowed, enhancing the thick black eyebrows that resembled raven's wings on an angular glide. His nostrils flared, subtle fleshy expansions possessing a life of their own at the bottom of his long, slender nose. His wavy hair, dark as night and shoulder length in his days with the band, now displayed peek-a-boo scattering of gray in a brushed-back, gelled sort of way that, to Sean, symbolized the slickness of the modern era.

"I'm just trying to make a point," Rocco said, resuming his harsh tone. "You haven't changed since we toured. Everything had to be your way or the highway back then, too."

"It was my band, dammit," Sean replied. "'The Sean Hightower Band,' remember?"

"We stuck it out with you through some lean times, man," Rocco answered, his eyes never wavering from Sean's. "We deserved more respect."

Sean leaned back in the chair and looked at Rocco, enjoying an extended drag from the cigarette. "Well, we broke up, right? You didn't have to put up with me anymore."

"You wanted to go solo anyway," Rocco said. "The label was sold and you figured your time had come to break away and sign with the big boys."

Sean shrugged and nodded. "Guilty as charged," he replied.

"At least you admit it," Rocco said. "I was pissed off—we all were—but that was a long time ago. I've let those old feelings pass, but you haven't changed. You still have trouble thinking of anyone but yourself."

"What's that supposed to mean?"

Rocco glared at Sean. "It may have been *your* band back then, but this is *my* place now, and I've got a business to run. If you don't play by my rules and do what I expect, don't plan on singing here again." Jutting his chin toward Sean, he added, "And what did I tell you about smoking in here, man? It stinks up my office!"

"What are you talking about, 'don't plan on singing here again'?" Sean asked, sitting up and dropping his cigarette into the cup. "You're not serious, are you?"

"The hell I'm not! These aren't the carefree band days anymore, my friend. I've got big-time responsibilities now. Employees to pay, insurance costs. A son in college next year." Rocco turned his hands palm-side up, his long, thin, bass-playing fingers gesturing toward the walls. "And did I mention the mortgage on this place? The one I pay each month to the Bank of the Lord and Master? If your bullshit turns enough people away, I'll lose money. You better believe I'm serious."

Sean grabbed some M&M's from a candy dish and rose from his chair. "*Shit!*" he muttered, grimacing and clutching his right hip.

"What happened?" Rocco asked.

Sean shook his head, remaining silent for several moments. "Fifty years old last month and my doctor says I have arthritis." Rolling his eyes, he laughed to himself. "Can you fucking believe it?"

Rocco furrowed his thick black eyebrows. "I thought arthritis was for old people."

"I guess some of us age faster than others, dude." Returning to an erect position, he exhaled a stream of air audibly from his nostrils. "I had a physical today and you'll be happy to know he told me to quit smoking." Sean chuckled. "Like that's gonna happen. I'm just glad he renewed my sleeping pill prescription. If it's not the shooting pains keeping me up, it's that I think too goddamn much."

"Great," Rocco replied, "another addiction to go with your fucking nicotine bullshit."

Sean waved his hand, as if shooing away a fly. "Nah, it's not like you think. I only take 'em two, three times a week." He rubbed his tongue across his mouth to create saliva as a sour dryness invaded the back of his throat. Reaching at first for another cigarette in his jacket pocket, he glanced at Rocco before turning his attention to the candy bowl. "Life's a bitch," he muttered, popping the round, multicolored shells into his mouth.

Rocco performed a quick imitation of a violin player.

"A fact's a fact, Rocco," Sean shot back. "Getting older *sucks*. I've gone from a high school track star to a goddamn cripple. Hell, even my sex drive ain't what it used to be, and you know how crazy I was back in the day. Most nights now I just smoke some weed with Merissa, down a couple of beers, and watch TV."

"Did your doctor say anything else?" Rocco asked. "Other than having arthritis and lungs like a barbeque grill?"

With both middle fingers held high, Sean stared at his friend before dropping both his arms to the sides. "I'll let you know in a week or two," he told him. "Doc took off for a vacation back East." He threw his chin upward as he turned to look at old band photos hanging on the wall.

"Those were the good old days, weren't they, Rocco?" he said, smiling as he approached the pictures. "Man, look how skinny you were. Do you remember what we used to call you?"

Rocco nodded. "The Italian Scallion."

Sean laughed, but his emotion felt bittersweet. He reflected on a younger and slimmer and, admittedly, more handsome Sean Hightower, before the paunch and jowl formations, when his dark blond, shaggy locks fell to his shoulders like a honeyed waterfall, thicker and longer than the thinning, gray-flecked shorter style of today. His unwrinkled face seemed so boyish and innocent compared to the older man with the noticeable lines in his forehead and deepening crow's feet creeping further out from the corners of weakening eyelids starting their downward trek. Straightening his shoulders, he sucked in his stomach and stood upright, his six-foot, two-inch frame counteracting the slope-shouldered posture he walked with today.

"I was twenty-seven years old when 'Looking Glass' started kicking ass," he said. "That's the same age when Brian Jones, Jimi Hendrix, Jim Morrison, Janis Joplin, and Kurt Cobain all died." With a finger resting on his lips, he nodded his head a couple of times in a slow, meditative manner. "Weird, huh? And Pete Ham, too. Their lives ended when mine was supposed to be taking off."

"Who's Pete Ham?" Rocco asked.

"Lead singer and songwriter for Badfinger. The guy committed suicide three days before his twenty-eighth birthday."

Sean's eyes narrowed as he continued looking at the photograph. "Now they'll live on forever in death, while I die a little every day from regret." He tightened his lips and took a slow, deep breath. "Dreams die hard, damn it," he muttered. "And those days were the best. It makes me understand suicide a little bit more, I think."

"Don't be an idiot."

Rocco approached Sean, focusing on the photos. "Yeah, we had some exciting times, I'm not denying it," he said. "But I like my life now, too."

"Don't tell me you don't miss it," Sean replied, his eyes remaining fixed on the photo of the group. "Other than making good music, the only responsibilities we had were getting sound checks straight and putting on a good show." He turned to face Rocco. "What did you know from mortgage and insurance costs? Don't you wish you could go back and do it again?"

"We reached our peak twenty-three years ago, Sean," he answered, "and that's a long time ago, so what's the use thinking like that?" Rocco pointed his finger to the photo of the band. "*That* was the 1980s." Extending his hands out toward the room, he added, "*This* is 2008."

Sean angled his head to the side, staring skeptically at his long-time friend. "And 2008's a fucked-up time," he grumbled. "It was an easier world back then, man. Life wasn't as serious."

"Life was always serious for people who took it seriously," Rocco countered. "You and I were different people in those days."

"It wasn't just us," Sean replied. His shoulders sagged as a smile of resignation crossed his face. "The world didn't seem as difficult and hateful, you know?" Walking back toward Rocco's desk, he removed the near-empty pack from his jacket pocket and slipped a cigarette into his mouth. "Once more, Rocco," he said, grabbing the lighter from the table and firing up before receiving a reply. Inhaling rather than puffing, Sean stared at the cigarette in his hand as the slow stream of smoke sifted from his nostrils. "You know something? When I look at the way life is today, it makes me very happy both my marriages ended before I had kids."

"The world we grew up in was pretty rough, too," Rocco told him. "You don't remember the nuclear arms race? The fucking Vietnam War? Civil rights demonstrations? The Iranian hostage bullshit? AIDs? C'mon, Sean, get real."

Sean stared at another picture, showing Rocco and a couple of the roadies making funny faces. "I can't remember the last time I had a good belly laugh," he said, taking another drag before continuing. "Maybe I'd feel different if I wrote another hit song, but right now too much of my reality is nothin' but a dark, bladder-shaped cloud pissing on my head."

Rocco shook his head and looked away for a moment before staring back at Sean. "You are one depressing dude, man," he said. "And will you please put out that fucking cancer stick?"

Sean strolled toward the desk, speed-sucking several more puffs before extinguishing the rest of the cigarette in the cup. "Can you blame me for my indulgences, Rocco? I haven't done shit since 'Looking Glass.' Once upon a time I had a platform, and people listened to the things I wrote about. Now I feel like I'm fading away. It's like the lines I wrote from a song called, 'Mark,' that almost seem omniscient now: 'A passionate man in a populated world. Seeking his voice. A flag to unfurl. Facing the worry of just growing old. Without a mark for baring your soul.'"

Sean took the few steps back to the chair and eased himself into the seat. Placing his right elbow down on the table, he rested his chin on the open hand of his extended arm.

"I shot my wad five minutes into my career and now I sell *cars* for a living. Can't get more exciting than that, huh, Rocco? Those movie companies are just *begging* for my life story." Sean picked up a pen and started doodling lines and circles on a yellow notepad. "Is that what I'm supposed to believe about myself?" Tossing the pen aside, he closed his eyes and pinched the bridge of his nose with his thumb and forefinger. "Am I supposed to think there's nothing wrong about being fifty and still dependent on my old man for money?" His head shook back and forth, a pendulum of self-incrimination. "Let's tell it like it is, man. I'm not all that good at what I do. The only reason I'm still working at the dealership is because I'm the owner's son." A soft chuckle born from bitterness escaped his lips. "So much for self-esteem."

"Selling cars hasn't stopped you from writing songs, Sean," Rocco responded. "If that's what you want to do, keep doing it."

"Yeah, but what good is it doing me?" he shot back. "I'm not just writing to jack myself off, Rocco. I want another hit!" Sean stared at the crushed tip of his cigarette inside the cup, sensitive in an appreciative way for the lingering aroma. "I want to record and tour again. Or maybe produce other acts and get my songs recorded that way." Rubbing his fingers together, he added, "But that takes money, you know?"

Sean stared at the bowl of M&M's, stroking his half-blond, half-gray goatee before reaching for another handful.

"Hey, save some for me, okay? That's the last of them."

Sean gobbled the round, hardshell chocolates as he rose from the chair. "I'm ready to go back out now," he said, grabbing his guitar.

"No way," Rocco replied, his tone leaving no room for debate. "Not after the scene you made."

Rocco strolled to the wall mirror to adjust his buttoned-down black silk shirt and gray sports jacket before dabbing his hands on the sides of his gelled black mane. He gazed at Sean, looking at him from his reflection in the background. "Lesson learned, Sean. The money I'm doling out tonight for those free meals and drinks won't be my loss, because you ain't gettin' paid. Go home to Merissa and be grateful that somebody still wants you around."

Sean stared narrow-eyed toward the mirror for several moments before breaking into a big grin. "See this smile on my face, Rocco?" he asked. "It's for two reasons. One is that I can't believe how fucking straitlaced and uptight you've become. Where's that hang-loose, bass-playing party animal I once knew? Your transformation's comical to me, man."

"What's the second reason?"

"What you said is true: I *am* grateful that Merissa still wants me around. I love that woman. She's the only thing that keeps me sane."

"You met her at work, right? At least something good came out of that."

"The one and only thing," he answered. "At first, I didn't think I stood a chance. Merissa's one of those feisty women who likes to give shit to men but not have it taken seriously, you know? She has poker nights at her place sometimes and invites guys from the dealership. When she asked me the first time, I figured I'd be another one of her boys to joke around with."

"Whose father happened to own the dealership," Rocco said.

Sean chuckled. "It's not like that thought didn't cross my mind," he replied. "But she soon learned my old man's the one with the money, not me. And I don't want to go into the business. If that was all she was looking for, we wouldn't have lasted this long."

Rocco approached the desk. "You may not be happy selling cars," he said, plucking Sean's cup of disposed cigarettes, "but having a good woman outshines everything else."

Sean watched Rocco head toward the bathroom with the cup.

"Merissa's not just a good woman, but a good person, too," he replied, sneaking another M&M into his mouth. "She does volunteer work at a place that helps kids from fucked-up homes. What I don't like is when she offers her apartment for nighttime meetings. It cuts into our time together."

Rocco flushed the cigarette remains down the toilet before exiting the bathroom holding a can of air freshener. Directing several mists in Sean's direction, he sat on the edge of the desk and stared, his expression quizzical. "It cuts into your time together? *Jesus*, how can you be so fucking selfish? Those meetings are for a good cause and they're probably only once in a while anyway, so what's the big deal?"

Shrugging, Sean offered no reply.

"Explain something to me," Rocco said. "You tell me you love her and she keeps you sane. Why aren't you living together?"

"You know where that would lead?" Sean asked, rolling his eyes. "Marriage." Shaking his head, he added, "I'm zero for two already when it comes to that stuff. Maybe it's fear of failure, but I don't want to strike out, you know what I mean?"

Rocco grimaced. "Man, you sound more like a self-centered twenty-year-old than someone who's fifty. Hey, here's a novel idea: think of someone *else* for a change."

Rocco looked at his watch and walked toward the door. Placing his hand on the knob, he fixed Sean with a defiant look as he opened the door a crack, allowing an immediate volume increase of the recorded music from the speakers in combination with the heightened voices from the tables. "Right now, I'm not sure I want you here next week," he said. "But if I give you another chance and they ask for 'Looking Glass,' you better fucking play it." Walking out, Rocco didn't look back.

Left alone, Sean surveyed the photos on the wall again; framed memories from the days when that song had made them stars. Those days were sweet indeed—a hit record, making good money, the opening act for Tom Petty on a nationwide tour, interviews in every city, and, of course, the girls. Man oh man, how awesome was that? From his unsettled thoughts echoed a hollow, sarcastic, chuckle. "How did it ever come to this?"

He'd been called an overnight sensation, ending 1985 with the fifth most-played single on Billboard's Top 100. He'd earned enough money to move from his dull, one-room Hollywood apartment to a three-bedroom, twenty-three-hundred-square-foot home with a pool on the west side, a mere twenty-minute drive from the beach. As more hit records seemed a foregone conclusion, his future and a chance for a much bigger house, seemed secure. How was he to foresee a larger company with more established groups purchasing the one he recorded for by the summer of the following year? Not only did his band get dropped from the label, a short time later, they'd imploded from the increasing discord and broken up.

Sean acknowledged the accuracy of Rocco's comments about him from those days after the split. He wanted to be the *man*, following in the successful singer-songwriter footsteps of superstars like Sting and Rod Stewart: artists who left a successful band to gain even greater fame and wealth on their own. But the time and money he'd spent writing and recording songs hoping for a career as a solo act had proved futile. Sean Hightower, one-time burgeoning rock star, never reveled in the glory of a chart-busting record again, and those lofty expectations of musical stardom had crashed like a lost meteorite in the unexceptional land of one-hit wonders.

Walking back toward the chair, he removed his final cigarette from the pack and fired up as Peter Gabriel's "Steam" played outside the office. The irony of hearing a Gabriel song, another artist who'd left a successful band to achieve great success as a solo artist, brought a self-pitying shake of the head. Listening in reflective isolation, he squeezed the cigarette between his two fingers like a vice, snuffing out the burning tobacco, and creating two indentations on both sides of the paper. Forced to use the lighter again, he reflected on the disagreeable phone conversation with his mother that morning and wondered if the lingering effects had set the foundation for his hostility tonight. He inhaled, jaw hard and tight, recalling how his tranquil mood had regressed into a quick-strike battle zone.

⁊ʒ⁊

Finishing his first cup of coffee, Sean poured another before lighting a second cigarette and sliding the window open for some fresh air. The late winter temperature hovered somewhere in the high sixties and the white, scattered clouds enhanced the magnetic azure hue of the morning sky. Returning the coffee cup to his lips, he turned back toward the room as the phone rang. Reading the name on the caller ID, he hesitated before deciding that whatever the reason for his mother's call, he'd rather deal with her now instead of later, especially if she planned to machine-gun him with her frustrating I-know-what's-best-for-you attitude.

"How ya doin', Mom?"

"I'm fine, honey," she replied. "You know me, getting worried when too much time passes without hearing from my children. I always like to feel there's things worth talking about."

Through the tone of her voice, Sean already sensed an ulterior motive for her alleged innocent reply. A suspect undertone of concern accompanied her voice, a certain leading-to-something sound that made him regret answering the phone. After a slight delay, she asked, "So, how are things with you?"

"The usual, Mom," he said. "Just taking life a day at a time."

"A day at a time is fine," she said, pausing, "as long as you don't lose sight of your future."

Sean closed his eyes and took a deep breath, waiting several moments to maintain his composure. "You don't have to worry about me, Mom," he told her. "I've always got my eyes on the prize."

"What exactly is the *prize*, Sean?" she asked, her tone growing teeth.

He rolled his tongue around his mouth and then scratched his ear in an unconscious gesture, thinking about what to say. "Mom,

I'm enjoying a peaceful morning on my day off, so don't ruin it, okay? I don't want to talk about this again."

His mother stayed silent for several uncomfortable moments. "Listen, dear," she said, her tone softening, "I didn't call to ruin your morning. But you're still only working three days a week, right? So don't play that day-off card with me."

Sean's grip tightened as he glared at the phone in his hand.

"First of all, Mom," he uttered between gritted teeth, "it's more like four to five days now. But I also have a music career, remember? All it takes is one hit song and I'll be back. As a matter of fact, I just finished one that might be the best thing I've ever written. It could be my comeback song."

A perceptible sigh sounded from the receiver.

"What?" Sean asked. "*What?*"

"You don't know how much it thrills your father to have you working at the dealership, to have one of his children following in his footsteps. You know that he—" His mother stopped in mid-sentence again.

This time Sean exhaled with an audible force. "Just say what you have to say, all right?"

Another long pause followed. Sean waited, impatient to hear his mother spit out what he already anticipated.

"Well," she said, "you know your father isn't getting any younger—but neither are you, honey. Don't you think it's best to finally forget the music and commit to learning the business full-time? What happens if your new song doesn't make it? Then what? It's such a cruel business, Sean. Why not move on and make a fresh start of things? You could be so good at the car business."

"How do you know, Mom?" he replied, his voice rising a notch. "You've never seen me sell a car. For all you know, I *suck* at it. How the hell do you know if I'm any good at it?"

"Because I believe in you, Sean. I think you've got a great future in the car business. But you're fifty years old now, and you can't keep chasing that music dream forever. You've given it long enough, don't you think? At least you can say you had a hit record once upon a time. How many people can make that claim?"

"Maybe I can also take out my Little League trophies, Mom. I mean, as long as we're talking past achievements, right? I'll put them right there on my office desk to let everyone see the kind of big shot they're dealing with."

Another breathy sigh sounded from his mother.

"Look, Sean," she said, "your father wants to give you the opportunity to take over the dealerships one day, to teach you everything you'll need to know. It's the kind of thing most people only dream about. And it could all be yours."

Sean remained motionless, lips pursed as he fixated on the welcoming distraction of the little neighbor girl sitting at her front yard lemonade stand.

He envisioned his mother's rosy scenario and compared it to the way he viewed himself, unsure whether to laugh or cry.

Sean Hightower, short-time rock star and longtime failure, running his daddy's car dealerships. Sean Hightower, the independent one of the family, full of expectations and promise, turning into a dependent, pathetic adult unable to make it on his own.

"I really don't want to talk about this anymore," he said, his voice cracking. "I have to go."

"Your father knows you're hurting, sweetheart," she told him, her words rushing out. "Emotionally *and* financially. He knows music was always your dream, always your passion, but you've got to face reality. He only wants what's best for you."

"*What's best for me?*" Sean shouted. "Don't you think I should get a say in what's best for me, Mom? It's my own goddamn life!"

"Please don't yell at me. I only meant—"

"You only meant that I'm a fucking failure, Mom. That I'm a fifty-year-old man who doesn't know how to do anything else!"

"Listen to me, honey," she said. "Your brother and sister have good jobs and are doing well now. But your father helped them through dry times and he wants to do the same for you."

"As long as I'm the boss's son, take advantage of it, right, Mom? *Right?*"

"Well…yes. What's wrong with that? You just can't keep pursuing the same dead-end dream for the rest of your life. You need to turn the page."

Sean closed his eyes, working his lower teeth against his upper lip. The time had come to hang up the phone, fetch his pot and pipe, and head out on the USS *Marijuana* as it navigated its way through his bloodstream, escorting him to the trouble-free land of I-Don't-Give-A-Shit.

ഞ്ഞ

As the intermingling sounds of music and muffled voices continued from the other room, Sean reflected on the reversal of fortune between himself and his two siblings. When "Looking Glass" started gaining airplay, David still toiled insane hours interning at a law office downtown, striving to win the hearts and minds of the suits reigning above him. And Rebecca waited on tables in New York, struggling to get something going as an aspiring fashion designer.

"Those tables sure turned, didn't they?" he whispered to himself. Rebecca had persevered through the early rejections and now kicked ass, making big bucks working for Broadway and television shows. David not only had won those hearts and minds but in time they'd made him a partner in the firm. Three kids and a twelve-year marriage later, he'd made his parents proud, just like Rebecca. And the third sibling? The *independent* one? The one who'd darted from the starting gate ahead of the other two? "Life's a bitch," he mumbled.

Puffing his way toward the end of his last cigarette, Sean stared at the old band photos again, lost in the time-machine memories of better days. Looking for a place to dispose of his ashes, he removed the cap from the air freshener, turned it upside down, and flicked the remains there before unfolding himself from the chair in a slow, cautious manner. Retrieving his guitar, he placed it in the case and headed for the parking lot—but not before snatching the rest of the M&M's.

Chapter 3

Apart from their sibling relationship and living in Los Angeles, Sean and his brother David possessed little in common. David's personality resided on the conservative side of the behavioral fence, acting more like a third parent than a brother and confidante. That was why Sean disagreed with—or, at best, ignored—most of David's advice on things, especially adverse opinions about his lifestyle. With David's own life revolving around work, wife, kids, and more work, the brothers rarely conversed, and outside of family gatherings, didn't socialize either. So when Sean arrived at his car and called home before starting the engine to check his voice mail, the sound of David's voice surprised him.

"Hi, Sean," the message started, "David here. Don't know when you'll get this message, but it's almost nine o'clock now and I just left the office. Call me on my cell up until about ten or so. I've got some very interesting news for you. I'll be in meetings all day tomorrow, so hopefully you'll call me tonight. Talk to you later."

Sean's phone showed the time as nine forty-one, so after opening another pack of cigarettes retrieved from his glove compartment, he followed David's instructions and called his number, more for the curiosity factor than any expectation of "interesting news."

"I almost gave up on you," David said, disregarding the opening pleasantries of "Hello, Sean," or "How ya doin', Sean."

Sean took a rapid puff, shaking his head at David's typical off-putting manner as the smoke meandered out his car window. "What's up, David?" he asked, impatient already. "Claire pregnant again?"

"Hell no!" David laughed. "This is all about you, bro. And it's real good news."

Gazing through his windshield at the lights on the street, he chuckled at the idea of his brother possessing the ability as the bearer of anything Sean deemed "real good."

"You have real good news that's all about me?" he asked, playing along. "I'm sorry, I thought I was talking to my brother, David. I must have dialed the wrong number."

"Listen to me, you cynical bastard. What if I told you that by pure, dumb luck, you have a chance to make some pretty good money again?"

Sean narrowed his brow, wondering what the hell his brother meant.

"All right," he replied, sitting up. "I'm listening."

"We're representing a new client," he said. "It's a Canadian corporation with a subsidiary that makes a cleaning product called Wally's Window Wipes. They want to break into the American market and run a six-month advertising blitz this summer. They'll target the demographic that watches the afternoon soaps and talk shows—you know, mothers in their thirties and forties with the kids and dirty dishes and messy homes. You with me so far?"

Sean's bafflement grew, knowing he had as much in common with stay-at-home mothers as an Osbourne had with an Osmond. "Is the next part where I come in?"

A momentary pause preceded David's exuberance. "Ready for this?" he exclaimed. "They want to use 'Looking Glass' as their song to market the product! Can you believe it, Sean? Is that the break you've been looking for or *what*?"

"*What?*" Sean shouted.

David continued talking, the enthusiasm in his voice underscoring every word. "When the big shots in the firm found out the Hightower who wrote the song is my own damn brother, they couldn't fucking believe it! I'm so happy for you, bro. Who knows where this could lead? A renewed popularity of the song and subsequent airplay again, right? And maybe this time somebody may actually record a cover version instead of fucking killing himself!"

David's last remark sealed Sean's eyes into tight pockets of painful reminiscence as he bit his lower lip and tilted his head upward, recalling the moment he'd discovered his chance at musical resurrection had crashed and burned. In August of 1993 he'd met Kurt Cobain, co-founder of Nirvana, a group whose previous album, *Nevermind*, had sold millions worldwide and produced a couple of major hits, "Smells Like Teen Spirit" and "Come As You Are." One night, with drunken enthusiasm at a downtown L.A. bar, Cobain had talked about the following month's release of their next album, *In Utero*, but spoke in greater length about his love for "Looking Glass," and how the *whole* band wanted to record it for their next record, praising the lyrics as a "no-bullshit look at life," and describing unique instrumental dynamics to make the song "a Nirvana tribute to the original." Sean had viewed this as analogous to the recipient of insider trading, privy to an inevitable cash bonanza few people knew about; the financial stepping stone he needed to get back in the game.

A daunting legal problem, however, stood in his way.

Bypassing the 1976 Copyright Act seemed an impossible hurdle, stipulating as it did that a songwriter must wait thirty-five years to reacquire the rights, something Sean had given away as a provision for signing his record contract. But the same week he'd met Cobain, thanks to the fortuitous cocaine arrest of the daughter of the record executive with whom he'd signed that contract, some beautiful quid pro quo maneuvering occurred through the partner of his father's lawyer, and within a whirlwind two weeks, as part of the agreement for getting the case dropped, Sean regained sole ownership of "Looking Glass." From a roadblock to a rebirth, the middle finger of fate had been transformed into an apparent victory sign.

Or so he'd thought.

After the release of *In Utero*, another Nirvana album destined to sell many millions, Kurt Cobain died from an apparent suicide in April of 1994. *In Utero* turned out to be the band's last studio album, causing the dreams of Sean's career revival to shatter into pathetic pieces of what-could-have-been.

"I know things haven't gone your way for a while," David said, "so it's about time you caught a fucking break. I sure as hell know you could use the money."

Sean felt a burning sensation pulsating from the back of his eyes and in utter frustration started pounding his fist against the dashboard. Pain and anger bubbled inside him as he witnessed the last shredded vestiges of his professional reputation ridiculed and minimized.

"*No!*" he shouted. "*No! No! No!*" His hands twisted into a white-knuckled grip on the steering wheel. "I won't do it, David! *No way* will I ever let that happen!"

A long moment of silence followed on the other end.

"What the *hell* is your problem, Sean?" David asked, his shock obvious by his tone. "I thought you'd be ecstatic about this. Don't you realize how much money you stand to make?"

"Goddammit, David! 'Looking Glass' is a song about confusion and disillusionment as we grow up. Don't you understand how I feel? I'll be going from someone who actually wrote a song of substance into some brainless asshole writing about a window cleaner!"

"Oh, give me a break, Sean. People don't think about that stuff. All the company wants to do is highlight the line about being stuck inside the looking glass when someone looks through a dirty window. I give them a lot of credit for picking out your song and running with it."

Sean stamped his feet, the dull echo of the floor mat accentuating his downfall. With his hand shrouding his face, he asked, "Do you know who John Densmore is, David?"

Sean heard a loud sigh through the phone.

"No."

"He was the drummer for The Doors. The other two guys want to sell their songs to the big companies, but not him. He remembers his rock 'n roll roots, and I respect the hell out of him for that." He nodded to himself. "I'm pretty sure Jim Morrison would, too."

"You're forgetting something," David said. "The Doors were one of the most successful bands of all time and John Densmore doesn't have to sell cars for a living."

His shoulders sagging at that painful reminder, Sean listened to the rest of his brother's comments.

"You told me yourself there isn't much money to be made anymore from 'Looking Glass,' so what are you acting so high and mighty for? Even your heroes like Pete Townshend and Bob Dylan have let their songs be played for products. Why not you, too?"

Sean shook his head in disgust. "'Bargain' is one of my favorite Who songs," he said. "A meaningful rocker about spiritual enlightenment, and Townshend let it be used to sell fucking *cars*, can you believe it?" Without waiting for a reply, he continued. "And Dylan? Don't remind me. I still remember the first time I heard 'The Times They Are a-Changin'' on a commercial for Kaiser Permanente.

Man, I couldn't believe it! *Kaiser Permanente*. One of the most inspiring and influential songs of the sixties being used to remind that same generation they're getting old and creaky. Every time I think about it I want to puke."

A few moments of silence followed. "Well, bro," David said, "it's been a long day, I'm beat, and I can't begin to tell you how disappointed I am by your reaction. But I'm going to do you a favor. I'll keep this conversation a secret and hope you come to your senses. It's a great opportunity that's still open, so I don't have to let them know about your refusal right now. But I'll be embarrassed as hell if you don't change your mind on this."

Sean took a final drag on his cigarette before tossing the burning stub on the ground. "There's a song by Tom Petty called 'Money Becomes King,'" he said. "It shows how the corporate mentality has taken over rock 'n roll. How it's all about money and not the soul anymore. At the end of the song he expresses the feeling of a fan that went to see his hero in concert but realized things would never be the same, and how the only thing he thought about after the show was downing a light beer that the singer was now doing a commercial for. You should listen to it, David. You might understand where I'm coming from."

"Welcome to the real world, Sean," David said. "The *corporate* world. Whatever you would make out of this may be dirty money to you, but a whole lot of songwriters wish they were in your shoes right now."

Sean acknowledged David's accuracy about one thing: the corporate world ruled the roost, and when they pull and tug, the puppets are the ones forced to dance. Too many great songwriters sacrificed integrity for the all-mighty dollar by allowing the significance of their songs to catapult from distinctive to destructive.

When the conversation ended, he remained in the parking lot, taking deep, slow drags on another cigarette. Once upon a time, Sean Hightower's songwriting echoed pride and independence, but if he followed his brother's urging, his self-respect stood to dangle like a stripped carcass, another casualty to the new world order. David was all about the money, incapable of understanding the emptiness Sean felt as his dignity floated away on a cold, cruel breeze. He thought of lines he wrote about people like his brother who viewed the world from a perspective that failed to consider individual differences:

The answers are clear, in black and white
Don't waste my time with gray
Just keep it simple, it's alright
So much easier that way.

Chapter 4

Getting the boot from Rocco had its upside. Instead of arriving at Merissa's place in the early a.m. to find her asleep, she'd still be awake at this hour.

He called her at home and on her cell as he walked to the car, repeating his attempts leaving the parking lot. With no voice mail messages on his cell or home phone, his bewilderment increased.

"Where is she?" he wondered aloud.

His need for her love and companionship took on an added urgency after David's news about "Looking Glass."

"What a day," he whispered, voicing his feelings about the exasperating conversations with his mother and brother and that whole annoying scene at Rocco's.

Thinking about his family depressed him. He felt exiled much of the time because none of them shared his sensibilities about the value of life. Money represented the center of their universe, but to Sean, love and self-respect mattered more in the end. Merissa understood that, he loved her for it, and tonight he'd make love to her with a passion he longed to express. He shook his head and chuckled, thinking about Rocco's admonishment over his refusal to consider marriage.

Most weekends they alternated staying at each other's place, so after stopping at home to collect some clothes, a toothbrush, and his dog, Hendrix, he figured to arrive at her place in about an hour. He couldn't shake his anxiety, battling disorientation from his inability to contact her or know her whereabouts, but he had a key even if she wasn't there. Driving through the street-to-street signal lights of late night Los Angeles, Sean reflected again on more regrets.

When "Looking Glass" entered the top ten, the corks had popped on the bubbly, and by the end of the evening he'd asked his girlfriend to marry him. Why not? Valerie not only appeared to be his lucky charm, she had a gorgeous face, a perfect body, and wanted sex anytime, anywhere. Young and stupid, Sean expected the good times to last forever. When they made their vows a few months later, however, the song had dropped from the charts, a second single wasn't released, and rumors swirled of an impending buyout of his record company.

In the midst of this discouraging period, Valerie had started talking kids, but Sean convinced her to postpone that idea until he signed a new record deal, providing the financial security they'd need. As his career stalled, their frustrations mounted. In less than three years another type of signing occurred: divorce papers. His dwindling savings took a hit from the settlement and Sean promised himself he'd never make such a foolish mistake again. Another foolish mistake later, the curtain dropped on that second marriage like a bad play.

He met Merissa on his first day of work at the dealership and, within a few weeks, had spent a memorable night at her place. More than a year into the relationship, they carried on like a happily married couple, but without the rings or sharing the same living space. Merissa broached the subject of marriage a time or two, but Sean avoided any kind of serious discussion. In his mind, the situation seemed perfect. Each had a key to the other's place and they came and went as they pleased. Discovering Merissa in this look-at-me-but-don't-touch impersonal city offered him a chance at love again, something he hadn't thought possible.

As he drove down the short ramp into the garage, Sean smiled but shook his head when he spotted Merissa's metallic blue Mustang. "What do you think, Hendrix?" he asked, addressing his dog in the front seat. "Was it asking too much of her to call me back?" Gathering his things in one hand, he clutched Hendrix to his chest and walked up the stairs to the first floor. His hands full, he knocked on the door and waited, listening to the muted sound of the television. Sean rapped his knuckles on the door again, but Merissa still didn't open up. "Must be in the bathroom," he whispered, placing his bag on the ground. Removing his keys, he found the right one and stepped inside.

As Hendrix squirmed to be freed, Sean released the dog from his grip, enjoying the thought of her furry little friend making the announcement of his arrival. Heading toward the refrigerator for a beer, a sudden series of unusual, rapid-fire barks emanating from Merissa's room startled him, and he scurried down the hallway in sudden concern.

Several minutes later, through his tattered awareness of time and space, he heard another type of sound.

Sirens.

Chapter 5

Sean sat stone-faced on the couch with Hendrix's black muzzle perched on his lap, preferring seclusion rather than listening to the inane bullshit from Roger and Adam, his two friends from the dealership. Right now, their good intentions mattered little to him and helped as much as a cup of water tossed on a forest fire.

"We're never going to forget her, Sean," Roger said, "but right now we're thinking of you. We wanted to make sure you're all right."

"Whatever we can do for you, just name it," Adam added. "We want you back whenever you're ready."

Sean glanced at both of them, nodding his head in a single subtle motion of insincere acknowledgment. The overwhelming trauma from Merissa's rape and murder just two weeks before had rendered him drained of feeling about anything. If the entire world disappeared in a mushroom cloud tomorrow he wouldn't care. He covered his face in one hand, gripping hard as he slid his fingers down from his forehead to the unshaven stubble on his cheeks and chin.

"I'm not ready for much of anything right now," he said, his voice little more than a whisper.

Sean rose to his feet and walked to the window. He observed that lemonade-selling little girl again, noticeably frail, with a cream-colored beret, sitting on a chair on the sidewalk behind a rectangular folding table covered by a white cloth hanging down on both sides. A man, perhaps her father, neared completion of the stand assembled around her, stacking two upside-down piles of paper cups on each side of a large barrel-shaped red container. The family had moved in the previous month and Sean had spotted her selling lemonade a few times as he drove past. Looking closer now, with a chance to study her features, he realized she seemed quite pale, possessing no more than a few strands of hair under her cap. He surmised what he hadn't deduced before.

Just a little girl, he said to himself. *What the hell did she ever do to deserve that?* Sean closed his eyes, trying to shut out another reminder of life's cruelty. *It's getting harder to take.*

"Everyone from the bowling group wanted me to say hello," Adam said, piercing his thoughts like a spear.

"If you need anything for the house," Roger added, "Anita and I can do some shopping for you. It's no problem."

After a long silence, the hourglass of his patience released its final grain. "Thanks for coming, guys," he said, turning from the window, "but I've got something I need to do."

Before closing the door, he agreed to call them if needed, speaking the words without the slightest intention. He entered the spare bedroom where Merissa's clothes, that she brought and left at his house, remained stuffed in trash bags on the floor. Her sister, Megan, had suggested he bring them to the Donation Depot at the Directional Center where she did volunteer work for women and their children from problem homes. The bags lay bunched together at haphazard angles secured with twist ties except one. Sean stared at the sole item of clothing that didn't belong to Merissa, sickened by the acute awareness of its significance. His unfolded gray sweat top, strewn on the floor with her panties and his sweat pants that night, crested the top of the opened bag.

Through the choking mist of his memory, he remembered seeing that top by the bed and instinctively clutching it against his chest and then his face, knowing that his sweat suit had been a favorite item of hers to slip into after work. Without a second thought, he'd put the top on, zipping it all the way and not taking it off until he returned home.

Now he wanted to rid himself of that item of clothing forever but had delayed sealing it in the bag. That hooded top represented the last thing Merissa had worn, and he recalled how cute she looked in the oversize sleeves that hung past her hands. As he stood looking down at the crumpled gray material, he saw nothing but a silent reminder of the beautiful woman who'd once filled those empty cotton spaces.

Stooping to gather the hooded top in his hands, Sean cradled it against his chest. Tears surged from his eyes as another levy of restraint collapsed. He fell to his knees, wailing into the soft cotton now covering his face. "Why did this have to happen?" he asked out loud. "Why? Why?"

Sean's hands squeezed the sweat top until all color drained from his fingers, his anger shoving the tears aside. He leaped to his feet and clasped both hands around the crumpled hood, whipping the floor and walls as if wielding an ax, over and over in a rage of frustration and excruciating acceptance. He staggered toward all four sides of the room, swinging away toward anything that got in his way: a desk lamp, a framed photo of Hendrix and him, a stack of CDs, a long, newly used candle, a cigarette-filled ashtray, an empty coffee cup, and a Vin Scully bobblehead Dodger doll. He staggered forward and back, side to side, his disoriented state of sober reality rendering him weak and unable to catch his breath.

Sean grabbed the armrest of his wooden chair and crumpled into the seat, his suffocating anger disintegrating into exhaustive helplessness. His glazed eyes, open and tearful, stared into the vacuum of his own desperate thoughts for several long moments. Or was it minutes? As he reentered the consciousness of his surroundings, his eyes lasered toward what appeared to be a playing card at the far end of the room. Walking over, he reached down.

"The Jack of Hearts," he whispered. Even through the cavernous depths of his grief, his discovery reminded him of one of his favorite Bob Dylan songs, "Lily, Rosemary and the Jack of Hearts." Sean turned the card over and peered at the recognizable Bicycle design found on many store-bought decks. *Was this in my sweatshirt?* he wondered. *Was it Merissa's?*

"Fuck it!" he shouted, flinging the card away like a mini Frisbee. "What goddamn difference does it make *now*?" Sean rushed to the open trash bag, shoved his sweat suit inside, and tied a double knot as fast as he could.

Chapter 6

Determined to place Merissa's volunteer days into his literal and figurative rear view mirror, Sean waved away an employee's attempt to speak with him as he dropped the bags onto the counter of the donation center and left. As he approached his car for a quick getaway, however, a man in a dark gray Honda Accord pulled into the parking lot, honking his horn and waving.

Sean's shoulders sagged as he whispered a curse, preparing for a few undesirable moments with the director of the Mid-Valley Youth and Family Directional Center, Elliot Hayden.

Elliot Hayden: part humanitarian working toward bettering problem family lives and part annoying know-it-all for working toward butting into everyone else's problems. Merissa respected him to the point of idolatry, but Sean disliked the man's seeming moral obligation to dissect decisions by others as his to analyze, accept, or reject.

Standing approximately six foot, four inches, Elliot reminded him of a haughty college professor peering down at you from atop his lectern.

Opinions, wanted or not, sprang from his mouth like a broken waterline.

After exchanging the usual pleasantries and Sean's explanation of his appearance at the center, Elliot wasted no time being...Elliot.

"You need a healthy outlet, Sean," he told him. "Something worthwhile."

Elliot removed his dark, silver-framed sunglasses and stared, the crow's-footed corners of his dark brown eyes lengthening into pronounced crinkles as he smiled. For a man in his mid-to-late fifties, his face remained boyish with a naturally bemused expression, punctuated by a stylish, silvery-white cropped beard matching the color of his full ponytailed head of hair. Merissa admired his LA cool style of dress, remarking more than once that he reminded her of an older male model out of the pages of *GQ*.

"Let's face it," he continued, tugging on the sleeves of his black corduroy jacket, "much of your work day is spent wooing potential buyers who think a car's ability to accelerate on the freeway or make a sharp turn is the most important thing on earth."

Sean angled his head downward, pinching the bridge of his nose as an added resentment crept over him. Elliot's lack of sensitivity and pompous preaching jack-hammered his tolerance into crumpled remains. "I don't want to hear any more of your holier-than-thou shit, Elliot," he said, his fingers stiffening from dangling hands. "I'm trying to find my way again, all right? You think you know what's best for me after what's happened? You have no fucking clue!"

Pivoting away, he hurried toward his car.

"Sean, wait! Wait!"

Sean heard the accelerating footsteps behind him but didn't stop. As he reached for his door handle, Elliot pushed his hand against the door.

"I'm sorry, Sean," he told him. "I'm very sorry. You're absolutely right. It's not my place to tell you what you need right now. All of us who knew Merissa are hurting, but nobody more than you. I can't even imagine." Elliot dropped his briefcase and extended his right hand. "Please forgive me."

Sean stared at Elliot's hand then glanced into his eyes for several moments before directing his attention toward the conciliatory hand again. Reaching out, he clasped it.

"It's all right," he said, his voice subdued. "Baby steps, you know what I mean?"

Elliot clasped his arm. "Yes, of course."

Standing back, Elliot nibbled on his upper lip and gazed into Sean's eyes, as deep as if intent on assessing the size of his pupils. "I know you want to go," he said, "but please let me say one more thing." A slight smile appeared as he paused before continuing. "You know how much Merissa cared about the clinic, how much it meant to her. Maybe it would help your healing to feel a part of that. I could always use an extra hand in the office. You could input names and records into our database, organize lists of donors, help us with contribution letters, make phone calls for event locations—things like that."

Sean started shaking his head before Elliot completed his sentence. "Forget it, okay? Just because I played a couple of fundraisers doesn't mean I want to devote more time to this place. The only reason I performed was because Merissa asked me to."

"But you know what we're about here. The people we help come from some of the same situations Merissa experienced herself. How could that not mean anything to you?"

An overwhelming weariness cocooned Sean's ability to continue. "I've gotta go," he said, opening his door.

"Just think about it, all right?" Elliot replied, grasping his briefcase. "Merissa did so much for us. Become a part of this place and see if it doesn't make you feel better."

જીજીજી

Returning home, Sean lifted the receiver and heard the repetitive, rapid-fire beeps signaling an awaiting voice mail. Craving a cigarette, he removed one from the pencil box he used to store them on the table next to his couch. With the lighter unused in his hand, he first listened with curiosity to the message left by Dr. Lodin's assistant, Beverly, asking for a return call, "today, if possible."

Having forgotten about his checkup from the week before, Sean assumed Dr. Lodin wanted to talk to him about the results of his blood and X-ray work but remained puzzled why he'd elected to bypass his usual method of making all non-emergency calls at the end of the day like he always did. Had he somehow heard about Merissa? Maybe he just wanted to offer his condolences.

"Hold on, Mr. Hightower," Beverly told him. "The doctor told me to let him know when you called."

Sean continued flicking his lighter on and off as he waited, staring at the reappearing flame in anticipation of fire and tobacco lovemaking.

"Hi, Sean," Lodin started. "As you know, I had to rush out of here after your examination so I wasn't able to look at your test results until this morning."

"Wouldn't you normally wait until you're done for the day before calling me to tell me I'm fine? Should I be worried?"

"It's too early to tell," Lodin told him.

Sean dropped the lighter on the table before running a hand over his mouth and chin. "Go on."

"Please understand that no conclusions can be drawn from this, but your X-rays show a shadowing, perhaps a widening, of the mediastinal structures in your chest. Perhaps it's nothing serious, but I want you to make an appointment for a CAT scan so we can get a closer look. Once we get those results back, I'll show them to an oncologist down the hall from our office. Her name's Karen Jillson, and we've worked together on scans a number of times."

Shadowing? Perhaps it isn't serious? Sean heard those words but not much else. In his mind, what else mattered? One plus one equals two, and *shadowing* plus *serious* equals…only one thing.

Closing his eyes, he massaged his forehead, listening for a few moments to his own breathing. A sudden dryness overtook his throat as he prepared to ask the question. "Are you telling me…I have…cancer?"

"What I'm telling you, Sean," Lodin replied, his unyielding seriousness making the room's temperature rise, "is that we don't know anything for sure right now. False alarms happen all the time, and we'll certainly hope this is the case with you. Let me see what Dr. Jillson has to say, and we'll go from there."

"Even for a thirty-year chain smoker like me?" Sean asked, almost to himself. "Do we have false alarms, too?"

"Stay on the line," Lodin said. "I'll transfer you to Beverly and she'll set you up for an appointment."

"No…no, I'll call back, okay?"

"Sean, listen to me"

"Not now, Dr. Lodin," Sean said, his head spinning in confusion. "I don't want to deal with this right now. Tell Beverly I'll call her next week."

At the end of the phone call, Sean realized the cigarette he'd planned to smoke lay crushed and twisted on the floor with pieces of shredded tobacco scattered around it.

Lifting his eyes from the floor, his attention moved from the pencil box toward the kitchen, where four unopened cartons, the sirens of nicotine, cradled his consciousness in a comforting, hypnotic allure.

"Cancer," he whispered. "Cancer," he repeated out loud. "*Cancer!*" he shouted.

Sean felt powerless, an impotent creature of this heartless life whose apparent intent to spare neither the victim nor the loved one continued unabated. Having already succumbed to nightmare images of Merissa's bloodied and disfigured face, he sensed a creeping madness challenging his sanity. Now the probability of cancer left him teetering on the edge.

He placed a hand over his misty eyes, wanting to feel the release of an explosive, pent-up sob, but nothing came. He felt detached from himself, the hanging judge of his own pessimistic thoughts—the woman he loved raped and killed, his career a sham, and now a guaranteed death sentence. Grabbing a cigarette, he fired up and called Hendrix over, cradling him to his body as he dropped on his couch. He gritted his teeth from the flash of pain passing through his hip, feeling angry over this now irrelevant intrusion to his greater concern.

"You're my best friend, little guy," he told him, stroking his head. "But there's nothing you can do for me now."

ᏚᏓᏚᏗ

Six empty beer bottles on Sean's nightstand stood like backup singers behind an ashtray filled with a night's worth of cigarettes. Sitting on the bedcovers within the darkness of his room, he continued yo-yoing his thumb on the remote button until sunrise. He acknowledged arriving at the right answer, finding his sudden peace of mind as the determining confirmation to his decision, the one logical resolution to his private mayhem, yet he first wanted to go somewhere to bid a final goodbye.

Pulling a sweatshirt over the clothes he still wore from the night before, Sean drove the twenty-minute early morning drive to the beach in a silent, trance-like state, his dependable dark blue convertible providing a brisk top-down ride for his friend in need. Exiting the car, he removed his shoes and socks when he reached the sand and, looking toward the water, listened with a concentrated clarity to the incomparable rhythm of the waves.

Nerve endings tingling like never before, he inhaled the unique smell of the cool, salty air brushing his face as he headed toward the shoreline, drawing an enhanced contentment from each barefoot step.

How many inspirational moments had enveloped Sean Hightower through the years as he marveled at the oceanic expanse, transporting himself toward the vast entrance of that sweet, glorious horizon? How often had he welcomed the mystery of it all, unsolved yet beckoning, offering his soul a chance to soar and his heart a place to dream, validating his life as an occasion for endless possibilities?

But as Sean's feet touched the wet, foamy sand, he stared in dismay at an unforeseen and alarming reality. That inspirational expanse had transformed into an unkind, ominous stretch of water, and the glorious horizon now offered nothing more than a suffocating, impenetrable wall.

Recognition of finality encased his entire being, leaving him struggling against a claustrophobic barricade overwhelming his senses. Forced to turn away, he gazed at the granular clumps around his feet, reminded of the chorus from his song "Hourglass:"

> *You're in an hourglass, no place to retreat*
> *Quicksand everywhere beneath your feet.*

Reality shouted at him from within, puncturing his soul with the force of undeniable truth. Sean had nothing to believe in anymore.

Above all, not even himself.

Chapter 7

He showered in slow motion, an automaton responding to the wires and springs, a repetitive and robotic shell of himself preparing for the conclusion of his life. When he shaved, the razor became a paintbrush, stroking smooth, precise lines around his goatee, working the angles of his previously stubbled jaw and chin like a master sculptor. After slipping on his favorite pair of jeans and flannel shirt, he studied the final product in the mirror, satisfied in the knowledge he'd go out looking good for his last performance, unlike some of his rock 'n roll heroes whose physical demise contradicted their illustrious careers.

Sean stared at the lone visible cloud in an otherwise clear, sunny sky, a floating white island offering a soft seduction and escape from the harshness he occupied below. A flock of birds crossed his vantage point, flying away in perfect unison and sense of purpose as a passing breeze summoned him toward his own distant freedom. He stood there in respectful silence, tearfully relishing one last act of spiritual lovemaking to the uncomplicated gifts of life he'd known since childhood.

He stared at that same hardworking little girl next door, selling her lemonade again and making a sale to a passerby reaching into her purse for money. He couldn't help but notice the determined expression of this puny, odd-looking kid with the egg-shaped face as she pulled the spigot on the lemonade container—a child whose simple accomplishments of youth might be the highlights of her short life.

Sitting on the couch, Sean lit a cigarette and picked up the prescription bottle from the table. A sense of relief washed over him as he envisioned the white flag sanctuary of his barbiturates. Using light from the window to look through the plastic orange container, he shook the pills as a bartender mixes a drink, consoled by the rattling death knell of acceptance. For the third time, he reviewed the note written to his parents.

Dear Mom and Dad,

Let me start by saying I'm at peace with this decision. By the time you finish reading this letter, my ultimate wish is that you eventually find understanding and comfort in what I've done. But I know that you stand no chance of this unless I succeed in explaining my reasons. So here I go.

My life has reached a crossroads: I could move in the direction you want for me and take over the business one day, a disheartening thought I can't fathom, or continue chasing my elusive dream in music. The success I achieved as a man in his twenties led me to believe that the best was yet to come and that my destiny was set. I guess when you're that age and feeling cocky it's easy to think like that.

Twenty years later, the verdict is in: I'm a complete failure and an even bigger fool. My music mutated into a siren's song, enticing me further into the illusion of promising waters, hypnotizing me into thinking this fossil still had a future. But at least I had Merissa, right? She was my safe harbor, a sanctuary of cool, healing serenity within that sea of chaos and uncertainty. She inspired me and kept my dying dream alive, and I thought we'd be together forever. But I was just deceiving myself...again. She's gone, taken from me in the cruelest, most unimaginable of ways. I know I'll never recover from what happened to her. Never. Just as I might never recover from the probable cancer Dr. Lodin told me about yesterday.

When hope takes enough punches to the gut, reality finally conquers us and knocks us to the ground, mocking and tormenting us in its victory dance. And so I finally give up. There's nothing worth living for anymore. When you receive this letter, I will have left the world behind. No more pain. No more failure. No more disappointments. No more cancer. A success at last.

All my love and gratitude,
Sean

He took another swig of beer, satisfied at writing everything necessary and then adding a request for them to care for Hendrix.

He uncapped the bottle of yellow pills and poured them on the table, staring in calm contentment at his merciful assassins.

"That ought to do it," he whispered, recounting the last of the twenty-one.

Leaving the pills in ready position, he placed the letter inside the stamped envelope and rose to his feet, intent on completing his mission from couch to mailbox to couch again. A bittersweet smile ensued as he looked at his guitar case leaning against a corner near the front door. It housed a former friend, now untouched and unwanted. He slipped the letter in his back pocket and opened the case.

Stroking the honey-colored wood grain finish, he stared at the finger-worn frets stationed along the darkened neck, loyal soldiers in an open casket.

The sudden ring of the telephone jolted Sean's tranquility, making his heart race from the unexpected sound. Glancing at the caller screen, his eyebrows arched in surprise at the letters LAPD. His arm reached out after the second ring, but he pulled back, clenching his fist with indecision.

After another ring, and nearing the moment his voice mail recording answered, he lifted the receiver and spoke, his voice hesitant and soft.

"Mr. Hightower," the caller said, "it's Detective Ray Maldonado from the LAPD." After a slight pause, he added, "I'm the one who talked with you the night of Merissa Franklin's murder."

Sean remembered, despite the delirium of his shock and grief that had seemed to swallow him whole. "Yeah," he uttered.

"I need you to come down to the station so we can talk. And the sooner the better because it's very important."

Sean stared across the room at the pills scattered on the table, anxious to finalize his exclusively personal, and final, plan. It didn't matter what the detective had to say; he couldn't bring Merissa back. "I can't make it today," he answered.

"Tomorrow?" Maldonado asked.

Sean realized he'd better say what Maldonado wanted to hear to end the call as quickly as possible. "Sure," he said, "whatever."

"Great," he said. "If you want to meet before or after work, that's fine. What's a good time?"

"Um, I don't know. I'm not working right now, okay?"

"In that case can you be here tomorrow morning at ten?"

"Yeah…sure…okay," Sean mumbled. "Is that it?"

"Just one more thing," Maldonado said. "The reason for our meeting tomorrow? We think you can help us find Ms. Franklin's killer."

☙☙☙

Placing the phone on the table, Sean pulled the chord from the wall socket, determined to guarantee a quiet ending. Whatever inconsequential ideas Detective Maldonado wanted to discuss didn't matter anymore. The time for concerning himself with this life and all its horrors had expired.

He noticed one of Hendrix's toys on the floor and realized his spoiled little lapdog hadn't been in the house for a while. Intending on having his loving friend with him during his slide into unconsciousness, Sean had prepared two big bowls of kibble and two bigger ones with water to ensure his survival. Holding the envelope in his left hand, he opened the door to the backyard, expecting Hendrix to come running.

"Hendrix!" he shouted. Receiving no response, he whistled and then called out again. "Hendrix!

Sensing trouble, Sean hurried straight toward the side gate and discovered that his idiotic pool man had failed to close the latch again, allowing an opening for Hendrix to wander out as he'd done before. With visions of ramming the man's head through a wall, Sean rushed through the gate toward the front yard, looking straight ahead but seeing nothing. Veering right, he took several rapid steps before coming to an abrupt halt.

Sitting on her knees with a passive, unsure expression, the girl from the lemonade stand was rubbing her hand over Hendrix's belly as the dog lay sprawled at her feet. A dark-haired woman in a navy blue pants suit crouched beside her, observing and smiling. They both looked up when Sean approached.

"Is this your dog?" the woman asked.

Sean struggled to answer, nodding at first.

"Yeah," he replied. "Sorry if he's bothering you."

"I was a little concerned when he came running toward us," she said, "but as you can see, everything's fine."

The girl gasped and lurched back a bit when her hand movement triggered a piston-like reaction from the black, furry little leg of Hendrix.

The woman giggled and patted the girl on the leg. "It's okay, honey," she told her, "dogs do that sometimes when you scratch their tummy."

"What's his name?" the girl asked, tilting her head up again.

Sean's first opportunity to observe the girl up close confirmed the illness he'd suspected before. He noticed how her cookie-round head appeared too large for her frail upper frame and that the fuzz of hair under her purple and gold Lakers cap offered no clue as to whether the strands were coming or going. The thin straps of her oversized Lakers jersey accentuated the bony shoulders, almost skeletal in their lack of a natural round form. Her right eyelid held itself at a partially closed three-quarter position, creating an unhealthy peek-a-boo effect in combination with the normal-sized left one. She continued looking at him, tightening her mouth and revealing two prominent dimples on her puffy, pale cheeks.

Sean cleared his throat. "Hendrix," he answered.

Offering him no more than a blank expression, she returned her attention to the dog, now lying on his stomach as the woman scratched his head.

"Hi, Hendrix," the girl murmured.

"I guess you already know we're your new neighbors," the woman said, rising to her feet and extending her hand. "My name's Stephanie Michaels, and this is my daughter, Kayleigh."

"Hello," he said, hesitating before offering his hand.

"You're Sean Hightower, right?" Stephanie asked.

"Yeah."

"When our real estate agent asked me if I'd heard of you, I told her 'Looking Glass' was a favorite song of mine back in college. I still turn it up whenever I hear it on the radio. "'Confusion,'" she started to sing, "'don't know right from wrong. Confusion, don't know weak from strong. Am I lost for good or will this feeling pass? It's like I'm stuck inside the looking glass.'"

"Sorry, Mrs. Party Food," Kayleigh said, displaying her first sign of emotion by looking pained, "but you don't sing too good."

Stephanie laughed. "Sorry about that, Sean."

"Mrs. Party Food?" he asked.

Stephanie rolled her eyes and grinned. "I run a catering business," she said. "That's a name Kayleigh's given me. She got the idea from Mr. Clean and Mr. Coffee. My husband is Mr. Flowers because he owns a couple of landscape nurseries, one in Montebello and another in Tustin."

"My half brother, Anthony, is Mr. Marine," Kayleigh explained. "He used to be Mr. Computer, 'cause he's really smart with that stuff. But now he's Mr. Marine."

Stephanie offered a tight smile that seemed shaped in sadness. "Anthony's my oldest son," she explained, "from a previous marriage. He was a tough kid who gave me a lot trouble, but when Kayleigh was born it was love at first sight. He was like a third parent. And when she got sick…" Clearing her throat, her eyes narrowed as she bit her lip, pausing for a moment before continuing. "When she got sick, the fevers, the pain, the bleeding, the fatigue, his life really turned around after that."

"Is he over in the Middle East?"

"No," she said, shaking her head, "he's stationed in Twentynine Palms for now. But it's impossible not to worry about it. You never know, right?"

Sean kept his passionate opposition to the Iraq war to himself.

"I miss him, Mama," Kayleigh said, her voice almost too low to be heard.

"I know you do, honey," she said, reaching out to stroke her daughter's arm. "We all miss him." Brushing a strand of hair back from her forehead, Stephanie looked back at Sean. "Anthony wants to become a software developer. The Marine Corps offers great job opportunities in computer science, and this was his chance to get a degree."

Kayleigh, her increasing comfort level now apparent, approached Sean almost shoetop to shoetop. "Anthony taught me how to use the Internet," she said. "I can find things all by myself now."

Sean looked down at the pale, zero-shaped face, noticing the skin rash around her right cheekbone and upper forehead for the first time.

"That's great," he said, offering a quick nod of his head.

"Thanks," she replied. "My other brother's name is Randy," she told him. "He likes to ride his skateboard all the time. Do you know what I call him?"

"Mr. Skateboard?" Sean asked.

Kayleigh's mouth opened in obvious surprise. "Yeah!"

"Mom!" a boy's voice yelled from the window. "Dr. Maginnis is on the phone."

The woman looked back at Kayleigh before returning her attention to the boy at the window. "Randy," she called back, "come out here and stay with your sister."

"But I'm busy with something!" he cried out.

"Randy!" Stephanie shouted. "Randy!" Getting no response, her shoulders sagged for a moment before she spun around and looked at Sean. "I'm going to kill that kid, Sean," she said, "but it's Kayleigh's doctor, and I've been waiting to hear about some test results. Would it be all right if you stayed with her for a few minutes? I'll stand by the window to make sure everything's okay."

The request caught him off guard.

"Wanna buy some lemonade?" Kayleigh asked.

Sean hesitated, his jaw tightening as his mind raced in confusion, transported from a decisive clarity of purpose just a few minutes before to a forced, unintended deviation. The woman needed to take the doctor's call, and her stupid son refused to come outside. What else could he do?

Chapter 8

Lifting Hendrix, he clutched the dog to his chest before extending his free hand to help Kayleigh to her feet.

Her initial unsteady gait reminded him of those videos he'd seen of foals when they first stand. Plopping herself in the chair, she took a Styrofoam cup from the stack.

"I've seen you a few times out here," he said.

"Uh-huh," she replied, releasing lemonade from the spigot with the studied concentration of a lab technician.

"Are you saving your money for something?"

"Uh-huh," she repeated. "The money's not for me, though. Did you see the big sign my daddy taped on the front of the table?"

Sean took a few steps forward to look.

"Why does it say 'Alex's Lemonade Stand' instead of 'Kayleigh's Lemonade Stand'?"

Kayleigh's mouth opened, and for a moment Sean thought she might drop the cup. "You don't know about Alex's Lemonade Stand?"

"Never heard of it," he said, taking the drink from her hand.

"It raises money for doctors so they can cure cancer," she explained. "To help kids like me."

Sean nodded. "And a guy named Alex started it?"

"Alex wasn't a guy, silly," she replied, rolling her eyes at Sean's question. "It's named after a girl named Alexandra Scott. She sold lemonade in front of her house and got real famous. Now Alex's Lemonade Stands are all over the world."

"The world?" Sean repeated, surprised at the fact. "She must be very proud of herself."

"I guess she was," Kayleigh answered, her voice subdued and distant. "But she died when she was eight years old." Kayleigh looked down at the ground for a moment before raising her head to look at Sean. "She had cancer, too."

Sean studied Kayleigh's expression, which, to him, seemed like a mix of sadness and defiance.

"How old are you?" he asked.

"Ten," she answered.

"When's your birthday?"

Kayleigh held her gaze on Sean, a grin spreading across her face. "Guess," she told him.

Sean shrugged. "I don't know."

"November fifteenth!"

Grasping his cup, he held it under his chin, placing the rim against his skin.

"Near Thanksgiving, huh? That's a nice time for a birthday."

"You know what I want?" she asked.

He shook his head. "I have no idea."

"Guess."

"A pony?"

Sean felt a sense of amusement when Kayleigh's mouth opened wide in a silent, shocked reaction.

"No!" she exclaimed, giggling. "Not a pony. A cell phone, silly!"

His eyebrows arched in surprise. "A cell phone?" he repeated. "Do you really think a ten-year-old girl needs one?"

"Mr. Marine says if I get one we can send messages to each other," she explained. Pursing her lips, her thin, watery milk skin scrunched together in tight lines. "But my mommy and daddy told me I'm not ready yet."

Sean took several sips and found the lemonade too sugary and not as cold as it should be. "Tastes great," he told her.

Kayleigh smiled at Sean and extended her hand, palm side up.

"That will be fifty cents, please."

"Sorry, my money's in the house. I'll give it to you later, okay?"

"Promise?"

"Promise," he replied, his reflexive answer holding no guarantees.

Sean kneeled on the grass near Kayleigh's chair and released Hendrix. For no apparent reason, the dog started running in circles, first in one direction then the other.

Kayleigh laughed. "He's funny!" she said.

"So," he said, pointing to her jersey and cap, "you're a Lakers fan, huh?"

"The Lakers are my favorite team in the whole wide world," she replied.

"Do you have a favorite player?"

"Oh yeah," she answered, nodding her head. "It's Coby for sure."

Sean nodded back. "I guess he's most people's favorite."

Kayleigh smiled. "I bet you think I meant Kobe Bryant."

"Well...yeah," Sean said. "Of course."

"But I'm not talking about Kobe Bryant," she said. "My favorite Laker is Coby *Karl!*"

Sean's eyebrows raised in surprise at the mention of a forgettable guy who hardly played and didn't even suit up for a lot of the games. Coby Karl had been on the team for one year, but he rarely ever played.

"Why him?"

"He had cancer, too," she said. "And now he's on the Lakers. My daddy says if he can do it, so can I."

Sean stared at this sick, fragile child, wondering if she'd even see another year.

"Your dad's right, because what Coby's doing is sending a message."

Her eyes blinked several times as her expression turned blank.

"A text message?" she asked. "To who?"

Sean held up a hand. "No...that's not what I meant. *Sending a message* is an expression. In Coby's case, the message he's sending is that he's showing you and everyone else with cancer that things can turn out okay, so don't give up."

For a fleeting moment, Sean considered the echo of his comment as it pertained to himself.

Kayleigh's mouth graduated into a tiny smile. "I like that expression," she said. "Do you know that on March seventh Coby had his best game of the year? He made two-for-four shooting, and two-for-two from the free throw line. That means he scored six whole points!"

"You remember all that, huh?"

"Yep," she said, nodding her head in prideful acknowledgment. "My mommy says I remember things better than anyone she knows." She cocked her head and leaned toward Sean. "Well, don't you want to know the score of the game?"

"I'm just waiting for you to tell me."

"One-hundred-nineteen to eighty-two!"

Kayleigh turned around so he could see the back of her jersey.

"See my number?" she asked. "It's fourteen. That's because my daddy calls me 'The Fourteenth Laker.' You know why?"

Sean shook his head.

"Because only twelve players put on their uniforms for the games and most times Coby is the thirteenth. That's why he's in his regular clothes a lot. My daddy says after Coby, I'm next."

"Look out, Kobe Bryant," Sean said, winking. "Here comes the fourteenth Laker, Kayleigh Michaels!"

Kayleigh's one healthy eye opened wide and the other one fluttered slightly. "I like that!" she said, giggling.

They both watched in silence as Hendrix rolled around on the grass.

"Are you really a rock 'n roll star?" she asked.

Somehow this question didn't trouble him, coming from her. "For a little while," he told her. "When your mom was in college, I guess."

"Wow!" she said, looking amazed. "That was like, forever ago!"

Sean closed his eyes and placed a hand over his face, finding her comment humorous.

"Do you listen to music?" he asked.

"Uh-huh," she answered. "How come you're not a rock star anymore?"

"I don't know," he said, shrugging. "I'd still like to be."

"That would be great," she exclaimed. "Then I could tell everyone I live next door to you!"

"What kind of music do you like?"

"I love Hannah Montana," she answered. "And The Cheetah Girls, too!"

"And your mom and dad listen to the forever-ago music, right?"

Kayleigh smiled and nodded her head.

"Do you like anything they listen to?"

Kayleigh squinted and looked up at the sky before answering. "I like the Beatles," she said. "Especially that song, 'Yellow Submarine.'"

"Everybody likes the Beatles," he told her. "Kids know who they are because grown-ups like your parents still listen to them. And most of their songs are over forty years old."

"Forty..." she mouthed, soundless and wide-eyed. "Wow! That's really old!" Her wispy, nearly colorless eyebrows furrowed as she looked at Sean. "I wonder if my mommy and daddy listen to new music. Maybe they'd like that, too."

Sean looked at her in surprise. "I like the way you think, Kayleigh, but most adults don't seem to care about new music."

"Why not?"

"Why not?" he repeated. Sean pondered the question for a few moments. "Let's say you and I each coach a basketball team, okay?"

"You mean, like Phil Jackson?"

"Yeah, like Phil Jackson," he replied. "But instead of regular names on the back of the jerseys, like Bryant, or Karl, there'd be the name of a rock 'n roll band instead. Okay?"

"Uh-huh."

"Now let's say you coach the team with the jerseys that have music names from today and I coach the team with the jerseys that have music names from forever ago."

"Like the Beatles?"

"Like the Beatles," he answered. "I guarantee you, if the players on my team played basketball as good as those bands play rock 'n roll, adults like your parents would think my team was better than yours without even watching them play the game. You know why?"

Kayleigh's head shook back and forth.

"Because the music on the back of my jerseys is all they listen to. And the problem with that is, if they don't listen to any of the music on the backs of *your* jerseys, how will they know if your team is any good or not?"

Sean studied Kayleigh's confused expression, realizing his analogy had missed its mark by the width of a galaxy. *What the hell do I know about talking to a kid anyway?*

"I bet my team can beat yours," she told him, scrunching her nose into a mass of wrinkled flesh and causing her right eyelid to shut like a fallen curtain.

He looked back toward the house, but Stephanie remained inside.

Kayleigh grabbed a paper napkin and wiped the top of the spigot. "Tell me all the names on your jerseys," she said.

Turning back in her direction, he continued the conversation. "Oh, there'd be lots of names on my team, but I'd take the Beatles first. Even though most of their music was from the 1960s, when I was just a little older than you are now, they're still my all-time favorite rock 'n roll band." Sean smiled, thinking back to those days. "The sixties was the music I first fell in love with. If I picked a basketball team from the bands back then, my starting five could all be from England: The Beatles, The Rolling Stones, The Who, The Kinks, and Led Zeppelin."

"Those are really funny names," she said. "Is that because they're all from England?"

"No, that's not the reason," he answered. "I guess they wanted names people would remember. But I could also have a starting five from America that would be really, really good: Hendrix is named after a great guitarist named Jimi Hendrix, and his band was called The Jimi Hendrix Experience. They'd be on my team for sure. Then there's The Doors, Creedence Clearwater Revival, The Beach Boys, and...maybe The Allman Brothers Band. Their first album came out in 1969 like Led Zeppelin, so they just made the sixties team, too."

Kayleigh stood motionless, staring at Sean with a dazed expression. "That's a lot of people on your team!"

"And that's not all," he told her. "Just like the Lakers, I need good players off the bench, right? There'd be Jethro Tull, Cream, Santana, The Byrds, Deep Purple, Jefferson Airplane, Traffic, The Moody Blues, The Animals, Pink Floyd, the brilliant but short-lived Buffalo Springfield..."

Kayleigh's eyes widened.

"They have funny names, too."

"Maybe so, but the only thing that really matters is their great music." Sean looked away for a moment before bouncing his hand off his forehead and turning back to look at her. "Wow, I almost forgot about The Grateful Dead! You can't leave *them* off the team."

"The Grateful Dead?"

"Oh yeah," he said. "Jerry Garcia, Bob Weir, Mickey Hart...those guys were great."

"I don't understand," she said. "Why would somebody be grateful if they're dead?"

Sean's thoughts ground to a halt as he stared back at Kayleigh's unhealthy, questioning face.

"Um...well, yeah, you're right, Kayleigh. It's just a silly name, that's all."

"Well, I don't like..."

"Want to hear some more names?"

"Yeah, okay," she replied, her enthusiasm lessened.

"All right," he said, "let's move into the seventies. I could have a starting five of Tom Petty and the Heartbreakers, Bruce Springsteen and the E Street Band, The Eagles, Queen, and The Clash. Bob Seger and The Silver Bullet Band's another one. Seger started in the sixties with The Bob Seger System, but when he formed the Silver Bullet band they really took off. Same thing with Fleetwood Mac. There's also other great bands like Van Halen, Elvis Costello and the Attractions, Talking Heads, Supertramp, Aerosmith...what's the matter?"

Kayleigh looked at him with a puzzled expression, her hands clasping her hips.

"You have so many players," she said. "How are they all gonna play?"

He looked at her and opened his hands palm side up.

"I guess we need more basketball courts," he answered. "Hey, I haven't even talked about the eighties and nineties yet. A starting five from the eighties could be The Pretenders, REM, Red Hot Chili Peppers..."

"Red Hot *Chili Peppers*?" she blurted out, her one-and-three-quarter gaze widening again. "That's really their name?"

"Are you ready for this, Kayleigh? One of the band members is named Flea."

Kayleigh's jaw dropped. "*Flea*?" she repeated. "Like on a dog?"

"Do you know who could also be in that top five?" he asked.

"Who?"

"The Sean Hightower Band!"

Kayleigh smiled and clapped. "Hooray for Sean!"

"Gimme a high five!" he shouted, holding up his hand to shoulder level.

Kayleigh's right eye disappeared under creased flesh as her smile extended to its farthest points. Raising her arm and rearing it back like a pitcher ready to throw a fast one, her noticeable lack of power produced nothing more than a soft thud.

Sean spotted Stephanie walking toward them, this time with sunglasses on.

"Thank you, Sean," Stephanie said, her voice noticeably subdued. "I hope I wasn't gone too long."

"Gee, Mama," Kayleigh said, "I never met *anybody* who knows more about music than Sean. Do you know how to play 'Yellow Submarine'?"

"Sure do," he answered.

"Can you play it for me?"

"*Kayleigh*," Stephanie said, showing displeasure. "I'm sorry, Sean. I didn't see that one coming."

"But it's my favorite Beatles' song, Mama," she explained, her voice a slight whine. "And Sean was a rock 'n roll star!'

"We'll talk about it later," Stephanie exclaimed, her mouth tightening.

Kayleigh's shoulders sagged. "Okay," she said, her tone coated in dejection.

"It was nice to finally meet you, Sean," Stephanie said, extending her hand. "And thanks again for staying with Kayleigh."

"Yeah, thanks, Mr. Music."

"*Mr. Music*?" he replied.

"Well, well," Stephanie said, a small smile appearing on her face. "Looks like you're the newest member of the Nickname Club, Sean."

"Is that so?" he said, smirking. "I approve."

Changing the subject as if pushing the button on a TV remote, Kayleigh asked, "Do you want to see my travel pictures, Mr. Music? I've got really, really neat ones from all over the world."

Sean looked at Stephanie, perplexed. "Travel pictures?"

"Photos and cutouts of all the places Kayleigh wants to see one day," she explained.

He noticed the slight cracking sound in her voice.

"I put up a picture of the Eiffel Tower this morning," Kayleigh said.

Sean called Hendrix over from a nearby resting spot on the lawn.

"I'm sorry, but I can't right now," he answered. "Another time, okay?"

⌘

He returned home. Closing the door with a gentle hesitancy, he studied his surroundings, steeped in dark uncertainty, as if revisiting a hometown burdened with anguished memories. He stared across the room at the scattered remnants of his deadly plans and trudged the short, dizzying path to the table. He stood there pensive and dreamlike, gazing beyond those twenty-one hit men into the depths of his soul. Moments later, or perhaps minutes, he returned the pills to their bottle and grasped the envelope from his pocket. The same hands that felt stable and firm in suicidal preparation now shook as he read his parents' names and address through the blurred and burning vision of his tears.

With a sudden violent motion, he ripped the envelope in half, and then again into quarters. His shredded message no longer seemed inviting or inevitable, and his thoughts resided neither on the blackness of the recent past nor the bleakness of the immediate future.

He nodded, recalling a song he'd written called, "Red Life, Green Life," after the breakup of his band when his life seemed at a crossroads.

I stop, I go, I stop, I go
Don't know why or what roads I'll pass
Fast and slow, fast and slow
Living in moments never meant to last

Here and now, Sean's one craving centered on his desire to feel and taste a cigarette, inhaling each savory puff deep into his lungs as the soothing sensation of the tobacco percolated and circulated through his membranes in a slow, blissful manner before culminating in a smoky release of wispy, hypnotizing reminders of reminiscences and farewells.

After all, having decided to quit smoking, his final cigarette may as well be a memorable one.

Chapter 9

Lying in bed with his eyes still shut, Sean listened to the familiar morning sound of his automatic sprinklers. His thoughts latched on to the previous day's events like barnacles to a ship, replaying the images of what had transpired. Writing the letter to his parents, counting out the twenty-one sleeping pills, the near...*suicide*.

An icy blade of recollection jabbed the pit of his stomach as he contemplated how convincing the decision seemed, the nearness of its consummation. He dry-scrubbed his face with both hands, leaving his eyes open to stare at the white blankness above him. Sean sensed a shadowy component remaining from yesterday he may have forgotten but found difficulty breaking down the details. After all, when a person's mind is focused on taking his life, what else matters? Still, he reviewed everything again.

I made a pot of coffee and wrote my note. I showered, shaved, and put on the clothes I wanted to be photographed in. I read the note again, made some changes, and then got the pills from the medicine cabinet. I grabbed a beer from the fridge and looked at the note again before putting it in the envelope. I got up from the couch, looked at my guitar in the case, and—

Sean catapulted from his flat position to a ninety-degree angle. "Shit!" he blurted. "Detective Maldonado!"

He looked at his clock: eight-seventeen. Remaining in the same sitting position, he reflected on what Maldonado had told him: "We think you can help us find Ms. Franklin's killer." The thought unnerved him. *What the hell could I ever do?*

Walking into the station a few minutes past ten, Sean asked for Maldonado and waited at the front desk. His blank-slate state of mind from the night of the murder had prevented him from remembering any specifics of the detective's appearance, so when a square-jawed Latino with a thick salt and pepper colored mustache approached him with an extended hand, engulfing Sean's like a human talon, it seemed more like an introduction.

Perhaps two or three inches smaller than Sean, the man possessed wide shoulders and a thick neck. His face bore a vertical scar on the left side of his forehead, running in a downward curve like the map of a river. Extending from his silvery-gray hairline to the charcoal-smeared bush of an eyebrow, additional smaller scars dotted the landscape.

His intense gaze seemed heightened by the bowling ball blackness of his eyes, which, in turn, seemed held aloft by the fleshy pouches underneath. And in the center of it all, Maldonado's wide, fleshy nose tailed slightly to the right, like a plane starting to spin out of control, a possible indication of a previous break. One immediate fact struck Sean—the face he gazed upon defined experience.

Maldonado led the way down a corridor. "I've been wondering how you are," he said, his baritone voice sounding as if he should be speaking from a stage rather than a police station. "Are you talking with a medical professional as I suggested? Seeking any help?"

"No," Sean answered, unaware of any recommendation. "But I took a leave of absence from work. That's helped a little."

"What have you been doing with your time?"

"Nothing, really," he said. "Just staying at home mostly."

"That doesn't sound too healthy if you ask me," Maldonado said. "Shutting yourself off from the world like that."

"With all due respect, Detective, I didn't ask you or anyone else what's best for me. Shutting myself off from the world is exactly what I want right now."

Maldonado turned on the lights to what appeared to be a conference room, exposing a rectangular dark wooden table surrounded by three black vinyl chairs on each side and one at the far end. "Take a seat, Sean," he said. "There's a coffee machine around the corner. Tell me how you like yours, and I'll go get us some." A few minutes later, he returned with a cup in each hand and a manila envelope tucked under his arm. He slid his chair closer to Sean and placed the envelope on the table. Sipping from the cup before placing it on the table, he nibbled on his lip and squinted, staring at Sean as if looking through him. "I'm glad you're here," he said, "but this isn't something I've been looking forward to." Wiping his lip with the back of his hand he continued. "Not only do I need you to revisit the night of your girlfriend's murder, I'm also going to discuss a couple of other things that may upset you."

Sean fingered the rim of his cup, battling the urge to vent and wail again. "I don't know how much more upset I can possibly get," he said, surprising himself with the calmness of his reply. "I sure as hell can't bring Merissa back, can I? Or go back in time to prevent it from happening. The only thing I *can* do is wait for the day that fucking monster gets what's coming to him." This time Sean's eyes tightened to a squint as he stared back at Maldonado. "And if I can help make that happen sooner than later," he told him, "then anything goes."

Maldonado leaned forward in his chair as a small smile appeared on his face. He gulped some coffee and pointed toward the envelope.

"Before I show you what's in here," he said, "I'm going to tell you something about Ms. Franklin's murderer that we've known from the beginning." Rolling his tongue around the inside of his mouth, he looked away for a moment before returning his attention to Sean. "Do you recall the writing on the two pieces of paper above the headboard?"

Sean had tried his best to tear the grotesque image of Merissa's blood-soaked face from his mind. He rubbed his hand across his eyes as if to erase the visual and focused on the answer to the question. Yes, he remembered what was there. "One paper had 'hello' written on it," he answered. "The other one, 'goodbye.'"

"You're a rock 'n roll guy," Maldonado said. "Do those two words sound familiar?"

"Only if you're talking about the Beatles' song," he answered.

Maldonado nodded. "That's exactly what I'm talking about, Sean. The same man who raped and murdered Ms. Franklin has done this identical thing seven other times, dating back six years. He's a serial killer the press has dubbed, 'The Beatles' Song Murderer.' You ever heard of him?"

Sean stared dumbfounded and silent for several moments before shaking his head.

"He's left pieces of paper with the name of a different Beatles' song every time. The first killing we know of occurred in Bakersfield, the second about thirty miles north in a town called Delano, and the last six in different parts of northern and western LA County."

Sean found great difficulty registering this information, his mind's defense system erecting an impenetrable wall resistant to the bacterial blather of outlandish information. The news of a serial killer raping and killing the woman he loved left him numb. These kinds of things happened to other people, not to Merissa. "The Beatles' Song Murderer," he muttered under his breath. "I can't believe it."

"You told us that you let yourself in with your key that night, is that correct?"

"Yes."

"You also told us that you didn't open the sliding door to her balcony."

Sean nodded as he stared at the side of his white Styrofoam cup. "That's right."

Maldonado tilted back in his chair and folded his hands. "Ms. Franklin's apartment only had two ways of getting inside. For someone to have come in through the balcony they'd have to climb twenty feet above the garage. The risk of being spotted would have been pretty high. Even so, we searched the area. No crushed shrubbery, no scuff marks on the wall, no footprints on the ground. Nothing. The fact that Ms. Franklin's front door was locked and her house key was missing from her key chain leads us to believe that the killer left the balcony door open as a decoy, and that he not only exited through the front door, he *entered* through the front door as well."

"Entered?" Sean said. "You mean the killer stole her house key and got in that way?"

"That's a possibility," Maldonado replied. "Or perhaps he somehow obtained a copy of her house key and let himself in."

Sean pursed his lips, adamant in his belief that Merissa's street smarts invalidated that possibility.

"I don't believe she'd let that happen," he told him. "Merissa lived on her own her entire adult life and didn't make those kinds of mistakes."

Maldonado raised his cat-fur eyebrows, the points triangulating like two ascending birds on a collision course. "Okay, fine," he said. "Let's say you're right. That leaves only one other possibility I can think of, and it's the reason I called you here."

Sean remained silent, confused and unable to think of any other logical answers. Maldonado manipulated the envelope on the table, feeling the contents inside. He sat up in his chair again, downed a large swallow of his coffee, and hurriedly rubbed his hands across his mouth.

Looking at Sean, he held his gaze for several seconds before speaking.

"I think Ms. Franklin let the killer in because she *knew* him."

The idea took a while to sink in, working its way through the speculation of likelihood into a dark hole of disbelief.

"What are you getting at?" Sean asked. "That Merissa might have been friendly with this sick asshole?"

Maldonado moved his thumbnail along the side of his cup before answering. "Not just her, Sean," he replied. "You, too."

Sean leaned back in the chair and pondered the detective's comment. "That's *crazy*," he said, shaking his head. "Maybe there's someone out there I don't know about, but she and I were together long enough that I know every one of her friends. And believe me, none of them are who you're looking for."

"All right," Maldonado said, reaching for the envelope, "but let's go through these anyway, okay?"

Sean watched in curiosity as he removed what appeared to be a group of photographs. To his surprise, the picture on top showed an employee from the dealership standing outside the building where Merissa's service had been held.

"Are all of those going to be pictures from the funeral?" he asked.

"I had two men stationed with telephotos." He leaned over toward Sean. "I'm sorry," he told him, his voice soft, yet firm. "I know it's not respectful, but it's something we had to do."

Sean looked at Maldonado for a few moments before glancing down at the photograph. "Why?" he asked. "What could you possibly want with pictures of people from the service? You don't really think that..."

"What I think is what I said before," Maldonado said. "There's a very good possibility that Ms. Franklin knew the killer well enough to let him in willingly."

"You didn't waste any time with your suspicions, did you?" Sean replied, disgusted at the thought.

"Suspicion is part of my job," Maldonado said. "And it may interest you to know that in the other seven cases I mentioned, there weren't any signs of forced entry either."

Sean looked away and shook his head in denial. The idea of somebody making a copy of Merissa's key started to make more sense. "Everyone who came to Merissa's funeral was there for the right reasons," he said. "I won't believe there's any more to it than that."

Maldonado crossed his arms and pressed his weight against them near the edge of the table. A degree of irritation showed in his expression. "My job is catching scum like this and bringing them to justice," he told him, his voice rising, "so I don't care how off-track you think I am. Serial killers don't have horns or fangs, Sean. They're able to avoid detection because they look and act like regular members of society. They talk sports with the bartender, ask their produce guy which watermelon is ripe, and talk shit about the boss with their co-workers." Maldonado seized the photos and shook them at Sean. "Are you going to tell me about these guys or not?"

Sean stared at Maldonado then at the envelope in his hand. One certainty remained clear—they both shared the same goal of finding Merissa's murderer. He was in over his head here. What did he know about investigative work? "Okay," he replied, angling his chair. "Let's look at them."

Maldonado placed the first photo in front of Sean.

"That's our head mechanic, Carlos Carrillo. He and Merissa were friendly. Carlos used to service her car after hours in exchange for her famous homemade brownies."

"Do you know if he ever went to her place for any reason?"

Sean pondered the question and nodded. "Actually, yeah," he said, "one time I remember. Carlos's brother runs a mobile car washing service on weekends. He did Merissa's car a few times, but a couple of months ago Carlos showed up instead because his brother was sick."

Maldonado nodded slightly, turned Carlos's photo over, marked a check in the center with the name, and wrote the word *brother*, followed by a question mark.

"I recognize those guys from our bowling nights," Sean said, looking at the next picture of two men standing together. "Merissa loved to bowl and was one of the organizers of Wednesday matches every other week with the workers from the Chevy dealership across the street, so I guess they work there. But that's all I know. She never mentioned anything about them before."

Maldonado marked a straight line on the back and put the picture aside.

"That's Elliot Hayden and his partner," Sean said, looking at the third picture. "He runs a guidance center that's part family counseling, part school for at-risk youth. Merissa did volunteer work for him. She'd invite the staff over for pizza and meetings sometimes, so it's probable Elliot was there."

"You never saw him come over?"

"She'd have them at night when I was performing somewhere and wouldn't be home until late, so I wouldn't know for sure. But like I said, it's likely he was there."

"When you describe this other man as his partner, are you talking business or love life?"

"Merissa told me that Elliot's gay, so I'm assuming the guy's his partner. I remember him from a couple of fund-raisers I performed at. They arrived together, sat together, walked around together, et cetera, et cetera."

"Do you know anything about him?"

"No, nothing," Sean answered. "I was introduced to him after the service, but I don't even remember his name."

"You said you're *assuming* they're partners, so you don't know for sure?"

Sean stared at the photo again, observing the shoulder-to-shoulder togetherness of the two men and the concerned expression on the partner's face as he looked at Elliot, dabbing his eye with a handkerchief. Crossing his arms, he squirmed and shook his head. "It's hard enough getting me to believe that anyone at Merissa's service, people we know, could have done this," Sean said. Turning away to cough several times, he continued. "Now you're asking me to think that a couple of gay guys are suspects? Can I see the next one, please?"

Writing the word *gay* on the back of the picture, Maldonado included a question mark before moving on to the fourth photo—a gray-haired man in a dark suit, walking away from the others with his arm around a woman.

"That's Tom Claiborne, our general manager," Sean said, "with his wife, Arleen."

"What kind of relationship did he have with Ms. Franklin?"

"Not much to speak of. Tom's a nice enough guy, but he's all business when it comes to his employees. He was friendly with Merissa, but never more than that."

"Never went to her place?"

"Not that I know. If he had, I'm sure Merissa would have mentioned it to me."

"She worked there before you, so it's possible, right?"

Sean shrugged his shoulders and nodded. "I suppose, but I don't see any reason for it."

Maldonado marked the back of the photo with a check before moving on to the next picture.

Three men and two women stood in a group.

"They're all from Merissa's department at work," Sean explained. "I only know one of the men's full name—Hank Sendowski. He's the one on the right. Travis is standing between the two women, and Arnie's on the left. They were all friendly with her but only in a co-worker kind of way. I doubt any of them were ever at Merissa's place."

"But you're not sure?"

"No, I'm not sure."

Maldonado's next photo showed his friend, Adam, standing with his wife, Eleanor, holding what appeared to be a Bible cradled in her arms. Eleanor's reputation as a Jesus-spouting human megaphone made her someone to avoid at every holiday party.

"That's Adam McBride," Sean said. "He's one of our car salesmen. We all call him Saint Adam because he's a religiously conservative, play-by-the-rules type. Definitely too prim and proper for my taste, but a good guy. Merissa always called him 'sweetie,' which he seemed to like. I know he's one of the guys Merissa invited for her poker nights, so I guess you can go ahead and put another check on the back."

Maldonado looked at Sean with a smirk. "I see you're catching on," he said, checking off the photo before moving on to the next one. Two men stood together, one with his arm around the other in an apparent attempt at comfort. Sean felt particularly saddened by the captured scene.

"The man who's crying was Merissa's hairdresser, Dino. I go to him, too. He's on a leave of absence right now because of what happened." Sean paused, swallowed hard, and waited to regain his composure. "Dino really loved Merissa. He must have told me a hundred times how lucky I was to have her." Grasping his cup, Sean took a few moments to stare at the black liquid before taking a sip. Directing his gaze upward, he kept the coffee in his mouth for several moments before drawing a deep breath and continuing. "The other man is Dino's partner...his *boyfriend*, Leander. They also played poker at Merissa's, but just like Elliot and his partner, these two don't count."

"Let me be the judge of that, okay?" Maldonado replied, keeping the photo front and center. "Do you know if Dino or Leander ever went to Ms. Franklin's place?"

"I have no idea. But one thing I'm sure of is that if you ever met Dino, you'd cross him off your suspect list real fast. Let's just leave it at that."

Turning the picture over, Maldonado wrote the word *gay* before adding it with the other suspects already discussed. "I'm not ruling anybody out right now," he told him.

Sean brought the cup within several inches of his face and stared ahead, rubbing his forehead with his fingertips. His brain felt like the cerebral equivalent of a punctured tire, flattened and impossible to revive.

Maldonado grasped the last two unseen photos simultaneously, raising them to eye level. "Just some group photos taken when the service ended," he said. "It's an opportune time to take these shots, when people converse afterward. There's one more new face, the guy with his arm around the tall redhead. Do you know him?"

"That's Roger Peterson," he told him, "another one of our salesman. He and Merissa were real friendly with each other from the time I first met them. I actually thought they had a thing going, even though Roger was married." Sean stared in compassion at Anita Peterson, a woman he'd known from his schooldays, when she hung out with his sister, Rebecca. Anita was always funny and cool, but she'd landed in an unhappy marriage. "Roger's one of the guys who bowls with us, so there's another one for you."

"Were you ever at Ms. Franklin's home during the card games?" Maldonado asked.

"Like those meetings for the guidance center where she volunteered, Merissa used to invite people over to play poker when she knew I'd be home late from a gig," he explained. "By the time I'd come back, they were pretty much done."

Maldonado reached over and set the pictures on top of the others. "That's it for the men at the service," he said. "Can you recall any other person we may have missed? Maybe some others from those poker games?"

Sean mulled the question, plopping his elbows on the table, his chin on top of clenched fists. He recalled just a few card games played in the time they dated, so remembering men other than Adam, Roger, Dino, and Leander didn't seem a difficult task.

"No, I don't believe so," Sean replied. "Merissa also invited some of her girlfriends, but they always came alone." Sean glanced at the top photo on the pile, a group shot of Elliot and his partner standing with Roger and Anita. As his eyes targeted Roger, he slowly shook his head.

"Why the face?" Maldonado asked, looking at the photo.

"Roger and his wife were separated for a while but they're back together again," he told him. "Let's just say it's more than his eyes that wander. I think he came to those card games more intent on getting laid than playing poker." Sean shook his head again, exhaling for an extended period as if blowing out smoke. "But that's irrelevant to what we're talking about here."

"Maybe," Maldonado said. "Was everyone still there when you got back?"

"Depends how late it was," Sean replied, eyeing the detective. "Why?"

"Simple reasoning," Maldonado said "If you're one of the last to leave, that means you're in no rush to go. And if you're a man, that probably means good looking women, plentiful liquor, and/or tasty food. Merissa may have been your girlfriend, but that kind of thing wouldn't stop a lot of guys from planning for the future in case things headed south."

Sean nodded, his eyes glazed over from the overwhelming possibilities. And two other photos still remained on the table.

"You got some others there?" he asked.

Maldonado reached over and grabbed them in one hand, spread like playing cards. One of the photos showed Elliot, his partner, Roger, Anita, and two women Sean didn't recognize in a semicircle around Dino and Leander, with one of the women's hands placed behind Dino's neck. The other one included Roger and Anita again, his arm draped around her shoulder, standing and apparently conversing with Adam, Eleanor, Hank, and Carlos.

"These are a couple of group shots, but nobody we haven't covered already, as you can see."

Sean placed his hands together as if to pray before letting his fingers slide between each and dropping his forehead to rest on them. The entire experience with Detective Maldonado salted his unhealed wound, leaving him glum and heavy-hearted. The revelation that the man who'd raped and killed Merissa might be someone he knew left him unable to think straight.

"You okay, Sean?"

"No," Sean answered, his voice close to a whisper. "Why should I be?"

Maldonado kept silent and stationary before leaning forward in his chair. "We need your help," he said. "It's something you're in the best position to do for us."

Sean remained in the same head-on-hands position as he spoke.

"I'm listening," he said.

"We want to find out what the people in these photos were doing the night of Ms. Franklin's murder. Where were they? Who were they with? But the last thing we want them to think is that we suspect them, and that's what'll happen if I'm the one asking those questions. If one of the men is really The Beatles' Song Murderer, and they realize there's a chance of being discovered, they'll work extra hard to keep from being caught." Maldonado placed his hand on Sean's shoulder. "Do you see where I'm heading with this?"

Sean inhaled until his lungs reached full capacity, exhaling in a slow, meditative manner. Now he saw the big picture. "You want me to ask them for you," he said, facing the detective as his stomach churned in anguish. "You want me to somehow bring up a night nobody wants to talk about, especially me. And not just once, but with *each* of them?" Sean shook his head and stared at the blank wall across the room, his tears threatening to overwhelm his eyelid dams. "And when you get your answers, you'll be through with me, right? Then you'll wish me luck and send this fucked-up man on his way, hoping he doesn't try to head-butt a speeding car."

Maldonado reached out and clamped an unyielding grip on Sean's forearm. "I have no intention of using you like a roll of goddamn toilet paper," he said, his scolding expression matching his harsh tone. "Dealing with tragedies is part of my job, but that doesn't mean I've grown callous to the people affected by them." He narrowed his eyes and reviewed the photographs of the possible suspects. "There's only one thing we can do to put this nightmare behind us, and that's finding the bastard who killed Ms. Franklin."

Sean wiped the tears away as he listened to Maldonado. Like people who dealt with the loss of a limb, he'd learn to face life despite the hardship, but he couldn't live with himself if the echoes of her cries grew faint and went unheeded. He still couldn't believe, wouldn't believe, that anyone he knew was The Beatles' Song Murderer, but doing something to help, *anything*, offered him a chance at purging the unrelenting sense of helplessness that continued to overwhelm him.

Sean rubbed his face in his hands, sat up, and looked into Maldonado's eyes. "You keep referring to Merissa as Ms. Franklin," he said. "She was Merissa, all right? *Ms. Franklin* wasn't the woman I loved and lost."

Maldonado stared back at Sean, unwavering. "That's exactly right," he said. "To you, she was and always will be Merissa. But I didn't know her, did I? And out of respect to her, and to you, I'm not going to call her by her first name, as if we were friends. Do I make myself clear?"

Sean pondered the response and smiled. "Yes," he said, "you make yourself clear. And for Merissa's sake, I'll do as you ask."

Maldonado nodded his head one time and leaned forward to clasp Sean's shoulder. "Thank you," he said. "I know what I'm asking you to do is extremely difficult, but if I didn't feel strongly about this—"

"Wait!" Sean blurted, turning his head toward the photos. Gathering them in his hand, he studied each one separately, focusing on the people in the background. Seeing the same main characters as the other pictures, or some random girlfriends of Merissa's, he tossed each one aside until none remained.

"I take it you didn't find what you were looking for?" Maldonado asked.

"You mean, *who* I was looking for," Sean replied. "The strange thing is, I wouldn't even know him if I saw his face."

Maldonado furrowed those distinctive sparrow eyebrows into a high, angular arch.

"What am I missing here?" he asked.

Glancing at the photos one more time, Sean narrowed his eyes in thought and paused a moment before nodding his head, convinced that one relevant person remained a no-show.

"You asked me earlier if there was someone else from those poker games we may have missed," he said. "I forgot about this guy because he only came to the last one." Sean leaned back and smiled to himself. "It was actually pretty funny. When I came home, Merissa, Roger, and Adam came up to me at the same time, wanting to show me what this guy, Amazing Stan the Magic Man, had taught them."

"Amazing Stan the Magic Man, huh?" Maldonado's lips curled into a tight line, causing most of his mouth to disappear under that bristle-broom mustache. "What was his relationship with Ms. Franklin?"

Sean leaned over, placing his weight on the right armrest. "I have no idea. He showed up one time, did his thing, and was never mentioned to me again by anybody."

"Not even Adam or Roger at work?"

"Not that I recall," he answered.

Maldonado removed a notepad from his coat pocket. "Amazing Stan the Magic Man," he repeated, writing down the name. Tossing the pad on the table, he leaned back, crossed the fingers from both hands together, and stretched his arms outward. "Looks like we got us another suspect."

Chapter 10

Halfway through a Big Mac and still thinking about the meeting with Detective Maldonado, the sound of his doorbell interrupted Sean's thoughts. Peering through the peephole, he spotted the purple and gold Lakers cap at the bottom of his viewing angle.

Kayleigh stood there with a smile on her face and an outstretched hand.

"You promised!" she told him.

"What are you talking about?" he asked.

She flashed a look of disbelief. "My fifty cents, remember?"

Sean felt a flush of heated embarrassment.

"Hey, I'm really sorry," he told her. "I'll give you a dollar, okay?"

"Wow! Thanks, Mr. Music."

Sean returned from his bedroom with the money and saw Kayleigh staring at his guitar case from the doorway. "Could I hear you play something?" she asked.

"*No*," he replied, handing her the dollar. He realized his tone sounded harsh, his answer rushed. "I'm sorry, Kayleigh," he said. "I don't play anymore."

She looked surprised. "Why not?"

"I don't know," he lied. "I lost my inspiration, I guess."

Kayleigh squinted as she looked at him, her rounded left eye remaining larger than the heavy-lidded right one. After several seconds, her frail shoulders registered the slightest of shrugs as she gazed back toward the closed case.

"I sure wish I knew how to play."

"Take some lessons and learn, like I did," he told her, anxious to return to his hamburger and privacy.

"But why won't *you* teach me, Mr. Music? I thought we were friends."

The prickly heat of exasperation started to creep up the back of Sean's neck. "We *are* friends," he replied, "but that has nothing to do with it."

"Please teach me, Mr. Music, *pleease*?"

"Look, Kayleigh," he said, his voice stern and steady, "when somebody tells you no, you have to respect it and accept the answer, okay?"

"But you could teach me 'Yellow Submarine,' and we could"

"*No!*" he shouted, leaning down closer to her face. "No 'Yellow Submarine'! No Beatles! No nothing! Do you understand?"

The instant he finished talking, Sean regretted his overreaction but couldn't undo the damage. Kayleigh's expression shifted from sweet hope to stunning shock. Moments later, her pale, almost transparent flesh contorted into twisted lines of extreme hurt. Hanging her moon-shaped face down toward the ground, she started to weep.

An unfamiliar voice cried out from the direction of her house.

"Kayleigh! *Kayleigh!*"

"I have to go, Mr. Music."

The distraught little girl turned from the doorway and started to walk away, dragging her feet as if she wore leaden shoes. Sean felt like a complete ass, covering his face with his hand and squeezing his temples in frustration. Kayleigh deserved an apology, but a private one seemed out of the question now that someone appeared heading their way.

He observed an auburn-haired woman with a ponytail, wearing jeans and a red sweater, slow her approach, shoot him an accusatory gaze, and stop in her tracks to stoop to her knees when she reached Kayleigh. Sean hurried out to the two of them.

"Why did you yell at my niece?" she asked, her brows furrowed and jaw tight.

"Because I'm an idiot, and I lost my temper," he told her. Sean walked behind the woman to face the tearful little girl. "I'm really sorry, Kayleigh," he said. "I acted like a jerk."

"I agree," her aunt replied, staring into his eyes.

Sean held her gaze for several seconds before responding. "I—I've had a rough time of it lately, and I guess Kayleigh caught me at a bad moment. She's a great kid and we struck up a nice little friendship yesterday at her lemonade stand." He reached down and offered a gentle squeeze on her shoulder. "Me *and* my dog."

The woman continued to stare at Sean. After several moments, he saw the hardness retreat from her face, replaced by a sudden calm. She grasped Kayleigh by the sides of her head and dislodged the girl's face from the burrowed depths of the red sweater. "Is that true, honey?" she asked, looking in to her eyes. "Should we forgive your friend this time?"

Sean lowered his right knee to the ground, ignoring the twinge of pain in his hip as he placed his face close to hers. "Isn't that right, Fourteenth Laker?" he asked. "You and Mr. Music are pals now."

Sliding her hand under her wet nose, she nodded.

"Look, Aunt Jenny," she said, reaching into her pocket. "Mr. Music gave me a whole dollar for his cup of lemonade!"

Sean offered a small smile. "If I hadn't forgotten to pay my debt yesterday, none of this would have happened."

"He owed me fifty cents so I wanted to come get it," Kayleigh said.

"But you can't just disappear like that, honey," her aunt replied, brushing her fingers across Kayleigh's cheek. "It's just you and me in that house, and I didn't know where you were." She turned from Kayleigh to look at Sean. "I'm looking after her right now and I panic easily, I guess."

"I didn't mean to scare you, Aunt Jenny."

Placing her hand over Kayleigh's face, she pinched her cheek. "Now you know better, all right?"

As Kayleigh stood, Jenny and Sean rose simultaneously.

"Jenny," she said, extending her hand.

"And I'm Kayleigh's diabolical neighbor, Sean."

As Jenny laughed, Sean observed her features for the first time, recognizing her attractiveness in, appropriately, a girl-next-door way. Specks of green flirted in her light brown eyes, offering a soothing kindness within their almond shape. Her nose, starting thin between the eyes, widened a bit heading downward, but worked in harmony with her wide mouth. Angular dimple lines extended from both sides of her nose, highlighting her light pink cheeks. With her hair pulled back in a ponytail, Sean viewed the wide, smooth forehead and dark brown eyebrows that followed the curve of her upper eye area. As they stood facing each other, her head reached two or three inches below his chin.

"My sister told me you were living here," she said. "You were one of her favorites. I was the nerd of the family. Give me Mozart, Bach, or Telemann and I'm happy."

"Are they on your basketball team, too, Mr. Music?" Kayleigh asked.

Jenny smiled and narrowed her gaze in apparent confusion. "I heard about your new name for Sean," she said, "but what do you mean, his basketball team?"

Sean smiled at Kayleigh. "Just something we talked about yesterday," he replied.

"Well, young lady," Jenny said, glancing at her watch, "you've avoided your homework long enough. Time to study your arithmetic."

Closing her eyes, she tightened her mouth in obvious displeasure. "I know," she mumbled. As they walked away, Kayleigh turned back to wave. "I'll see you soon, okay, Mr. Music?"

"For sure," he told her. In a louder voice, he added, "And talk to your parents about when we can start your guitar lessons."

Kayleigh stopped. Inch by inch, she rotated back toward Sean. "What did you say?" she asked, her one good eye widening as the other struggled catching up.

Jenny's expression seemed troubled as she took several long strides toward Sean. "Her parents can't afford it."

"There are three conditions you have to follow if I'm going to teach you how to play," he said, ignoring Jenny's comment while maintaining his focus on the girl.

Rocking back and forth like a metronome, she scrunched her nose, looking worried. "Three?"

"Yep," Sean said. "And here they are. Number one, you have to get your parents' permission, okay?"

Kayleigh's worried expression remained unchanged. "Okay," she said, not sounding confident.

"Number two, you have to make sure all your homework is done before you practice your guitar." Glancing at Jenny, he added, "Including your arithmetic."

Kayleigh looked confused. "But I don't have a guitar."

"I've got one you can borrow."

"Really?" she shouted. "Oh, boy, oh boy, oh boy! You're the greatest, Mr. Music!"

"But you haven't heard my third condition yet," he said. "Music lessons cost money, right?"

"Oh no," she said, looking dejected. "I forgot about that."

"*Sean*," Jenny said, taking a step closer, "they can't afford—"

"To pay for your lessons," he said, disregarding Jenny's plea again, "you'll take them at my house, and when we're finished, you'll play with Hendrix. My dog's getting fat and needs the exercise."

"*What?*" Kayleigh shouted in obvious disbelief. "You don't want any money?"

"So what do you think, Aunt Jenny?" he asked. "Is the price affordable?"

Kayleigh balled her teacup-sized fists and shook them over her head. "Yes!" she hollered. "Yes, yes, yes!"

Jenny sidled up to him with an expression one-hundred-eighty degrees different from her angry introduction several minutes before. "That's very generous of you, Sean," she said. "Thank you for all three conditions."

Alone again with the other half of his microwaved hamburger, Sean contemplated his agreement to teach Kayleigh, knowing the offer stemmed from guilt over his behavior rather than a true desire to teach her. Although he disliked the thought of picking up a guitar again, showing her a few chords seemed tolerable. One thing she'd have to accept, however, centering on an unstated fourth condition, rose above the others as the most determining one of all.

No Beatles' songs.

Chapter 11

I t's still tough coming to work," Sean said, talking to Roger between bites of his turkey sandwich. "I see the windows of the
showroom and picture Merissa at her desk." Offering a tight-
lipped smile and a distant gaze, he added, "It's going to take a
while, I guess."

Roger Peterson, an ex-collegiate basketball player who still retained an athletic frame and a youthful face, sat arrow straight as he
lowered a cheeseburger from his mouth with one hand while the
other reached for a Coke. Although a scant eleven months separated their birth dates, Sean acknowledged the appearance of a greater
age difference. Roger's face remained relatively unlined, and his
thick, brushed-back, sandy-brown hair with a high pompadour reminded Sean of Warren Zevon's reference to perfect hair from the
song "Werewolf of London." He sat silent for a moment before
placing his drink back on the table. The deep-set intensity of his
dark-eyed gaze commanded attention with its expressive sincerity.

"We'll all miss her, Sean," Roger replied. "Your relationship
was different, of course, but she was a friend to everyone." Roger
dipped a french fry into the ketchup on his plate and held it aloft.
"It must hurt like hell, but you still have a life to live. Merissa
would want you to move on from this."

Sean wanted to check Roger off the list of potential suspects as
soon as possible, just like all the others, but did his you-still-have-
a-life-to-live advice sound a bit too clichéd and cavalier? *Merissa
would want you to move on from this?* Was that the best he could
come up with? He took a deep, silent breath, his front teeth clenching his lower lip.

"Just be thankful you didn't see what I saw that night," Sean
said. He paused, stone-like, flashing back on that recurring, horrific

image. "Let's just say I'm getting better, but there's a long way to go."

Roger nodded in silence.

"Were you at work when you heard about Merissa?" Sean asked, rubbing his thigh before gripping his knee and holding tight, waiting for the answer.

"No," Roger said. "Adam called me before I got in that morning."

"How'd *he* find out?"

"I don't know, I didn't ask."

Sean squirmed in his seat. Looking down at his half-eaten sandwich, he pushed the bread aside and looked back at Roger.

"It must have been a pretty surreal sensation, knowing you were at home, relaxing, the night she was killed," he said.

Roger finished the last of his burger and took a large swig of his soda, focusing on Sean the entire time. He picked up his napkin and dabbed the corners of his mouth before responding. "Actually," he began, "I wasn't home. A couple of my old fraternity brothers were in town and we met for some drinks and dinner."

Sean envisioned Maldonado's suspicious expression after hearing Roger's answer. But why should a straightforward explanation like that raise skepticism? "How's Anita doing?" he asked, eager to change the subject.

Roger reached for his glass again, despite having put his drink down mere moments before. Leaning forward a bit, he placed his elbows on the table and offered a wide-eyed expression that seemed almost childlike. "I've got a confession to make, Sean," he said. "What I just told you about where I was that night is bullshit—but I'm telling you this for a reason."

Sean's stomach tightened and his skin felt a sudden rush of heat.

"I guess it was an open secret why Anita and I separated for a while," he said, eyeing a passing waitress. "I played around on the side and finally got caught."

"What's this got to do with where you were that night?" Sean asked.

Roger held up a hand and stared for several wordless moments. "Like I said, I'm bringing this up for a reason. When we got back together, I truly believed my cheating days were over, and up until the night of Merissa's murder, I was the perfect husband. But that night..." He raised his hands, palms up. "My dental hygienist, can you believe that?" As Roger looked down to pluck another fry, Sean caught a slight upward motion from the corners of his mouth. "Anyway, what I told you about meeting a couple of college buddies is the excuse I gave Anita." In a sudden rapid motion, Roger threw his hand out toward Sean. "*But*," he said, almost shouting, "my conscience caught up to me after a while. I only screwed her one time and was back home by eleven."

Sean's legs bounced up and down under the tablecloth as his mind raced. Roger's philandering seemed to show no signs of abating, continuing to make a victim of poor Anita, but that didn't mean Sean had a right to think anything more than that.

"Now everything's different," Roger said. "I realize how quickly something can be taken away, how fast things can change." Balling his hands into fists, he brought them down on the table with a degree of force before leaning in toward Sean. "I appreciate Anita more than ever before. It took a tragedy, Sean, your terrible, terrible loss, to slap me in the face and give me the perspective I needed."

Sean took a sip of water and felt the glass shake in his hand. The pain of revisiting his nightmare left him devoid of anything to say.

Remaining silent, he glanced at his watch. "I'm happy for you, Roger," he said at last, his voice low and feeble. "Come on. It's time to go."

"Hey," Roger said, reaching for a final french fry, "admittedly I was a hound when it came to hot women, but tell me you weren't shocked when you heard what happened to good ol' monogamous Adam."

"What are you talking about?"

Roger looked surprised, his eyes opening wide. "You don't know? Haven't you noticed he hasn't been around the last couple of weeks?"

"I just figured he was on vacation."

Roger's shit-eating grin preceded a slow shake of his head.

"A woman accused Adam of touching her tits during the test drive," Roger said, laughing. "Adam swore he was only helping her adjust the seat belt, but the bitch threatened to sue for sexual harassment until disciplinary action was taken."

Sean stared at Roger, expecting a stupid punch line to a joke.

No punch line. No joke.

"I can't *believe* it," he muttered. "Saint Adam was fired over one person's accusation?"

"He wasn't fired," Roger replied, "at least, not for now. Maybe his years at the dealership and his pristine reputation gave him the benefit of the doubt. They transferred him to Van Nuys."

Sean looked away for several seconds and shook his head in reflective gratitude that he worked a couple of miles from the beach instead of the furnace at the Van Nuys location.

"Well, that sure sucks, doesn't it?" he said. "From the ocean breezes of Santa Monica to the sweatbox of Van Nuys."

Roger leaned back and placed his hands in his lap. His eyes narrowed as a tiny smile appeared, frozen in place as he stared into Sean's eyes like a soothsayer possessing unforeseen knowledge. "I don't find the allegation surprising at all," he said. "How many evangelicals have been busted through the years for sexual shit? Or those conservative, holier-than-thou politicians with all their affairs? Hell, some of them get caught with another man!" Roger chuckled to himself as he rolled his eyes. "Some of those guys make anything I've ever done look tame. And do I even need to mention the sleazy-ass history of all those priests in the Catholic Church?"

"Oh, come on, Roger, give me a break," Sean squawked, his face scrunched in denial. "Don't start equating Adam with any of those assholes. There's no way he's capable of that shit!"

Roger lifted his arms from the table and threw his hands out in apparent frustration. "And how many times did those *assholes* get away with *that shit* because they were supposedly incapable of it?" Maintaining his focus on Sean, he leaned in again, placing one hand on top of the other at the edge of the table. "Take it from someone who's gotten away with lots of things, Sean," he told him. "If you really want something bad enough, you do whatever it takes to get it."

Chapter 12

Kayleigh's family invited Sean to watch the first game of the NBA Finals between the Los Angeles Lakers and the Boston Celtics. As he waited in line at the bakery counter to order a dessert to bring, a sudden voice from behind startled him.

"I *thought* I saw you, Sean." Looking back over his shoulder, he stared into the self-assured eyes of the center's director, Elliot Hayden.

Sean's jeans, sweatshirt, and sneakers matched most of the casual Sunday afternoon attire in the market, but Elliot looked debonair in his khaki-colored slacks, open-collared polo shirt, tan sports coat, and brown leather loafers.

"Hello, Elliot," Sean said, hoping for the social version of a twenty-four-second clock.

"I must say you look a lot healthier than the last time I saw you," Elliot remarked, extending his hand. Pointing at the various pastry selections on display, he chuckled. "If that's your secret, maybe I should forget all those fruits and veggies I eat and go for the sweet stuff."

Sean smiled before turning back toward the counter.

Elliot took another step closer. "Got any shows coming up?"

"Nope," he replied, a single turn of his head to left and right. "Those days are over." He continued fixing his gaze on the women working behind the pastry counter, well aware of Elliot's desire to continue the conversation.

"From what I figure, Sean, it's what you love to do. I mean, look at your history. No matter what nonchalance you displayed at our shows, I knew better." Elliot approached from the left side to resume eye contact. "The way I see it, the sooner you get out there again, the better."

Sean took a deep, silent breath, wondering how people like El-liot convinced themselves they knew what was best for everyone else. "I'll keep that in mind."

The petite uniformed Latina with dark-rimmed glasses and ex-pressive eyes called Sean's number. As he ordered the cookies, El-liot remained by his side. Removing his cell phone from his pocket, Sean pretended to read and respond to a text, hoping that might cause the man to move on and take care of his own marketing needs.

"You haven't stopped playing completely, have you?"

Sean tightened his grip on the phone, working to remain calm, subduing the itchy sensation pin-pricking the back of his neck. He remained quiet, taking longer than usual to place the phone back in his pocket. Looking up again, his eyes narrowed. "You just said a minute ago I look a lot better, right?"

"Yes," Elliot answered, "and it's true."

"So that should tell you whatever I'm doing lately must be okay. I'm fine and getting on with my life. The only time I pick up a gui-tar is to give occasional lessons to a girl next door. That's it."

Elliot's eyes widened. "Private lessons from someone with *your* background? That's a lucky girl."

"Sure, if you call having cancer *lucky*." Sean felt an empower-ing sense of satisfaction deriding the remark, but Elliot just nodded. Sean handed money to the woman, anxious to finalize the transac-tion as he watched her head for the cash register. "What time is it?" he asked, knowing the answer from his cell phone.

Elliot glanced at his shiny silver watch. "Four twenty-seven."

"*Really*? I better get home and shower. I'm invited to the girl's house to have dinner and watch the Lakers game with the family." Returning at the perfect time, the woman handed him his change. "Take care, Elliot," Sean said, turning away.

With the freedom of a parking-lot escape within reach, Elliot caught up to him as he took his first step outside.

"You gave me an idea," he said. "Could I run something by you before you go?"

The only running that interested Sean concerned escaping from Elliot. "Another time, okay? I'm in a hurry."

"You know I also deal with unlucky kids," he said, positioning himself between Sean and his car. "I'm not saying they have cancer, but a number of them come from abusive backgrounds. When we can bring a little sunshine into their lives, it's the greatest feeling in the world."

"What's that got to do with me?" Sean asked, resigned to Elliot's persistence.

"We're having a talent show the last Saturday in July. I need someone to play the guitar for the kids who are going to sing."

Sean's eyes grew wide for a moment before shutting closed as he shook his head back and forth. "No way!" he cried out. "You want me to play corny-ass songs for nervous little kids?" Shaking his head, he reached for the door. "Give me a fucking break."

"You're looking at it all wrong, Sean," Elliot said, a pleading tone to his voice. "You'd be doing a good deed, something impactful for these poor kids, just like you are now with that sick girl. And who knows? Maybe she'd like to come to the show. I bet she'd love it, watching her teacher play the guitar."

Sean glared at Elliot. "Don't call that playing, all right? It's not even close."

"Well, compared to what you used to do, of course it's not the same. I didn't mean to imply—"

"But I'll give you this," Sean said, his voice lower, "I know how much your place meant to Merissa, so I'll think about it."

Elliot smiled and patted Sean on the shoulder. "That's wonderful," he exclaimed. "I'll only need you for that final week. A little practice time with the kids and then the show. That's it!"

Sean wagged his finger at Elliot. "I'm still not agreeing to anything, understand?"

"I understand," Elliot replied. "We still have some time, but all I ask is that you let me know sooner rather than later. It may not be a rock concert, but there's still a lot we have to plan for."

Across the street, Sean noticed a cop writing out a ticket, leading him to think of Detective Maldonado and his list of suspects. Ridiculous as it seemed considering the man's homosexuality, why not take advantage of the moment to mark someone else off the list? Now it's my turn to ask you a question," he said.

Elliot gave a slight tilt of his head.

Sean paused, gathering his thoughts for a lie that required a convincing storyline. "According to you, I look better, so thank you," he said. "But I've been told that part of my healing process is to picture the location of Merissa's close friends the night of her murder. It's supposed to help remind me that their normal lives were also affected, that it wasn't just me. One of our salesmen said he was at a bar with some friends. The GM said he was helping his kid with her homework." Attempting to show his best unassuming demeanor, he added, "So, if you don't mind me asking…"

Elliot bit his upper lip and stared at Sean, his eyes tightening and blinking in rapid succession. "You mentioned the Lakers earlier, so it's a sad coincidence that you're asking me this question. Martin—my partner—is a big basketball fan and was given a couple of tickets for the Lakers game that night. About an hour before we were supposed to leave, I got a call from a board member, asking what time I'd be arriving at a charity affair I thought was the next night. It was sponsored by one of our major donors and there was no way I couldn't attend—not if I didn't want to jeopardize seeing another check from him again."

Sean stroked his goatee and nodded in silent acknowledgment. A quiet, sarcastic chuckle followed. "I imagine Martin wasn't too happy about missing the game."

"Oh!" Elliot exclaimed, raising his right hand as if taking an oath. "I insisted he go to the game anyway." His expression changed in an instant as he looked down on the blacktop, somewhere in the space between the two of them. "Who would have thought?" he asked, shaking his head in a solemn back-and-forth manner. With a moist sheen in his eyes, he pinched the tip of his nose and held his hand there for several moments before dropping his arm back to his side. "Guess there's nothing more to say about it." Taking a deep, visible breath, he rubbed his right palm across his right eye. "Please think about doing the show, okay?" Reaching into his pocket, Elliot removed a business card from a small gold case. "Here's how to reach me."

On the way home, Sean dug his nails into the leather passenger seat, disgusted with himself for utilizing the same phony excuse to accommodate Maldonado's request.

"Jesus," he whispered. "My *healing process*? How 'bout a lobotomy? That might help my healing process."

Carlos, Dino, and Adam remained the last on Maldonado's original list, but after overhearing Carlos's conversation with Tom about visiting his family in Guatemala during the week of Merissa's murder, the detective had told him he'd get confirmation from the airlines and to just finish up with Dino and Adam.

Dino and Adam: two *suspects* who made no sense whatsoever. Dino's current leave of absence from the hair salon prevented Sean from speaking to him now, but he anticipated seeing Adam at the next bowling night. When Roger informed him about the woman's groping allegation, the claim had seemed preposterous. Picturing that straight, clean-cut guy as a closet pervert, or even worse, didn't compute. Sean expected to encounter the same empty feeling with Adam as with the others—the proverbial dog barking up the wrong Beatles' tree.

Chapter 13

When the final horn sounded, Kayleigh rose from the couch, her shoulders slumped and her head lowered. Her Lakers jersey seemed to hang like a purple and gold curtain, a closing curtain, draping much of her frail body.

"It's just the first game, honey," her father said. "Remember, you have to win four of them."

"Yeah, I know," she said, her voice sounding pained. "But we gotta make more baskets. We only scored eighty-eight points!"

"The Celtics play really good defense," Sean said, "but you're right. The Lakers need to shoot a lot better."

"Do you think Coby will ever play, Daddy?" she asked.

"I don't think so, Kayleigh," he answered. "When it comes to playing for the championship, only the top twelve are going to suit up." He smiled. "You know the way it is. Coby is the thirteenth Laker."

"And I'm the fourteenth!" she trumpeted.

"And don't you forget it!" her father cheered.

Sean rose to his feet to say his goodbyes, but Kayleigh approached him before he uttered a word, standing at his feet and looking up.

"Can I show you my travel pictures now, Mr. Music?"

He gazed down at the circular, pallid face, housing one and three-quarters eyes of hopefulness. Her cracked, thin lips curled into a slight, encouraging smile.

"Lead the way," he answered.

The first object capturing his attention didn't involve the many wall photos but, rather, the table by her bed, with several prescription bottles, a large container of antibacterial soap, and a green and yellow box that read "disposable vomit bags" lined up.

"Look!" she shouted, rushing up to the wall on his right. "Here's my newest one. It's Cinderella's Castle at Disney World." She absorbed the photo in silence as her eyes gazed in wonder. "Isn't it beautiful?" Kayleigh stared a few moments longer before directing Sean to a photograph of Mount Rushmore. "I bet you know what that is," she said. "Everybody does! How could somebody do that to a mountain? Isn't it amazing?"

Changing direction as if the floor tilted back and forth, Kayleigh continued to veer toward one side of the room and then the other, twice standing on her bed and pointing to various square, round, multiple-sized pictures with a *joie de vivre* that seemed alien to him. A diminishing amount of wall space remained from the bumper-to-bumper traffic jam of worldwide photos taped alongside one another. Her small bedroom-tour exuberance never waned as she showed off her pictures of the Egyptian pyramids, the Grand Canyon, the Eiffel Tower, a Hawaiian sunset, the Great Wall of China, a German castle overlooking the Rhine, the snow-covered Alps with a village below, an ornate Thai temple, and the Statue of Liberty, among a number of others.

"My daddy says if you want to see the Statue of Liberty up close you have to go on a boat." Her face contracted into a wrinkled grimace. "I don't want to get seasick."

"I don't think you will," Sean said. "It's an easy boat ride."

"Really?" she asked, her tone buoyant.

"Really."

Kayleigh breathed an exaggerated sigh of relief. "I *hate* throwing up." Her solemn tone seemed a complete disconnect from the previous minute. "Like after my treatments."

Sean studied her expression as a fleeting look of sadness passed over like a dark cloud blowing across the sun. "It looks like you've got a lot of adventures ahead of you," he said, turning back to scan the walls.

"I've had a lot of 'em already."

"You have?"

"Uh-huh," she said, nodding up and down, up and down, as if her head connected to a spring. "I can go wherever I want to."

"I don't understand."

"I just look at a picture and pretend I'm there," she explained. "I'll show you."

Kayleigh examined the various pictures on the walls until her gaze zeroed in on a poster of a lush mountain forest parted to expose a towering waterfall hurtling down into a crystal blue lake far below. He watched as she hurried over and stood with her eyes closed and an ear pressed against the paper.

"Close your eyes, Mr. Music," she told him. "Can you hear how loud the water is?"

Sean gazed for a moment at the little dreamer in front of him before shutting his eyes as she requested. "Yep," he told her. "I can hear it now."

Kayleigh turned to face the poster with her eyes still closed. She placed both hands on her face, caressing and stroking her cheeks. "I can feel the mist on my skin. It's cold and wet, but it feels good." She stood silent for several seconds before continuing. "And now I feel the branches and leaves around me," she said, extending her arms to the side. "Everything is so green and pretty!" She started moving her hands back and forth, as if petting a dog. "Now I'm feeling how slippery the rocks are."

Sean watched Kayleigh inhale, her delicate, bony shoulders rising several inches in a momentary holding pattern before dropping down.

"Smell how clean the air is." With a sudden upward motion, Kayleigh tilted her head back, her eyes remaining closed. "Look, Mr. Music!" she cried, pointing at something only she could observe. "See that? There's a big, colorful butterfly above you."

Sean found himself staring at the blank ceiling.

"It's got orange and purple wings with black stripes and yellow spots. Isn't it beautiful?"

Sean studied Kayleigh, contemplating the difference between her immense imagination and the straitjacket limitations inhibiting his own.

As she stood transfixed in front of the waterfall, a young girl immersed in the vibrant hues of belief and transported on the winds of hope and infinite expectation, he realized that his dreams, relegated to the safety of the harbor, remained cautious in scope and confined by life experience.

He felt a simultaneous sensation of being an old man and a child—a limbo-like state of knowing too much and too little. Several lines from his song, "Tug of War" seemed appropriate, even biographical, at that moment.

Innocence of youth
Innocence of truth
Is it better knowing so much more?
The why's, the how's, the reasons for?
Sometimes yes, sometimes no
Back and forth I go
Just like a tug of war

The reality seemed obvious. Kayleigh's strength and determination to fight her battle and live life to the fullest far outweighed his own. He didn't want to die, of course, but he waited three weeks to make the appointment for a CAT-scan, fearful to face the future over what lay ahead when...*if*...that test scheduled for next week revealed the truth he'd brought upon himself. The certain cigarette truth.

Chapter 14

Entering Adam's driveway, Sean struggled to control the double-trouble despondency blanketing his thoughts. His possible cancer prognosis constituted a relentless whiplashing to his focus and sense of normalcy, but the irritating call he'd received that afternoon from his exasperated brother, telling Sean to "get off his high horse" and "accept the damn offer already" compounded his problems. "The deadline for signing the paperwork is almost up," he told him. David went on to explain the pressure he faced at the firm, that no one had anticipated a problem after learning of the sibling relationship, but now they've started asking questions about the delay.

"So answer me this," he said. "How do you think it will make me look if I have to tell our new money-making, great-for-the-firm client that we can't use the jingle they want because the owner of the song, my own damn brother, won't agree to it?" Attempting to lighten the mood, he wound up making Sean feel worse by uttering a shard-of-glass comment penetrating his sensibilities.

"Everybody's looking forward to the cleanser hitting the American market in August," he explained, "and as the company has *personally* told me, 'Looking Glass' will help ensure that 'windows across the USA get cleaned the Wally Way!'"

David's shameless recitation of the cleanser's insipid slogan disgusted him, but he now recognized the burden placed on his brother. His partners at the firm figured the jingle part of the deal was a case-closed, slam-dunk situation, but what did those assholes know, or care, about maintaining one's integrity? They were lawyers!

David reminded Sean again about needing the extra money, capping the conversation off with a clichéd lecture about second chances. He reiterated his argument about major artists selling their songs to sell products, but Sean believed that to be an asinine line of reasoning. Guys like Dylan, or Seger, or Townsend, had a shit-load of hits to be remembered by: one song-turned-jingle didn't affect them or their reputation.

David's entire focus centered on Sean's future earnings, but "Looking Glass" remained his one and only success, his lone badge of honor as a serious artist. In return for the money, he'd sacrifice his self-esteem and end up a corporate stooge.

Sean honked twice and waited. By a stroke of luck, Adam had called him at work the day before, asking for a ride to the bowling center. The situation presented the perfect opportunity to ask the same painful, prickly question he'd presented to the others on Maldonado's list.

"Thanks for picking me up, Sean," Adam said, easing himself into the seat. "When I found out Nancy needed my car tonight, I figured I'd be stuck at home." Locking in his seat belt, he added, "I owe you one."

"No, you don't," Sean replied. "Now we have a chance to catch up and see what's new."

Adam uttered a forced, brief laugh. "What's new?" he echoed. "You know what happened to me, right? Why I'm not at the Santa Monica dealership anymore?"

"Yeah, I heard." Glancing to his right, Sean shook his head. "Freakin' unbelievable."

"I'm sure God has a plan, but I still can't understand why that woman accused me of touching her like that," Adam said.

Sean shrugged. "Who knows?"

"I don't mean to be disrespectful, but she must have been six feet tall, with a chest out to here," Adam said, holding his arms out and his hands turned inward for emphasis. "Was it my fault she couldn't unhook her shoulder strap? I was only trying to help, but there wasn't much room to reach around. I guess I brushed up against her, and she went ballistic."

"I'll talk with my father if you want me to," Sean said. "If I explain what happened, maybe he'll bring you back."

"Thanks, but I don't want to stir the pot any more than I have already." Crossing his chest, he added, "Thank God, I still have a job."

From the moment Sean had met Adam at the dealership, he'd reminded him of a roadie he'd befriended in his touring days. Both men stood an inch or two under six feet, with long necks and skinny physiques, and their ears, not much larger than poker chips, stuck out like a human version of Mr. Potato Head. Each combed their thinning red hair in a slight downward angle from left to right in a failed attempt to cover up their widening foreheads, pale and lineless like the rest of their face, which seemed to accentuate the deep blue of their eyes.

Although they both resembled a nerdy high school teacher whose students made fun of him behind his back as he wrote math equations on the blackboard, that was where the similarities ended.

Whereas Sean scored much of his weed and blow on the road from Red, the band's nickname for the roadie, Adam's idea of rebelliousness centered on such risky behavior as ordering a fattening dessert at lunch without his wife's knowledge, or stepping off the curb to cross the street before the walk sign turned green.

"How are Eleanor and the kids?"

"They're great. Luke's playing little league and starting piano lessons and Nancy's on the cheerleading squad at high school. There's a game tonight, so she needed my car."

"What about Eleanor's car?"

"It's Bible study night. Every other week a church group gathers at someone's house to discuss passages. She loves those things so it's only right that I didn't ask to use hers."

"I know you're into your religion and everything, Adam, but you don't appear to be as deeply involved in that stuff as she is."

Adam nodded several times before answering. "I believe deeply in the Lord," he replied, "but Eleanor leads more of an active life when it comes to His teachings."

"So I guess you and her have found a way to work it out," Sean said. "I mean, here you are joining your beer drinking, rowdy friends to go bowling, even bet a little money, while your wife's at a Bible study."

Adam looked out through his window, gripping his thighs with each hand.

"Eleanor doesn't ask too many questions."

Sean waited for an elaboration, but none came.

"I never really thanked you and Eleanor for your support and friendship after Merissa's death," he said, keeping his eyes straight ahead. "I tried to keep people away, but you guys dropped by any-way to see how I was." He looked at Adam and patted his shoulder. "You even brought food for my dog. That was a pretty cool thing to do."

Adam turned back to the left, angling himself toward Sean. "A friend in need, right?" he replied. "We *wanted* to help, Sean. We couldn't just sit around doing nothing."

"Well, it must have hit you hard, too," he said. "You were friends with Merissa before I even met her."

"Yeah, I was, but things changed after she met you. Not that I didn't understand, but a fact's a fact." Adam turned to look out the side window. "Not that it matters now, but admittedly I was hurt a bit."

Neither man spoke for a while, but when Sean did, he dove right into the question he needed to ask.

"I guess you were with Eleanor the night of the murder," he said. "Probably having a peaceful evening doing whatever, right?"

The ensuing silence coerced him to look at Adam. Sean's surprised open eyes met Adam's narrowing ones.

"That's a strange thing to ask," he said. "What we were doing that night isn't even worth talking about."

Sean clenched his jaw in an uncomfortable moment of silence. "I only meant it as a comment about how unpredictable life can be," he said, responding with the first excuse he could think of. "I'm sorry I brought it up. It's just that…"

"Just *what*?" Adam snapped.

"It's just that…" Sean tightened his grip on the steering wheel, stumbling over his thoughts. "It gives me the chance to close the door on everything about that night." He felt defensive and needed to say more. "You're not the only one I've asked. I've talked to some of the other guys at work, too. Roger and I talked about it at lunch recently."

Adam took an audible sigh. "All right," he said. "Sorry if I got a little uptight, but I've avoided thinking about Merissa for my own good. We all handle things differently, I guess."

"Let's drop the subject, okay?" Sean said, reaching for the radio dial. "It's bowling night, my man!"

When Sean parked his car in the lot, Adam reached over and placed his hand on Sean's shoulder. "Just so you know," he said, his voice calm and steady, "you were right about the peaceful evening. I was home that night with Eleanor, watching TV."

శోఎోఎ

Aided by Sean's three-holed cannonball scattering the two and seven pins to finish with a spare on his final throw of the night, McDougal's Ford Marauders defeated Tolbert's Chevy Terrors by a narrow margin. After dollars were collected and the trash talk faded, groups of twos and threes returned to the parking lot and dispersed to their cars. Sean remained behind with Adam, chatting inside about the pros and cons of the new floor models until Eleanor's text announced her arrival. As the two of them walked toward her car, Sean waved.

"How are you, Sean?" she asked, her tone revealing unwanted pity.

"Doing well, Eleanor," he replied, his lighthearted response a forced one. "How are you?"

"I'm fine, thank God," she answered, crossing her chest. "The Lord tests us in many ways, but he who has faith will always be in His hands."

Her answer validated his feelings about Eleanor's probable disapproval of the wagering and beer drinking. Adam only ordered sodas but threw his money down like everyone else.

He said she didn't ask many questions, so maybe Eleanor didn't know.

"Sorry, honey," Adam said, "but suddenly I have to pee real bad. Talk with Sean until I come back."

Sean hoped Adam's leak time turned out to be shorter than his comment inferred.

"So tell me, Sean," she said, her brows furrowed, "have you moved on again? Are things better?"

"I'm fine, Eleanor," he replied, patting her arm.

"That's good to hear," she said. "I've prayed every day, asking the Lord to watch over you."

"Well," he said, nodding his head in acknowledgment, "keep those prayers coming, okay? I could use all the help I can get."

Eleanor glanced toward the doors. "There's something personal I want to tell you that Adam wouldn't want you to know." Eleanor leaned her head outside the window and stared at Sean. "The tragedy you suffered affected us more than you realize. Before it happened, we started seeing a marriage counselor because…well…let's just say we were having problems and needed help." Closing her eyes for a moment, she bit her upper lip and inhaled deeply. "Things were at their worst the night Merissa was killed. Adam didn't even come home until a quarter to one. He told me he picked up a dinner and just sat in his car somewhere, but it doesn't matter now. After what happened that night, the Lord helped guide us and make it clear what's really important and how much we appreciate what we have." She crossed herself again and looked skyward. Offering a tiny smile, she added, "I just wanted you to know."

Gripping the open portion of the window, Sean leaned forward, looking down at Eleanor. "Adam wasn't with you that night?"

"No," she answered, shaking her head.

"Then why did he tell me he was watching TV with you?" he asked, confusion mixing with anger. "Why would he lie to me?"

Eleanor placed a hand under her chin, pursing her lips as she looked into his eyes.

"My husband's a proud man, Sean. He probably didn't want you or anybody else knowing about the problems we were having. Knowing my dear Adam like I do, he might have thought people wouldn't think the same of him."

Sean didn't respond as he pondered Eleanor's reply. Her answer seemed logical but he felt troubled about the lie.

"Please don't say anything," she said. "If he told you he was with me, he must have had his reasons."

Chapter 15

Walking back to work with Roger after another lunch together, the familiar sound of a Stevie Ray Vaughan guitar riff announced an incoming call from Sean's cell phone. His stomach knotted as he read Dr. Lodin's name on the screen, and preferring to converse with him in private, he let the phone go to voicemail.

Returning to the dealership, he took several slow, calming breaths nearing his cubicle in preparation for the return call. Before he got the chance, however, the general manager, Tom Claiborne, approached him and pointed outside toward a couple reading the sticker on the window of a white Taurus.

"They asked for you," he told him. "The woman said she was a big fan of yours." Placing his hand on Sean's shoulder, he smiled and winked. "Hey, if it helps sell a car, sing 'em a damn song."

Sean lowered his head in underwhelming excitement. "I need to call my doctor, Tom," he said. "As soon as I'm done, okay?"

Claiborne's smile disappeared. "Can it wait?" he asked.

The two men stared at each other in silence for several moments.

"I don't want to lose any potential sales," Claiborne told him, "so make it quick and get out there."

Beverly answered on the second ring, sounding harassed as usual, but when she heard Sean's voice her tone changed to a softer and friendlier one. Biting his lip, Sean wondered if the softness and friendliness represented a reason for sympathy.

"Doctor Lodin is with a patient and has another three to see before the end of the day," she told him. "But he wanted me to call you to let you know he has the results and wants to talk about them today. Can you call back between four and five?"

Sean stared at his photo of Hendrix on the desk. "Can you tell me anything, Beverly?" he asked. "The good? The bad? The ugly?"

"No, Mr. Hightower," she answered. "And even if I knew something, it wouldn't be right of me to discuss it with you. I'm sorry."

"*Damn it,*" Sean muttered. Craving an answer but forced to wait, Sean felt alone and upset. He slid his chair back and grabbed his hip as he stood. The pain didn't jolt him as much as other times, but still registered on the discomfort meter. Moving in a slow, step-by-step manner toward the showroom doors, he walked outside and approached the couple, both appearing to be in their mid to late fifties, waiting in the shade by their car. A quick glance at their Bush/Cheney bumper sticker preceded the extension of his hand.

"Hello," he said, grasping the woman's hand first. "My name's Sean. I heard that you asked for my help."

The woman didn't say a word for several seconds before turning toward her husband. "It sure is, Wayne!" she exclaimed. "Sean Hightower!"

If Sean had the power at that moment to unleash a swarm of hornets on the woman's head he'd have done it with pleasure, but he smiled instead, keeping his dark thoughts to himself.

"I'm Margie Blankenship," she said, finishing the handshake. The man reached out and grasped Sean's hand. "I'm Margie's husband, Wayne," he told him. "Nice to meet you, Sean."

"'Looking Glass' was one of my favorite songs when it was playing on the radio," she told him. "I heard it all the time." With a slow shake of her head, she chirped, "Wait until I tell the girls in my reading group about this. They won't believe it!"

"So which car would you like to look at today?" he asked.

"Well," she said, dabbing her forehead with a tissue, "whatever we get needs to have a good air conditioner! It never seems to cool off in this city."

"First thing we'd like to do is test drive the Taurus SEL," Wayne told him. "It's come down to a choice between that one and the Chevrolet Malibu. We only drive American cars. Always have, always will."

During the test drive, Sean continued glancing at his watch, trying to will the time ahead. By the time they finished, he needed a beer, some weed, and a speed-of-light departure from Margie and Wayne Blankenship. His self-control reached a tipping point with these two complainers, and their disagreeable voices still echoed in his head.

'The seats aren't comfortable.'
'The air conditioning isn't strong enough.'
'There's not enough leg room.'
'There's no pick up when I accelerate.'
'I don't like the way it steers.'
'I feel the road too much.'
'The sound system isn't good.'

Sean expected the Blankenships to leave, happy that he'd never have to see them again.

"Well, Sean," Wayne said, "the car may not be perfect, but what the hell is nowadays, right?" He chuckled and then continued. "I don't want to get on my bandwagon, but let's just say we're heading into trouble if we don't protect America. We're getting soft, and buying American cars sends a message to those foreign car lovers that there's nothing wrong with the things we produce in this country. That's why we may be back."

Sean stared in disbelief. "Let me ask you something," he said, pointing toward their bumper sticker. "Do you really think those two guys invaded Iraq to protect America?"

The Blankenships looked at each other before turning their heads in unison toward Sean.

"As a matter of fact, I do!" Margie exclaimed, her dark eyebrows furrowing. Straightening the posture of her smallish frame, she tilted her chin upward, looking him in the eyes as wisps of her neck-length dark brown hair hung in limp, sweat-induced strands across her forehead. "And you and your liberal friends better hope God continues to bless those two men."

"And God bless those young men and women protecting our freedom," Wayne added.

"Protecting our *freedom*?" Sean repeated, his voice rising. "You've got to be kidding! Remember what Cheney told us back in 2003? That we'd be greeted as liberators? Five years later, seems more like *lubricators* to me. You know why? Because our military's getting screwed!" He shook his head and took a step closer, his eyes narrowing. "Remember Osama bin Laden? That bearded asshole sitting in a cave somewhere in Afghanistan with his Al Qaeda buddies? In case you don't remember, they're the ones who attacked us, not Saddam Hussein, and seven years later we haven't even caught him yet!" His eyes opening wide, a sarcastic smile emerged. "But, hey, why settle for one war dance when you have a chance for two?" Sean shuffled his feet forward one at a time before stepping back the same way. "Call it the Chickenhawk Cha-Cha!"

From seemingly out of nowhere, Roger appeared, placing himself between Sean and the Blankenships. "I'm very sorry," Roger said, easing him away. "My friend has been under some pressure and—"

"Hey, I forgot to ask," Sean shouted, "did they ever find those WMDs?"

Roger placed his arm around his friend's shoulder and steered him toward the showroom. "Calm down, buddy. Let's go inside." He brought a second chair to his cubicle and placed it next to his own. "Sit down here and don't go anywhere," he told him. "I've got to go upstairs to check on a lease and then I'll bring us some coffee, okay?"

Sean stared ahead, nodding in an almost indiscernible way.

Leaning forward, Roger placed his hand on his shoulder. "Not to say it wouldn't have been fun to see a little political punch-out, but I don't think Tom would take too kindly to it. Or your father."

As he walked away, Sean looked toward the door as the Blankenships rushed in, scowling and animated as they approached Vicky Hamlin's desk, a co-worker of theirs. Glancing in his direction, she said something to them before rising from her chair and walking toward the back.

Sean stared at a young guy in blue jeans and Green Day tee shirt looking at an F-150, and wondered if the kid would ever have cancer. Such a stupid thought, but he couldn't help himself. Looking at his watch, he decided not to wait until four o'clock and called Dr. Lodin's office again, perhaps catching him between patients. As Sean waited for Beverly to answer, he stared at framed photos of Roger's wife, Anita, and another of their son and daughter at Disneyland, standing on the left and right of someone in a Goofy costume.

"Hi, Beverly, it's Sean Hightower again," he said. "I'm wondering if Doctor—"

"Oh, Mister Hightower," she said, cutting him off. "Hold on, let me see if Doctor Lodin can talk with you now."

Sean felt his heartbeat increase as he attempted without success to stay calm. Strumming his fingers on the desk, his head swiveled from the ceiling, toward the doors, and at the black Escort on the showroom floor before the sound of the doctor's voice caused him to lurch forward in his chair.

"Hello, Sean," he said.

Sean swallowed what little saliva remained. The tone of Lodin's voice sounded as he expected; ominous and resigned. Placing his right elbow on the desk, he rested his head on his fist and closed his eyes, ready for the worst. "Okay," he said, his voice tight and raspy, "what's the news, Doctor?"

"You're fine, Sean," he replied. "That shadowing we originally saw in the X-rays turned out to be nothing more than a variant of the normal vasculature."

A rush of lightheadedness infiltrated his ability to speak for several moments. "I'm...fine?"

"Yes," he answered. "Apparently, those wider than average mediastinal structures are nothing more than a harmless anomaly you were born with. It caused me to think there might be something there." Lodin chuckled. "But as the saying goes, 'there's no there, there.'"

Sean felt a sense of momentary nothingness, as if his entire being consisted of little more than the surrounding air. He leaned back and stared at the ceiling, watching the blur of the overhead lights through the suddenness of watery eyes. A deep exhale preceded his response. "Wow," he whispered, wiping his hand across his eyes. "What an enormous relief."

"As it was for me, too," Lodin said. "Unfortunately, I've had to deliver the bad news to a number of others, but not this time."

Sean attempted to stand but his legs weakened as he descended back into his chair. "Thanks for the great news, Doctor Lodin. I better get back to work now."

"Before you do, wait on the line for Beverly. She needs to give you Dr. Jillson's office number. They asked us to have you call them for some information they need."

When Beverly greeted Sean again, he grabbed the pen on Roger's desk but found nothing to write on. Opening the drawer to his left, he spotted a notepad with something written across the top of the page. The moment he saw the message, Beverly's voice faded away and everything around him disappeared. In an instantaneous recognition of her swirling and angular style of handwriting, he read these words:

Roger, please forget whatever ideas you have about you and me. I love Sean. I also want to remind you that you're a married man.
Your friend, Merissa

Chapter 16

D o you remember which chord 'Feelin' Groovy' starts
with?" Sean asked, handing Kayleigh the guitar.
"Uh-huh," she replied, nodding her Lakers cap covered
cue ball head. "The D chord."

"So let's hear it."

Kayleigh wriggled in her chair until creating enough space from
the lemonade table to hold the guitar on her lap. Sean watched as
she simultaneously worked her bony fingers into the correct position while sliding the exposed tip of her tongue between her lips. A
hesitant, but not-so-bad-sounding D chord followed.

"Excellent, Kayleigh!" Sean exclaimed. "And after you strum
that chord, you sing the first word, '*slow*,' and then you go where?"

"The A chord," she answered, rearranging her fingers.

"You're a quick learner."

Kayleigh played the chord.

"...'*down, you*'...." Sean sang.

Kayleigh stared at Sean and bit her lip. "Sorry," she said, "I forgot what comes next."

Kneeling, he grasped one of her fingers and removed it from the
neck. "All you have to do now is leave these two fingers right
where they are. It's still an A chord, but a different kind. Now you
sing the next two words, '*move too*,' before putting that finger back
on like this and..."

"Let me do it, Mr. Music," she said, pushing his wrist away.
Producing an unsatisfactory muffled sound, she scrunched her face
and tried again. The pinging sound of a breaking guitar string startled her, causing Kayleigh to almost drop the instrument. "Oh, *no*!"
she cried out, visibly shaken. "I broke your guitar!" Tears welled
up in her eyes as she looked at Sean. "I'm sorry! I didn't mean it!"

"You didn't *break* the guitar, Kayleigh. It's just a string. I've done it a bunch of times."

"Real—really?" she asked, wiping her frail forearm across her eyes. "Can it be fixed?"

"Of course."

Kayleigh's head swiveled toward an approaching car slowing down to pull over and stop at the curb. "I hope he wants some lemonade!" she said, handing over the guitar.

Sean's head tilted in surprise when he saw the driver exit the car.

"Hey, mister, would you like some lemonade?"

"I sure would," Elliot said, giving Sean a wink.

Kayleigh pulled the spigot, filled the cup, and handed him his drink.

"That'll be fifty cents, please."

"Are you raising money for Alex's Lemonade Stand?" he asked, reaching into his pocket.

"Uh huh."

"I think that's great," Elliot replied, placing the cup down on the table. "You're doing something very special for a great cause." He reached into his inside jacket pocket, removed his wallet, and handed Kayleigh a ten-dollar bill. She stared at the money in her hand, looking confused and a bit upset.

"I'm sorry," she told him, "but I don't have enough money to give you back your change."

"What's your name?" he asked.

"Kayleigh Michaels."

"Nice to meet you, Kayleigh," he said. "My name's Elliot, and I want you keep the change. You're doing a wonderful thing and I know every dollar counts."

"Wow!" she shouted, staring at the money as if the tooth fairy herself sat on her palm. "Ten whole dollars!" She spun to her side, waving the bill in front of her. "Look what Elliot gave me, Mr. Music!"

Sean offered a tributary nod of acknowledgment but assumed no coincidence behind Elliot's sudden appearance. "That was very nice of you, Elliot," he said. "I guess I shouldn't be surprised that you know about Alex's Lemonade Stand."

"Of course I do. It's an amazing story."

"Elliot's a nice man, Mr. Music," Kayleigh said, continuing to stare in obvious delight at the money in her hand.

"Well, thank you, honey." Looking at Sean, he smiled and nodded his head. "Mr. Music, huh? I like that name for you."

"So what brings you out to my neck of the woods, Elliot? I didn't figure you knew where I lived."

"I'm a persistent man, Sean," he said. "We have the phone number and address of every person who's worked at the Center, even special guests like yourself that played for us."

Sean chuckled. "Maybe Kayleigh should start calling you, "Mr. Persistent."

Elliot stared at Sean, showing no change in expression as he sipped from his cup. "Our talent show is in three weeks and everything is setting up quite nicely except for one thing—we still need a guitar player. Know where I can find one?"

"Mr. Music plays the guitar!"

Both men turned toward Kayleigh.

"Tell him, Mr. Music," she said. "You could win any talent show. You're a rock 'n roll star!"

"That's not what he's talking about, Kayleigh," Sean replied, giving a quick shake of the head. "Elliot wants me to play for some kids in his talent show."

"Really?" she replied, her voice rising. "That's really neat!"

Elliot placed his hands on the front of the lemonade stand and leaned forward toward Kayleigh. "Tell you what, honey," he said, nodding his head toward Sean. "If your friend here agrees to play guitar for us, not only will you and your family be invited, but I'll give you a private tour of the Center before the show starts so you can see how we help other kids." Sean slumped into his chair as he watched Elliot work his charm, attempting to seal the deal with a wink and a smile. "I think a big-hearted girl like you will like what we do."

"Oh, boy!" she cried out. "Will you play, Mr. Music? Please? *Pleeease?*"

"You both forgot something," Sean said, staring at Elliot. "I don't play anymore." After another moment, he turned his gaze away and looked at Kayleigh. "We don't even know if it will be okay with your parents."

Her expression changed, an anticipatory smile eclipsed by a sudden tight-lipped look of doubt.

"I'll make you a deal, Kayleigh," Elliot said. "Even if Sean doesn't agree to play for us, you're still invited. But he's right about your parents. Would you like me to talk to them for you?"

"You would do that?" she asked, wide eyed.

"Of course. But if they don't want you to, you have to respect their answer and not give them a hard time. Agreed?"

He extended his hand toward Kayleigh.

"Okay," she said, grasping the tips of Elliot's long fingers.

Sean observed Kayleigh. His growing familiarity allowed him to study her in further depth. He marveled at her capacity to smile over simple things like most kids her age, while remaining enslaved to the decrees of King Cancer. He found himself travelling back in time to his own childhood, before the realities of life's progressive stages chipped away at his innocence like a perpetual sandstorm. Observing her bright, wholesome expression competing against the weight of those continual shadows clinging like twilight beneath her eyes, he decided if playing guitar in a kids' talent show excited her this much, he'd acquiesce this one time.

And it was a good bet those kids wouldn't be asking to sing a Beatles' song.

Chapter 17

It's been nine weeks to the day since you came here," Maldonado said, "and we've been able to narrow down the original list of suspects. Capturing a murderer never comes fast enough, but in this business, two steps forward to one step back is a preferred way to dance."

Sean watched in silence as Maldonado removed the photographs from the folder. Picking through them, he placed the group picture of Hank, Travis, and Arnie, three employees from the dealership, to the side. He proceeded to do the same for the head mechanic, Carlos Carrillo, his general manager, Tom Claiborne, and Merissa's hairdresser, Dino.

"I won't exclude them completely until we find who we're looking for," he said, pushing the photos farther away, "but I feel it's best to focus on the others for now."

Like Scrabble pieces, the detective laid the other photos in a left to right order on the table, allowing full exposure of the lingering Beatles' Song Murderer candidates. "The one other suspect not included here is Amazing Stan the Magic Man. We've actually come across several in the LA County area with that same nickname, but that doesn't surprise me. It's a big city with lots of professional magicians, and if you're name was Stan, what else would you call yourself, right?" Maldonado scanned the photos. "We'll certainly keep him in mind, but it appears he was just a one-time visitor at Ms. Franklin's." Maldonado looked up from the photos. "And I still have a strong hunch the murderer was a close acquaintance."

Sean leaned forward on his elbows and rubbed his hands together, glancing at the men Maldonado pushed aside—men Sean never suspected in the first place. Until yesterday, he also felt the same about the others, but the note he read and pocketed from Roger's drawer engulfed him in increasing waves of uncertainty—enough to phone Maldonado requesting another meeting.

"I looked around to make sure Roger wasn't there before putting the note in my pocket," he told him. "I swear, the doctor's assistant could have been speaking a foreign language at that point. I lost focus on her and everything around me."

Maldonado's cell phone rang. "Sorry, I have to take this."

Sean grasped the other photos and found the one with Roger and his wife, Anita. Studying the man's solemn face, he reflected on what transpired the day before at the dealership when Roger returned to his desk after the discovery of Merissa's note.

"Sean!" Roger said, his voice a loud whisper.

Sean's eyesight ascended from the desk to Roger's face.

"Tom wants to see you in his office. He's with that couple you got into it with." Rolling his eyes, Roger nibbled on his lower lip and stared. Sean couldn't be sure if Roger felt genuine concern or wanted to bust out laughing. "Sorry, buddy," he told him. "Good luck."

His urge to grab Roger by the neck and question him about the note, and maybe more, remained on hold as he walked down the hall toward Claiborne's office. His thoughts raced, wondering what Roger had been up to and for how long. For the many times he'd gone through the motions as a car salesman, feigning enthusiasm while answering third grade questions, Sean never lost his cool with a customer. And as trivial as the incident seemed compared to Merissa, or to his previous thoughts about having cancer, Tom Claiborne had a well-deserved reputation as a no-nonsense disciplinarian when it came to employee misconduct. As the owner's son, Sean didn't know if that mattered.

Sean kept his head lowered as the Blankenships passed him in silence outside the doorway, sensing their icy glare. He stood and didn't say a word until Claiborne motioned for him to sit in the chair across from him, his indecipherable expression leaving uncertainty about his fate.

"I called you in here for two reasons, Sean," he said, his voice cold and steady. "The first thing is, I want to make something very, very clear. If you ever pull that shit again, I won't care if you're God's son, you'll never work here another day." Claiborne's unwavering eyes seemed to bore a hole into Sean's skull. "Do you *understand* me?"

Sean nodded. "I'm sorry, Tom, I just—"

Sean's mouth clamped shut as Tom's hand shot up.

"Now for the second thing I want to talk about." Claiborne swiveled the leather chair to his left, looking out his window for a few moments at the empty hallway. He scratched his neck, stroked his chin, and then turned back, resuming his laser beam focus on Sean. "Your father told me to treat you like any other employee, which is fine, but no other employee of mine has gone through the hell that you did. That's the kind of thing that's going to affect you for a long time, and I understand that. The Sean Hightower who represented himself like an unprofessional asshole a few minutes ago isn't the man I know, and it's why you still have a job."

Sean shut his eyes for a moment and nodded. "Thank you, Tom."

"But there's something I want you to do first," he said. "Actually, let me rephrase that. There's something I insist that you do before resuming your employment." Claiborne leaned his upper body forward, hands and arms flat on the desk, staring at Sean with a look that showed neither anger nor compassion. "I want you to get away from here for a while and don't come back until you're ready. Use whatever vacation time you've accrued and, hopefully, you won't have to dig too much into your own savings, but however long it takes, I don't want you here until your mind's right."

While Maldonado's phone conversation continued, Sean's thoughts returned to the subject at hand as he glanced at the photos of the men who weren't deemed likely considerations anymore. Focusing on the one of Dino, not only did it remind him of the grieving man's extended leave of absence from the salon after Merissa's death, but also the need to make an appointment now that he had returned.

Redirecting his attention to two of the remaining suspects, his shoulders sagged from confusion and doubt as his eyes alternated between the faces of Roger and Adam.

He felt as if he'd been transported to some *Twilight Zone* episode where people he thought he knew might not be those same people. Plopping his elbows back on the table, Sean covered his face in his hands as Maldonado finished his call.

"You said you don't know those two guys from the Chevy dealership, right?" the detective asked, pointing at the third and fourth photos from the left. "But you've seen them at those bowling matches?"

Sean nodded. "The only thing I can say is that the guy on the left is the loud, obnoxious type who takes winning too seriously. The other one kind of blends into the background and doesn't say much at all."

Maldonado held his coffee cup to his mouth, staring at the two men. "Is this bowling thing you guys had still going on? Merissa was the ringleader, right?"

"More for the poker nights," he answered. "It took about four or five weeks but the teams are bowling again every other Wednesday like before." Sean ran his finger along the rim of his cup. "I didn't go to the first two, but went last week. I knew it was going to be awkward for everybody, but I enjoy the camaraderie so it had to happen sometime, right?" Leaning back, he offered Maldonado a tight-lipped smile. "It hurt like Hell, Ray. The memory of her laughter and the way she smack talked everybody...even her stupid-looking bowling motion..." Sean allowed his tears to fall without restraint, staring at the beige nothingness of the wall in front of him.

"You want some more coffee, Sean?"

"No thanks," he answered, his eyes remaining fixed on the wall. "Are we almost done?"

"You told me those bowling matches are every other Wednesday and you went last week. So a week from Wednesday's the next one?"

"That's right."

Maldonado picked up the photo of the two men whose names remained unknown.

"See what you can find out about these two guys," he said. "Starting with their names. Do they work at the Chevy dealer across the street? Do you see them with a wife or girlfriend?" Maldonado tossed the photo back on the table. "Any pertinent information would be helpful, like what you told me about that note in Roger Peterson's desk, or Adam McBride maybe copping a feel."

Sean sat up and looked at Maldonado, surprised at himself over forgetting to mention something "pertinent." His sudden change in expression must have seemed obvious because Maldonado sat up himself with a surprised expression of his own.

"What is it?" he asked, his wide-eyed look narrowing into a squint.

"I forgot to tell you," Sean said. "I'm helping Elliot Hayden with his fundraiser coming up at the end of the month, so I'll be going over there to work with some kids. Maybe there's nothing to it, but I figured it's worth mentioning."

Maldonado clasped his hands together, placing them against his stomach as he leaned back, shoulders pressed back against the chair. "That's good, that's good," he said, breaking into a smile. "Ms. Franklin apparently spent a lot of time at that place. There could be somebody we don't even know about. Somebody that should have their photo right here on this table."

Chapter 18

Dressed in a powder blue cashmere sweater, black polo shirt, and dark blue tailored jeans with loafers, Elliot greeted Sean at the entrance doors of the Valley Youth and Family Directional Center. As he approached him from the parking lot, Sean conceded how this oft-times overbearing individual represented the LA casual look with aplomb. The sole connection between his Domaine Chandon Napa Valley sweatshirt and Elliot's cashmere sweater involved the warmth they both provided on this chilly Friday morning.

"Before I show you what we do in here," Elliot said, placing his hand on Sean's shoulder, "let's take advantage of the fresh, morning air and walk the grounds."

Strolling along the sidewalk bordered by grass and small trees, they passed a fenced playground filled with sand and the usual things one sees for young children—a slide, a small jungle gym, various sized red rubber balls, and a couple of multicolored buckets laying on their side with a partially buried blue plastic shovel between them. What appeared to be a failed attempt at a sandcastle rose about a foot above the ground as a semi-crumbled remnant of an overnight historical ruin.

"The problems at home usually start with children as young as these," Elliot said, stopping and pointing toward the playground. "We have programs to help them get along with their peers and to prep them for the skills it takes for early education." He looked at Sean, grim faced. "Many believe, as do I, that if we lose a child at this age, we may never get them back, and they'll waste whatever potential they have."

Sean reflected on his childhood years in school, remembering the mediocre-at-best grades he received and the jealousy he felt toward his brother and sister's academic excellence. At a certain point, Sean stopped trying, ready to rebel from the frustration and feeling of inferiority. But his life changed forever when his eighth-grade music teacher, Mrs. Oglethorpe, introduced him to the guitar and taught him some chords. Perhaps she rescued the kind of potential Elliot referenced, because from that point on, Sean never looked back...until the realities of the music business forced him into his current 180-degree, twisted neck, chained-to-the past, futureless state.

From the children's playground, they walked another couple of minutes past two large rectangular concrete tables with benches before proceeding toward a patchy grassy area containing small trees and a half-filled flowerbed. Rounding a bend, they veered right and reached a separate building next to a basketball court. Several yards away, on a large section of dirt, a frayed net hung at an abused angle as a lone volleyball rested in solitude at the bottom of the pole.

Elliot pointed toward a triangular shaped one-story vanilla colored building with a pointed roof resembling a glider taking off into the sky to accommodate each extended wing of wood arching back in a forty-five-degree angle. The east and west sides consisted of a grooved vertical dark brown design, complimenting the ninety-degree angles of the stucco structure. Sean hadn't paid much attention to the surrounding generic architecture of the school, but the building standing before him seemed different—modern and more appealing.

"This is the library," Elliot explained, "our most recent addition to the facility. Two years ago last month to be exact. Words can't begin to describe how beneficial it's been to the children." He looked to his right, then back to his left, his eyes perusing the length of the building. "That's is why we work so hard in our fund-raising efforts, Sean. Between the money we raised and some help from the state, we were able to accomplish our goal." Elliot removed a set of keys from his pocket. "Come on, I'll show you what it looks like inside."

Unlocking the door, Elliot ushered Sean in and turned on the lights. Three round wooden tables, each surrounded by six chairs, commanded the middle of the room. Two computers, one against the wall on the left and the other against the right wall, sat on square laminated tables, each a few feet away from metal framed bookshelves lining a portion of each wall. One shelf contained a full row of books, others held just a few, while some remained empty.

"We know what they do at home," Elliot said. "They sit on their butts and play video games." Walking toward the center of the room, he looked around for a moment before turning back toward Sean. "But nothing like that here. What we try to do is introduce them to the wonderful world of their dreams. Video games don't get them to think about life and their role in it, but books do. They stimulate their dormant imaginations, and without that, whatever potential they have as people is ultimately stifled and unrealized."

Sean nodded, trying to remember the last book he read in its entirety.

Elliot pointed upward, moving his hand across the width of the ceiling at the row of lights hanging like yo-yos.

"Marty did a beautiful job installing the lights."

"Martin did this?" Sean asked, scanning the sleek, symmetrical overhead design. As his eyes moved down to a corner of the wall, he pointed to the initials of a sticker on the faceplate switch. "Is he the Boyd on that 'Boyd's Electronics' label?"

"Yes, that's his last name."

"I've seen trucks with that B-shaped plug design before."

"His company services all of LA and Orange County, so that's very possible. I keep telling him with his resemblance to Pierce Brosnan, he should put his handsome face on the truck instead."

"I could use some work at my house." Sean said.

"Even film companies use him now," Elliot told him, holding the door open as they headed outside. "Long days and late nights sometimes, but the money's good."

Arriving at the main entrance to the center, they walked down the tan colored tile hallway until arriving at a small, eggnog colored room housing a piano in the center and two acoustic guitars leaning against the wall. To the left of the piano, five chairs with a music stand for each completed the required assemblage.

"This is where you'll practice with the kids," he told him, extending his hand toward the room. "As we discussed before, I need you here on Monday, Wednesday, and Friday, from five to seven fifteen, forty-five minutes with each child."

As they headed toward the section of the building housing the office and conference rooms, Elliot explained how the school and directional center worked in harmony, each benefiting the child and families in an effectual, even synergistic, manner.

"Dysfunctional families come in all varieties," he said, "and these kids are victims of that dysfunction. The physical and emotional—"

"Excuse me, Elliot? Elliot?"

A dark-haired man wearing a long-sleeved black-and-red-flannel shirt with dark gray cargo pants appeared from one of the rooms without prior notice. He seemed to be a few years younger than Sean but taller by two or three inches and a good twenty pounds heavier. His face, with a nose that widened at the bottom like a bell, had an approximate two-day stubble, and his brown eyes resided in thin, cashew-shaped sockets. Although he kept his hair short, tight curls covered his scalp with wisps of liberated strands sticking up for their independence. He glanced at Sean, nodded in acknowledgment, and turned his attention to Elliot. "Sorry to interrupt," he said, "but I want to remind you that you'll only have me until eight o'clock. I've got that ritzy party I'm performing at."

"Which is why I want you here right from the start at six-thirty," Elliot told him. "You'll stroll among the guests and do your thing as they're arriving and eating their appetizers. But remember, ignore the people looking at the silent auction items. I need their complete attention."

"Six-thirty to eight is perfect," he said. "I can't be late. The woman who's hosting the party is offering me a very nice payday."

"Sean," Elliot said, "I'd like you to meet Amazing Stan the Magic Man. He'll be providing some entertainment for the fundraiser."

"Please," Stan said, extending his hand, "just call me Stan."

In an instant, Sean's alarm bell focus intensified. "I've heard about you, Stan," Sean told him, losing his hand within the man's oversized grip. "Sean Hightower. Nice to finally meet you."

The announcement of Sean's name appeared to startle the man. He shook his head for a brief moment, as if attempting to comprehend the echo of the name. "You're Sean Hightower?" he asked.

Sean felt a sudden irritability at the probability of another comment about "Looking Glass." But the abrupt transformation on Stan's face from contentment to seriousness proved his expectation untrue.

"Merissa and I often worked together on projects," Stan told him. He gazed at the ground for a moment before raising his head and flashing a small smile, looking at Sean with a resigned expression. "I just want to tell you she was a very lovely lady. A great person that I was honored to call my friend."

A few moments of silence followed as Sean attempted to regain his bearings. Stan's admission shot forth from the realm of the unexpected and his emotions teetered between sadness and gratitude. Elliot placed his arm around Sean's shoulder. "Let me introduce you to my staff," he said, attempting to nudge him forward. "Looking forward to Saturday, Stan."

Sean held his ground. "That was very nice of you to say." Extending his hand again, he said, "Thank you."

Stan smiled. "Of course," he replied.

"You came to one of Merissa's poker nights a few months back. I got back after you already left, but Amazing Stan the Magic Man was all anyone talked about. They were all pumped up about showing me the card tricks you taught them."

"It was really no big deal," he told him. "Merissa left her scarf here and I offered to bring it to her house on my way to a party I did that night."

Curling his right hand downward so that his fingers closed in toward his palm, Stan flicked his wrist upward and produced a card from seemingly out of nowhere, held between his thumb and forefinger.

"My card," he said, handing it over. "Here at the center, I'm just another guy helping out, but for those cynical disbelievers out there, I'm Amazing Stan the Magic Man."

Sean studied Stan's business card, impressed by the listing of LA's most renowned venue for magic, The Magic Castle, as his work place. In smaller letters, the card showed his other services for conventions, parties, and private lessons.

"I never know if he's coming or going," Elliot said. "Stan must keep an entire show's worth of stuff in his desk drawers. I wouldn't be surprised if he has a spare set of clothes stashed away some-where."

Stan laughed. "Give me time, Elliot." Returning his attention to Sean, he continued. "I often go to shows from here. Elliot's kind enough to let me keep work materials in my desk for those times when I get a last-minute call, which happens often." He chuckled. "Believe me, what I did at Merissa's house that night was from a beginner's class, but they still got excited over it."

୧୭୧୬୧୭

Sean tucked the card in his pocket as they walked away. "The Magic Castle, huh? Those guys are incredible."

"That's where I first met him," Elliot said. "When he found out about the Center, he asked to come visit, and not long after that he volunteered to help. Now he's a part-time employee. We have a running joke about using his magic to make more donors appear."

Walking through the main entrance, Sean noticed a large card-board poster on the right-side wall with a rectangular plaque above it that read, "Places We Go." Peering through the glass casing, he saw various ticket stubs taped at differing angles. Most of them showed movie theater designations, but he also spotted a couple for Magic Mountain, one for Universal Studios, three for a concert featuring a Latino singer he didn't know, and a few Dodger and Galaxy stubs. In an instant, a sudden dagger-like attention getter, isolated near the upper right corner, caught his eye. He gazed at the full, unused ticket next to another similar one with only the stub remaining. Staring in silence, his thoughts transported him onto a battleground between past and present.

"At the beginning of each year we remove everything and start fresh," Elliot explained. "For most of these kids, a day trip anywhere is new and exciting, so we like to highlight their memories. Even teachers participate, as long as it's something the kids can relate to and not some vacation out of town."

"Are those your Laker tickets you told me about?" Sean asked, his voice rendered closer to a whisper. "April eleventh?"

Elliot stared at Sean before staring through the casing for several long moments. When he finally answered, his voice sounded equally hushed. "Jesus," he said, "I'm sorry, Sean. What was I thinking?" He moved forward, his face now a few inches from the glass. "A lot of these kids know Martin because he helps out here in his free time. When they found out he went to a Lakers game, that was something really special to them. They insisted I put his ticket up there. I included mine to show them what a full ticket looks like. Kind of a before-and-after thing." Grasping the corner of the glass, he adjusted the angle a slight amount, correcting the slightly skewed position from before. Turning back, his eyes narrowed in a pained look of apparent embarrassment. "I guess I was thinking more about them than anything else."

Sean nodded several times, continuing to look at the Laker tickets. "Makes sense," he said. Patting Elliot's shoulder, he walked away.

After introducing Sean to his office staff, Elliot said goodbye to Sean, reiterating the practice days and times for the singers as he departed. Nearing his car, Sean recognized a woman in a ponytail and baseball cap standing in front of her open trunk with a large trash bag tucked under her right arm.

"Jenny, right?" he said, approaching her. "You're Kayleigh's aunt. I met you at my house, remember? I'm Sean Hightower, her neighbor."

Jenny's eyes widened. "Yes, of course." Adjusting the bag to her left arm, Jenny extended her right hand. "Wow, what a coincidence." She stared and smiled for several moments. "I'm moving into a new apartment and getting rid of things I don't use anymore. Are you here for the Donation Depot, too?"

"No, not for that," he answered. "They've got a fundraising event on Saturday and the director asked me to help some kids who are going to sing."

"That's very nice of you, Sean. Elliot must be so happy that you volunteered."

"How do you know Elliot?"

"I've dropped off items here before," she said. "That's where I met him. He introduced himself and thanked me for the donations. He's very passionate about the Center, and I admire him a lot for that." She gestured with her chin toward Sean. "I knew about the fundraiser, but I didn't know you'd be part of the entertainment."

Rolling his eyes, he smiled and shook his head. "After it's over, I don't know how many people will think they've been entertained. I'm not expecting much." He spotted a sealed box in her trunk. "Need help with that one?"

"Oh, that's heavy, so yes, please! There's an old CD player and receiver in there."

Jennie closed the trunk and they headed toward the shop.

"I guess you heard about the event from Stephanie?" Sean asked. "Or Kayleigh?"

An unusual amount of silence followed his question before Jenny answered. "No," she said. "They didn't say anything to me. Did you tell them recently?"

"To make a long story short, Elliot met Kayleigh when she was selling lemonade a little while ago and invited the whole family." He uttered a sarcastic laugh. "I think Kayleigh has it in her head that she's going to a rock concert. She's in for a big disappointment."

Jenny opened the door with her free hand, and Sean walked in first, easing the box on the counter. They stood and waited while a sweet-looking, gray-haired woman attended to someone else, writing the donated items on a sheet of paper. As Sean glanced at the thank you notes on the wall, Jenny reached over and placed her hand on his elbow.

"When you came up to me in the parking lot, do you recall that I mentioned what a coincidence it was?"

"Yeah, I remember."

Jenny's lips tightened as she stared into his eyes, seeming to hesitate before speaking. "When he found out you were living next door to Stephanie, and that we had met, he asked me not to tell you how long I've known him." Looking away for a moment, she stroked her ponytail and adjusted her cap. "But we had lunch together only yesterday, so this is too crazy."

Sean's eyes narrowed, his mind a combination of confusion and curiosity. "You've got the advantage here, Jenny. I don't know who you're talking about."

She snickered before responding. "I know I have to answer you, but promise not to say anything, okay? What's silly is that it's no big deal at all."

Sean spread his hands, palm side up. "And this mystery man is?"

"Adam," she exclaimed. "Adam McBride!"

Sean reared back, tilting his head and staring at Jenny. "You know Adam?" he asked. "Saint Adam McBride?"

Jenny's eyes and mouth opened wide. "*Saint* Adam McBride?" She laughed aloud. "Is that what you call him? That's hysterical!"

The gray-haired woman approached them. After Jenny described the various items, the woman told them she needed to categorize everything with her assistant in the back before writing a receipt. Sean carried the box and Jenny the trash bag into a small room behind a curtain before returning to the front of the store to wait and continue their conversation.

"Adam and I went to high school together," she explained. "Birmingham High in Van Nuys. I first saw him at our ten-year reunion, but it wasn't until our twentieth that we exchanged email addresses. Yesterday's lunch was the first time we did anything socially." Her eyes narrowed as she looked out the window in silence for several moments. "I can't believe how much he's changed. He's turned into a real serious religious guy." She looked back at Sean. "That's just not who I am."

"Now I know we're talking about the same guy," he remarked.

"I know this comment is coming out of nowhere, but I've grown up a lot over the last few years, and my faith is in myself. I had a marriage that lasted too long, and I put up with too much you-know-what. Now I run an online clothing and accessory business that's doing pretty well, and I feel good about myself again."

Sean nodded once. "Well, whatever you went through, you seem to be the stronger for it."

Smiling, she flexed her bicep and winked. "But getting back to Adam, I still don't understand his reasoning for wanting me to keep quiet about our past. He also told me that if his wife found out about our lunch date, she'd kill him. All he kept saying was how he values his privacy, whatever that means." Turning around, she crossed her arms and leaned back against the counter. "Everyone who's donated money is on the mailing list for these fundraisers, and that includes Adam and me. He's going with his wife Saturday night because she insists on it. He knows you went to one of these things before, so he's afraid the three of us might all be here." She shook her head, nibbling her upper lip in apparent bemusement. "You should have seen how relieved he looked when I told him I was going to a party that night."

Sean raised his arms and clasped his hands together in mock prayer before dropping them on top of his head. "Because the big, bad secret might get out?"

"Excuse me," she said, "do I know you?"

Sean laughed, rolling his eyes. "Uh, no," he replied, flashing a sudden mock seriousness. "Never seen you before in my life."

After a brief conversation about Jenny's online business, the woman returned with an invoice for the items. When they left the store and approached her car, she stopped and turned to face him. "Thank you for your help, Sean, and good luck with the show. I would like to have seen it."

Sean closed his eyes, smiled, and shook his head. "At least I'll be spared the indignity of having you witness the depths to which I've sunk," he said.

Jenny reached out to brush his arm. "I understand," she said. "But it's nice of you to help out for a good cause. Besides, I'm a classical music fan, remember? It's my sister, the Sean Hightower fan, you might need to explain things to."

"Long ago and far away, Jenny."

"I suppose," she replied, "but I would have enjoyed seeing you play for those kids anyway." Jenny looked away for a moment, laughing to herself.

"Was that a laugh at my expense?"

"No, that's not it," she replied. "I'm sorry. I'm just thinking of another coincidence that involves you, too."

Sean waited in silence.

"The man who invited me to the party is the magician that'll be here at the fundraiser."

"*Really*?" Sean replied, his eyebrows rising. "Amazing Stan the Magic Man?"

"Can you believe it?" she asked. "He asked me not to tell anybody, but seeing you here today, I just had to."

"Why the secrecy this time?"

Jenny took a deep breath, a sudden sheepish expression on her face. "I know it sounds like a soap opera cliché, but he's still married. He told me he's been separated since April but his wife won't grant him a divorce yet."

"Well, it's none of my business, but be careful."

Jenny nodded. "I know," she told him, "but I'm not looking for a relationship. Just some company and a little fun once in a while."

"Did you meet him here?"

"No, not here," she answered, pushing some loose strands of hair back under her cap. "I met him at a software convention a few weeks ago. Stan was hired to work the room and when he told me he'd seen me somewhere before, I thought it was just a stupid pick-up line. But when he mentioned the volunteer work he does here between his magic stuff, I figured I've donated enough things that he was telling the truth."

"Has Stan met Stephanie, yet?" he asked. "She's going to be seeing him here."

Jenny shook her head. "This will only be our second date, and he asked me not to say anything to anybody right now for obvious reasons." Her eyes widened as a large grin appeared on her face. Sean found her pronounced dimples appealing. "I forgot to tell you one other thing that Adam told me," she said. "He's taking magic lessons from Stan."

"That's cool. Maybe he'll do some card tricks for Jesus at the Second Coming."

Jenny smiled, but wagged her finger at Sean. "That was naughty," she said. "Apparently, they met at a party, and Adam got hooked after Stan performed some magic."

Sean remembered that night at Marissa's quite well.

"I can see it now," he said. "Saint Adam McBride and his Magic Carpet Ride."

Jenny giggled. "The last thing he said to me before we left the restaurant was how much he'd like to show me the tricks he's learned." She rolled her eyes. "I guess that means another secret rendezvous with Saint Adam McBride."

Chapter 19

Rocco sipped a beer as his right leg dangled over the armrest of Sean's living room chair. Watching and listening as his friend finished tuning an acoustic guitar, he remembered how he marveled at the dexterity and fluidity exemplifying his mastery of playing during their band days. Although his problems with Sean's ego and temper during that time remained an unpleasant memory, his past resentment never overshadowed the fact that the man handled his six-string with the talent of a true pro— moving his fingers like a ten-legged dancer, leaping and soaring in harmony and rhythm.

"You were made to play that thing," he told him. "I came here to tell you in person that I want you back at my place as long as you behave, but even if you never play there again, at least don't give it up, okay?"

Sean kept his head down, turning the peg for the B string. "This old acoustic was always one of my favorites." Clutching the guitar by the neck, he placed it next to him on the couch. "And now I'm going to surprise Kayleigh with it."

Rocco's eyes widened. "Wow, that's actually a *nice* thing to do," he exclaimed. "This is all too confusing for me. Will the real Scan Hightower please stand up?"

With a middle finger acknowledgment of the comment, Sean shook his head and chuckled. "Fuck you, Rocco."

"Now *that's* the Sean Hightower I know!"

"To answer your question, you sarcastic asshole, I know this will make the kid real happy, okay? That's all you need to know."

"Too bad you never had a daughter," Rocco said. "They steal your heart from the moment you first hold them."

"In Kayleigh's case, it's probably been as much breaking of the heart as stealing it," he replied. "Whenever I look at that sick kid's face smile at me…" Grabbing his bottle, Sean took a swig and turned away, staring through the sun-speckled window. "You know, Rocco," he said softly, "life's a fucking bitch."

Rocco chuckled.

As if on a swivel, Sean's head spun back to look at him with narrow, uncomprehending eyes. "What are you laughing at? There's nothing funny about that at all."

Rocco held up both hands in mock defense. "Jesus, Sean," he exclaimed, "I know that! I'm just amazed at how this kid seems to have changed you, and definitely for the better, I might add. Suddenly, the Tin Man has a heart!"

Pretending to sneeze, Sean replayed an old band joke by rearing his head, closing his eyes, and placing the back of his hand against his mouth. "Fuuuuuck you!"

Rocco reacted with a new response, repeating the same motions. "Iiiiit's true!"

Sean smiled, shrugged, and glanced at the clock. "I don't know if she's home, but I'm going there now. Want to come?"

"I really should go," he replied, "but I've never seen a real-life Beauty and the Beast."

Sean extended his arm toward Rocco, offering another middle finger response before attempting to rise from the couch. Grabbing his hip, he gritted his teeth and groaned. "Dammit!" he muttered.

"That arthritis you talked about?" Rocco asked.

Sean straightened up in a slow, balloon-filling manner. Grimacing at Rocco, he exhaled slowly and nodded. "I'm telling you, man, life's a bitch."

Approaching the front yard of the Michaels' house, Sean spotted Stephanie's black Nissan Altima in the driveway. When they arrived at the front door, he held the guitar case in his left hand and rang the doorbell. After waiting for about a minute, he pushed the button again.

"Doesn't look like anybody's home," Rocco said.

Sean kept his eyes on the door several moments longer. "I guess not," he answered.

Walking away, they both heard the sudden sound of the door unlocking. Turning back, Sean looked into the misty and puffy-eyed face of a disheveled Stephanie Michaels. She wore no makeup, and portions of her hair tumbled out from a Dodgers cap. Leaning against the half-opened door, she clutched the side with both hands and offered a small smile of recognition.

"Hello, Sean," she said, her raspy voice closer to a whisper. Redirecting her gaze toward Rocco, she said, "Hi."

Offering a quick wave, he said, "I'm Rocco."

Sean noticed Stephanie's eyes veer toward the guitar case.

"Was she supposed to have a lesson today? I'm sorry, I didn't know."

Sean took a few steps closer. "No lesson, Stephanie," he said. "I just want to give this to Kayleigh."

Holding the case from underneath as if presenting a gift on a platter, he encouraged her to hold it. With a tentative motion, Stephanie reached out to grasp it, allowing Sean to unlock the latch and show her the guitar inside. In a simultaneous reaction, tears welled and a full smile flashed forth as her bloodshot eyes moved up and down the instrument like fingers on the strings.

Wiping the tears away with the back of her hand, and then again with her palm, she handed the guitar back to Sean without saying a word for several moments before choking back a sob. "This is so nice of you."

"If now isn't a good time, I can always come back later."

A barely audible chuckle preceded her answer. "It's either a very good time or a very bad one." Stephanie nibbled her upper lip and looked back over her shoulder before opening the door further. "Come in and I'll explain."

The curtains remained drawn most of the way, leaving the house in a darkened state. Stephanie led them to the same room where they watched the Laker games, including the game-six loss to the Celtics for the championship. As if reading his mind, she said, "It took a lot of consoling, computer time, and an extra scoop of her favorite ice cream to dry her tears after that last game. But…" The tears formed again and fell from her eyes. Two-handing them from her cheeks, she shook her head and continued. "That night was *nothing* compared to what we go through, what *she* goes through, with the chemo treatments. We hoped she was finished with them, but the doctor felt she needed another round. That's where we were this morning."

"How's she doing?" Sean asked.

"For her sake, let's hope she's sleeping," Stephanie said, her bit-

terness reflected in her tone, "because it's Hell on Earth for my little girl after the chemo."

"I think we should go, Stephanie," Sean said. "I'll give Kayleigh
her present when she's feeling better." He looked at Rocco and received a nod of agreement.

"Maybe you're right," she told him, "but if she's awake and
having a few decent moments, your gift could be exactly what she
needs."

Jason Michaels, Stephanie's husband, called out from
Kayleigh's bedroom. "Steph," he cried, "need your help!"

Stephanie rushed away without looking back. Sean and Rocco
stood motionless as the jumbled sounds of Kayleigh's moans, vom-
iting, and cries permeated their room.

"We shouldn't be here, Sean," Rocco said. "Let's go."

Sean's face flushed with heat and his eyes watered as he placed
the guitar on the floor and listened to the agony of his little friend.
"In a minute," he replied. "I'll be right back."

Viewing the scene through the partial opening of her door, he
watched in helpless, gut- wrenching sorrow as Kayleigh's father
held the vomit bags while Stephanie cradled her daughter's shoulders. Kayleigh's eyes rolled upward in her swollen sockets and her
mouth remained open between each regurgitation. Her cries sliced
him up inside, a slashing combination of pain and suffering—a
branding iron image seared in his mind.

Another sound from behind caught his attention. Looking back,
he realized Rocco left and closed the door. Glancing back toward
the nightmarish scene from Kayleigh's room for another few moments, he turned away for good, grabbing the guitar case as he
rushed toward the door, knowing he didn't belong there.

Sean spotted Rocco, his back toward him, staring at the sky
from the sidewalk in front of his house. As he approached him, his
friend remained immobile—a statue in blue jeans and black leather
jacket. Sean lowered the case to the ground and covered his face
with his hands, leaving them there like a mask. Dropping his arms,
he gazed into the vast nothingness of the blacktop in the street, inhaling deeply before blowing the air out in a gust of anger and distress.

Rocco's voice, soft and pensive, penetrated the silence. "I was
raised to believe in a compassionate God," he said.

Sean glanced at him continuing to look skyward before returning his own vision toward the ground.

"But how do I justify those teachings when that kind of *shit* can happen to a little girl?"

When Sean lifted his eyes from the street, he saw that Rocco's gaze now zeroed in on him.

"You're right about something, Sean," he said. "Life *is* a bitch. But compared to what we just witnessed in there, how the hell would you know?"

Chapter 20

Two days before the Saturday night fundraiser and four more before he returned to work, Sean sat by his pool in the late afternoon, waiting for Roger and Anita. New employee handbooks needed to be reviewed and insurance forms filled out before Monday, so Roger offered to bring them to Sean's house, explaining to him over the phone that he and Anita had a five o'clock appointment not far from there.

Sipping on a beer, he gazed at a group of clouds braided like a horizontal question mark, symbolizing the instability of his current reality. Merissa's killer remained at large, he didn't write or even play music anymore, and he didn't have much of a social life. A slow nod of his head followed the realization that a chance to sell cars offered a welcome distraction and an opportunity to relieve the boredom.

The blues guitar cell phone ring redirected his thoughts back to the present moment.

"Hightower here," he answered, "but Roger isn't."

"We're pulling up now," Roger replied. "You still in the back?"

"Yep, side gate's open."

Sean heard the car approach and the motor cut off. Glancing at the time on his phone, he wondered why Roger needed to leave work early. Anita walked through the gate first, followed by Roger, apparently texting a message to someone. After a few moments spent greeting Hendrix, Anita approached Sean.

"Hi there, stranger" she said, extending her arms as he rose from the chair.

"Good to see you, Anita," he told her as they hugged.

"Well, well, well," Roger said, waving his hand toward the pool and then toward Sean's attire. "The retired life suits you, my friend."

"That's a shame," he replied. "On Monday, I'll be back offering summer deals and hoping the AC works on test drives."

Roger handed Sean the pamphlet. "Here you go, buddy, for your reading pleasure."

"Can I offer you something to drink?" Sean asked, looking at Anita.

"No thanks. We can't stay that long." Looking at the time on her watch, she lifted her eyes toward Roger. "In fact, we only have about five minutes."

Roger inhaled, nodded, and released the air in an extended exhale. "Okay, babe."

"Are those insurance forms in here?" Sean asked, thumbing through the pages.

Roger closed his eyes and shook his head, followed by a small chuckle. "Not when they're in my jacket pocket which happens to be in the backseat of my car."

After a few moments spent staring in her husband's direction as he hurried through the gate, Anita's eyes followed Hendrix trotting back from that direction. She dropped to one knee and petted him in silence before rising again to look at Sean.

"I've known you a long time, you know that?" she asked. "Rebecca and I were close friends in high school and you were her little brother who always liked to show off on the guitar."

Sean chuckled. "You could have been my first groupie."

Anita smiled, betrayed by eyes reflecting an obvious sadness.

"Something wrong, Anita?"

Staring at Hendrix, she answered Sean as if speaking to the dog. "I don't know how much you know about our marriage," she said, fiddling with her wedding ring, "but it hasn't been the smoothest journey, believe me." She looked at Sean, biting her lip in momentary silence. "We were even separated for a while." Turning away, she wiped a tear from her eye. "Sorry."

"Don't be," he replied.

Taking a deep breath, she continued. "It took a while, but we're finally meeting with a marriage counselor today." Imparting a partial smile, seemingly wistful, her shoulders rose and dropped with a resigned shrug. "I still love him. Even with the cheating, I still love him."

Sean reached out to touch her shoulder. "You're a good woman, Anita."

Anita uttered a quick, sarcastic sounding laugh. "Sorry, Sean," she said, "I appreciate that, I really do, but those were the exact words I remember hearing from Roger, and I apologize for bringing this up, the morning we found out about Merissa." She shook her head, staring at the ground for several moments before looking up again and then turning away to gaze into the pool. "He came home really late the night before, sometime after two. He had called me from work, telling me he was meeting up with some fraternity brothers for dinner and drinks, but something about the tone of his voice didn't seem right, didn't sound sincere. So that next morning, maybe because I felt so angry and sad after hearing about Merissa, I finally had the strength to confront him."

Anita's look seemed distant, her mouth tightening and her jaw growing rigid as she stared into Sean's eyes. "He admitted everything. But the most painful thing he told me was his final words before leaving for work." A tear fell from her eyes. "He said, 'You're a good woman.'"

Under normal circumstances, Anita's reference to Merissa's death may have wounded him, or embarrassed him after his botched attempt to sooth her with his comment, or perhaps make him feel uncomfortable by his exposure to her hurtful honesty, but after her remark about Roger's absence from the house that night until two o'clock, he couldn't help but wonder about a possible connection. Roger claimed he returned to his house around eleven after fucking his dental hygienist, but Anita said it was three hours later. Why did he lie? Was he trying to make Sean think he developed a conscience by coming home in time to kiss his wife goodnight? A little nobility to dilute the sleaze?

Or was there another reason?

Chapter 21

As planned, Elliot greeted the Michaels family at four-thirty, two hours before the guests were due to arrive. Sean arranged a final dress rehearsal at five o'clock with the three children, but got there at the same time because Kayleigh wanted to drive in his car. Dressed in a made-for-Los-Angeles-summer light gray suit and charcoal gray silk shirt with burgundy-hued tie, Elliot looked the part of a persuasive and charming pony-tailed fundraising host. After shaking hands with Jason, Stephanie, and Randy, he knelt in front of Kayleigh and extended his hands. With the right one he shook her hand, and with the left he held a gardenia flower with a safety pin on the back.

"This is for you, sweetie," he told her. "Smells great, huh?"

Kayleigh held the flower in her open palm, dipping her nose for a couple of extended sniffs as her face disappeared under the brim of her Lukers cap.

"What do you say, Kayleigh?" Jason asked.

"Thank you," she said, looking at her mother as Stephanie pinned the flower near her collar.

Elliot placed a gentle hand on her head. "Well, Kayleigh," he said, "how about that tour I promised you and your family?"

"What about the magic show?" she asked, her pale, peering face resembling a low rising moon.

Elliot smiled down and winked. "Don't you worry about that, okay?. We're saving the best for last. Amazing Stan the Magic Man is looking forward to giving all of you a private show before everybody gets here."

"Awesome!" Randy shouted.

Kayleigh giggled, her eyes transforming into slits as her pallid cheeks wrinkled like a deflated white balloon.

"Come on, everybody, we better get going," Elliot said, glancing at his watch. "Sean, feel free to join us, but your singers will be here in less than thirty minutes."

"I'll wait in the music room," he answered.

Despite the closed door, Sean noticed the bright lights through the overhead window as he neared the room. With a simultaneous knocking and turning of the knob, he peeked his head through the partial opening. Seeing nobody to his left, he opened the door enough to lean in and look toward his right. Sitting at the desk near the chairs and music stands, Stan held a deck of cards, appearing to work on a trick of some kind. Scattered on the desk was a large red scarf, a box of long stick matches, a watch with a shiny gold band, a brown paper bag, and a cell phone.

"Hi, Sean," he said, glancing up.

"How ya doin', Stan?" Sean lowered his guitar case to the floor by the nearest music stand. "Did Elliot tell you I'll need this room at five?"

"Yeah, no problem," he replied, shuffling the deck and turning the top card over. "*Whoa!*" Stan tilted his head and his eyebrows furrowed. "Something's wrong." Tossing the cards on the table in a rapid one by one sequence, he started nodding his head as the last few remained in his hand. "I knew it!"

"What's wrong?" Sean asked, approaching the desk.

"The deck's short a card," he mumbled, continuing to stare at the cards. "I'm lucky. Better to have happened now than when I'm performing a trick."

Sean spotted the identifiable Bicycle design on the back of the cards. His thoughts raced back to the day he found one on the floor when he packed Merissa's clothes—a card he recalled as similar to, if not the same as, the ones he was looking at now. As for which one it was, it had been too long, but for some reason he had a recollection of a familiar connection to something, or, perhaps, someone.

"Do you always need a full deck to do tricks?"

"No, but I do a number of them where I'll ask you to think of any card." He looked at Sean, standing to his right. "I wouldn't look very good if you chose the one that's missing."

Pulling a trash can out from underneath the desk, Stan scooped the cards in one clean sweep, his gold USC ring catching Sean's eye as the long fingers gripped the deck like a spider devouring his prey. "No use to me now."

Sean watched them disappear in an instant, culminating in a loud thudding sound.

"You work with Adam McBride, right?" Stan asked.

The question startled Sean, as that now made two different people at the Directional Center talking about Adam within the last few days. "Yeah...yeah, well...I used to. He works at the other dealership now. Why?"

"Because *he's* the reason that deck is fifty-two minus one."

"Adam?" Sean asked, squinting his eyes in confusion. "How the hell did that happen?"

Stan turned his upper body to the right and angled back in the chair to look at Sean. "Quick backstory," he said, "but it involves Merissa. Is that all right?"

Sean nodded his acceptance.

"Adam and I attend the same church. That night when I went to Merissa's house, I recognized him and we talked for a while." Stan chuckled. "I remember thinking Roger was this Sean guy she used to talk about because it seemed he was next to her the whole time."

"No surprise," Sean muttered. "So you and Roger are on a first name basis, too?"

"One of the things I do is teach private lessons," he said, "so after I handed out my business cards Adam and Roger both approached me about it. To save money, they take group lessons here at the Center with Elliot. It's just basic sleight of hand stuff but it makes them think they're the next Houdini."

"So you gave Adam that deck of cards to take home?"

"Yep," Stan answered, turning back again. "And you know why?" Rolling his eyes, he shook his head and looked away for moment before returning his attention to Sean. "You're not going to believe this. He tells me his wife doesn't allow cards in the house because they represent the whole evil gambling thing, so he wanted to practice during his lunch hour until he got good enough to entertain her. Then she'd see it was all in good fun."

"Oh, I believe it," Sean said, "not surprised at all. But why didn't he just go out and buy his own damn deck?"

Stan snorted an air of apparent disgust. "Logical question, Sean, but we're not dealing with a normal situation here. Adam flat out refused to buy his own cards until he felt he was ready. All right, fine, but now that I know he lost one of the cards without saying anything, it pisses me off. This is my profession, and it could have been very embarrassing if I was unaware the deck didn't have a full fifty-two."

"Maybe he didn't know."

Stan stroked his chin, his eyes zeroing in on Sean. "I don't obey the teachings of everything I'm taught on Sundays, but taking responsibility for one's own actions is something I definitely believe in. It was up to him to know." Rubbing his forehead with his fingertips, he looked down at the trashcan. "It just never crossed my mind the deck was short. I put it in my drawer with the other ones a few months ago and didn't use it again until today."

Stan rose from his chair and nudged the trash can back under the desk with his foot. Sean heard his chuckle before noticing how Stan's serious expression from the previous moment transformed into an amused one. "If you ask me," he said, "and please excuse the pun, sometimes Adam seems like he isn't always playing with a full deck."

Nodding in acknowledgment at the remark, Sean smiled and pointed to the other items remaining on the desk. "Are those part of your act for Kayleigh and her family?"

"Yes," Stan answered, reaching for the scarf. "Just a few basic 'how did he do that' tricks to entertain that poor little girl." Waving the scarf in the air, he snapped his wrist and suddenly held a red rose in his hand instead.

Sean responded with three soft hand claps. "Very nice!"

Stan followed with an extended half bow. "Thank you," he said. "I learned that one back in my early days, but it still has its moments."

When Stan's cell phone rang, Sean meandered over to admire a Carlos Santana concert poster on the back wall, recalling a time he saw him kick ass as the opening act for Bob Dylan at the Memorial Coliseum in Portland many years before. Unable to avoid overhearing the conversation within the modest confines of the room, his attention toward every spoken word from Stan soon heightened into full-blown concentration. Although Jenny's name hadn't yet been mentioned, Sean realized she was the one who called.

And thanks to the Santana poster, a sudden, clear recollection of the forgotten blue Bicycle playing card created an image in his mind as large as the poster itself. Now he needed to get to that trash can.

"That's right, when the clock strikes eight, I'll be finished here and should arrive at your place in about twenty to thirty minutes, depending on traffic...Yeah, it's going to be fun...Don't worry, you'll do fine...Hey, if you're going to be my lovely assistant and know what to do, you'll have to learn how I perform the tricks." After another pause, he laughed. "Exactly," he told her. "All right, I'll talk to you later."

"Hi, Sean."

Through a sticky breakaway from his eavesdropping state, Sean turned and recognized Leticia, one of the singers for the show.

"Um, hi, Leticia," he said, needing to clear his throat. "Go ahead and sit down, I'll be right with you."

Stan glanced at his watch before rising from his chair to gather his materials. "Good luck," he said, smiling at the girl on his way to the door. Turning back to Sean, he nodded and winked. "Good luck to you, too, my man. Nice talking with you."

When the door closed, Sean held his hand up toward Leticia. "Hang on a minute," he told her. Sliding out the trash can from under the desk, he gathered the cards and started to review each one.

With a few more remaining, Stan reentered the room without looking at Sean, walking toward the left to retrieve his jacket from a hook on the wall. As he turned back to leave, he spotted Sean holding the cards.

"What are you doing with those?"

"The *Jack of Hearts*," Sean said, speaking in a precise and deliberate manner. "That's the missing card."

Stan's eyes opened wide as he stood there, motionless and silent. After an exaggerated shrug of his shoulders, he smiled and nodded several times. "Well, well," he said, "now you know. For whatever good it does you, now you know."

Sean watched him leave, continuing to stare at the closed door. *You're right, Stan,* he thought, *I know about the Jack of Hearts, but what I don't know about is if Jenny's in danger.*

Chapter 22

S ean didn't believe in that overrated, overused, "things happen for a reason" nonsense, but, nonetheless, his chance meeting with Stan couldn't be discounted. Could the deck of cards he now held in his hand offer a link to Merissa's murder? He hadn't mentioned the Jack of Hearts discovery to Detective Maldonado, but now a connection seemed possible. As soon as he finished this final rehearsal with Leticia, Darryl, and Gabriella, he'd call him.

ↄ≻ↄ≻ↄ

The Anderson Club and Banquet Hall shared the same large parcel of land as The Mid-Valley Youth and Family Directional Center. Each time Elliot held a fundraiser, the club donated its facility for a bargain rate. Another benefit from this arrangement centered on the parking, providing everyone with easy access to the additional spaces. By arriving two hours early, Sean and the Michaels family received their prime pick of locations, choosing to park in areas directly between the doors to both buildings. Sean returned to his car at six-ten to talk privately with Detective Maldonado, providing a clear view of the occupants of the first car turning in from the street—Adam and Eleanor McBride.

Hoping they wouldn't notice him, he waited to make the call, but Adam's lingering expression of recognition as he spotted the vehicle preceded a big smile and wave of his hand before turning to say something to Eleanor. Moments later, Sean lowered his window as they both approached. "My, my," Sean said, working up a smile as he shook their hands. "Who is this beautiful couple? Look out for the paparazzi!"

Eleanor laughed as she clutched the collar of her sweater to ward off a sudden breeze. "Paparazzi don't seek out simple, God-fearing folks like us, Sean."

"Want us to wait for you?" Adam asked, holding his hair down with his hand.

Sean raised his cell phone in the air. "I've got to make a call first," he told them. "I'll see you inside."

Detective Maldonado sounded either tired, frustrated, or pissed off when he answered, making Sean question whether now was a good time to play Robin to his Batman.

"I was going to call you," he said.

"Why's that?"

Maldonado didn't say anything for several moments. "The Beatles' Song Murderer," he answered, his voice trailing off on the last word. "He struck again."

Sean's eyes slammed shut as his body collapsed against the seat. The tears returned from their hiatus as the world around him disappeared in a shroud of pain and sadness. He missed Merissa so much. And now another woman underwent the same torture. Another...*Merissa.*

"When? Where...where this time?" he asked, his voice a raspy whisper.

"Tuesday night in Simi Valley," Maldonado answered, identifying the city located about thirty miles northwest. "A residential street with apartments up and down the block. You'd hope there'd be some kind of lead, some kind of witness coming forward, but nothing so far."

Sean exhaled hard enough to blow out candles on a cake.

"No prints, no evidence, *nothing*...again!"

A few seconds of silence followed.

"Listen to me, Sean. You're not the only person I've spent time with whose life was torn apart from this guy, who got swallowed up by the immense grief that you did. It absolutely cuts me up inside. So trust me when I tell you that I want to catch this sick asshole as much as any of you. But in all my years chasing down scum like this, the most important thing I've learned is what I call 'minding your p's.'"

"And that means?"

"Patience plus persistence equals payoff. Believe me, okay? From the time I graduated from the academy, I got handed a badge and a gun, but nobody gave me the ability to read minds. The best quarterbacks complete their passes against all the schemes the defense throws at them by studying the playbook and being prepared. That's why we need every piece of evidence we can get, and why we need to figure out whatever clues may be out there for us to solve. So that when the opportunity strikes, we'll be ready to strike. Just don't give up hope."

Sean stared at the ground outside his window, his thoughts suspended by a fatigue of helplessness. "Thanks, Ray," he said. "The football analogy took me by surprise, but in this case, I found it appropriate."

"For whatever it's worth, we did find one thing at the crime scene that I'll mention—a bloody sliver of gray duct tape on the victim's tongue. We're speculating that she tried to remove it from her mouth with her teeth and bit the back of her lip in the process. The matching DNA proves the blood is hers, but other than that, it's the same residual markings from the tape across her mouth, and the red coloration and bruising on her wrists from the handcuffs."

Sean pictured Merissa in the same predicament—her mouth taped shut and her hands bound as she suffered. More teardrops advanced from behind closed lids.

"Duct tape on her tongue?" Sean repeated, wiping his cheeks with the back of his hand. "Does that help? Does it mean anything?"

"It tells us he used duct tape," Maldonado said. "Common, store-bought duct tape."

"What about security cameras?"

"Oh yeah, they had 'em all right," he told him. "Modern ones, too. But anybody who showed up in those frames during the approximate hours leading up to and after her death has been checked out and cleared. Ms. Franklin's place only had a couple of older cameras for the garage and pool areas, and nothing of consequence there, either. This guy apparently understands how to avoid detection. He knows when and where and how to strike." Maldonado exhaled a loud, extended breath, followed by a muted cough. "So why'd you call, Sean?"

His parched throat felt like an esophageal concrete passageway as he swallowed. He wiped his cheeks again and sat up, gazing out his windshield at the guests walking toward the banquet hall past the swaying trees in the lawn. "I never told you about finding that Jack of Hearts, did I?"

Silence.

"No, but you're about to."

Sean described the scene when he packed Merissa's clothes for the donation center. He explained how he'd waited until the end to deal with the final thing he wanted to rid himself of—his sweatshirt that she apparently had on that night. Sean explained how he put it on before the police arrived, not thinking about it as any piece of evidence but simply as the last thing Merissa wore. But after disposing of the memories represented by her belongings, the grief and anger overtook him, and he swung the sweatshirt repeatedly like a baseball bat, knocking over anything in the way.

"Sometime after that, I fell back into my chair and just stared into space for a while. That's when I noticed the card. What I'm thinking is that it must have been in one of the pockets and came out when I swung the sweatshirt around."

Another period of quiet followed, leading a frustrated Sean to wonder if he'd lost the connection. "Are you there?" he asked.

"*Jesus,*" Maldonado muttered, "we search the whole freakin' room for clues and you don't tell us you're wearing what might have had the biggest goddamn clue of all?" A loud exhaling sound preceded Maldonado's next comment. "I'm pissed off, Sean, but berating someone who was out of his head with shock and grief would be wrong. The problem now is it may be too late to get any fingerprints."

"Because they may have faded away?"

"A good chance of that, yeah," Maldonado answered. "But like I said, it *may* be too late. The good thing about playing cards when it comes to prints is that they're one of the better surfaces for print detection. That type of plastic retains film from sweat or oil longer than some other surfaces, so maybe we'll still be able to detect a discernible image."

Sean realized Maldonado expected him to still have the card.

"The length of time leaves everything up in the air at this point, not to mention how many different prints might be on that card. In addition to the killer's, we've got yours, for sure, and very possibly Ms. Franklin's." Maldonado made several tongue-clicking sounds. "Are you home, now? I'll send someone to go get it."

Sean squeezed the phone and scrunched his mouth, preparing to confess something he knew wouldn't be well received. "I don't know where it is," he told him. "It was months ago, and back then it didn't mean anything to me. Maybe I even tossed it."

"Shit," Maldonado muttered. "*Shit!*"

"I'm sorry Ray, I—"

"Well you better make goddamn sure, okay? We need all the help we can get right now."

"I will," he said, "but the reason I asked you the Jack of Hearts question is because something happened here a little while ago that may have shown me where that card came from. I didn't believe it at first, but you may be right when you told me The Beatles' Song Murderer could be someone I know."

"Slow down, Sean, slow down," Maldonado said. "First off, what do you mean, 'something happened *here*'? Where are you?"

"A fundraising event at the Valley Center that Elliot Hayden operates. It's the same place where Merissa did volunteer work, remember?"

"Of course, I remember."

"There's a guy here who used to work with Merissa. 'A great person who I was honored to call my friend,' is how he put it. And get this—he's the magician that came to her house one night and taught tricks to everyone."

"Stan, right?"

"Yes."

"Did you get his last name?"

"No, sorry," Sean answered. "I have his business card, but it only says, 'Amazing Stan the Magic Man.'"

"Find out for me."

"Will do, but what I wanted to tell you is a little while ago I saw him working with a deck of cards that was missing the Jack of Hearts."

"It *was*?" Maldonado asked. "Are you sure?"

"One hundred percent. He threw them in the trash can before he left the room, so I took them out and went through every card, ending with the fifty-first. I still have them in my pocket."

"That is *very* interesting news."

"And the cards have the same blue Bicycle design on the back."

"Okay…okay," Maldonado said, his voice taking on a sudden animated tone. "Tell me everything it says on the card."

Sean reached into his pocket, reading the card's entirety out loud.

"We'll run a second background check on that name. Maybe something noteworthy will show up that we missed the first time. The man does parties and conventions, so we'll need to take another look at the victims' backgrounds, things they may have attended in the days leading up to their murders. Let's see if any of them could have known him previously. It's a shot in the dark, but a possible lead nonetheless. Good work, Sean."

Sean leaned back and rested his head against the window as he eased his body between the door and the edge of his seat. Understanding that a short time ago he may have conversed face to face with Merissa's murderer turned his stomach into a logjam of knots and nerves.

"Are you really able to find out if they went to any conventions or parties or whatever it might be that had a magician? That sounds like a shitload of work."

"Do we have any other choice?" Maldonado shot back, his voice rising. "Welcome to the world of shitload, Sean. *This* is what it takes. *This* is what we need to do."

"Of course," Sean replied, his voice softening.

"Try to find that card, all right? We'll see if we can check it for prints and match them against the rest of the deck."

"When I get home tonight I'll look for it," he answered, spotting Anita Peterson, sans Roger, walking toward the entrance. He looked at the time on his phone and realized he needed to end the conversation. "I better go, Ray."

"Answer me something first," Maldonado said. "If you called to tell me about your suspicion of Stan, a guy you previously didn't know, then why'd you tell me I could be right about Miss Franklin's murderer being somebody you knew?"

Sean looked toward the club entrance and saw people arriving at a faster rate. "Because of what Stan told me about Adam."

"What *Stan* told you about him? Did you know they knew each other?"

"Not until today," he answered. "He told me they attend the same church. He also taught him card tricks." Closing his eyes, he shook his head in confusion and, as he recognized now, in fear as well. "Now I'm thinking Adam could also be the one."

Sean described what he'd been told—about the private magic lesson and how Adam returned Stan's deck of cards one Jack of Hearts short of a full fifty-two. The coincidence seemed too great to ignore and the detective agreed, intrigued by these new revelations and complimentary of Sean's help in uncovering them.

"It's about six-thirty now," Maldonado said. "Can you call me back at nine? I just want to know if you make any further observations tonight."

When the conversation ended, Sean remained in his car another few minutes attempting to calm his emotions. The lingering light of a breezy July early evening allowed an extended visibility of the guests continuing to arrive. Spotting Darryl, one of the singers performing that night, standing by the entrance as his parents approached him, he reminded himself that despite his current distractions, playing a few basic chords on an acoustic for a nervous kid at a fundraiser required nothing more than a small percentage of his focus. But as he reached for the door handle, engulfed by his sudden knife-edged distrust of Adam and Stan, he realized one percent might be all he had to give.

Chapter 23

After entering through the open-air overhang off the parking lot, Sean watched two staff workers greet a couple at the sign-in table. After presenting them with a Mid-Valley Youth and Family Directional Center coffee cup and ball cap, they directed them to the courtyard, pointing toward the walkway on the right side. Recognizing Sean, they smiled and wished him luck as he walked by, guitar case in hand. Rounding a corner to the courtyard, he observed groups of people milling around long rectangular tables as they perused the donations for the silent auction. Ever the salesman, Elliot stood among them, gesticulating, talking, and passing his hands over the various gifts. At the end of the table nearest Sean, the signing paper under a wrapped basket of what appeared to be kitchen supplies blew to the ground after another strong breeze. A bald man with a flowery shirt leaned down to grab it, but as he started to rise, another paper flew off. After tucking both sheets under their respective gifts, the man walked toward Elliot and started speaking with him, pointing to the area where he'd just been.

As Sean turned and headed for the stage, he saw the Michaels family waving their hands from one of the dining tables. Waving back, he started walking in their direction, glancing to his left as Stan performed a trick for two men and two women standing near him. Placing his guitar at the base of the microphone, he greeted the Michaels and told them he'd return after getting some food.

Closing the sliding lid to the lasagna platter, he looked toward the card on the table signifying what the next enclosed container held.

"Try the chicken wings," a familiar voice said. "They are messy but delicious."

Turning, he smiled at Anita Peterson, looking noticeably weary despite the makeup.

"Hi, Anita," he said. "I didn't know you'd be here tonight."

"It's for a good cause, so why not? We were here for the last one, too, thanks to…well…thanks to Merissa."

Sean acknowledged the remark with a smile and nod.

"I was in my car when I saw you walk in by yourself. Is Roger here?"

A sorrowful expression overtook her face.

"I told him I didn't want to be with him tonight," she explained. "He's supposed to be at home reflecting on what an asshole he can be, but who the hell knows? She looked down at his plate. "Oh, I'm sorry, Sean. Finish getting your dinner."

"I admit I better eat soon," he told her, glancing at his food. "I'm playing for some budding young superstars who'll be singing tonight."

"Looking forward to it," she said, offering his elbow a light squeeze. "Now go eat."

As she walked away, Sean realized he wanted to know. He *needed* to know.

"Anita, wait!" After she stopped and turned, Sean beckoned her with a tilt of his head.

"Need help finding the chicken wings?"

"So why's he at home?" he asked. "Tell me."

Anita stared at him, her expression a blank canvas. "Your food's getting cold, Sean."

He leaned forward, placing his face close to hers.

"Just tell me he forgot about your anniversary, or came home late when you cooked a special dinner for him, something like that, okay? Tell me that the marriage counselor stuff is working and your unhappy facial expression had nothing to do with his past bullshit."

A momentary appearance of moistness appeared in her eyes, transforming into a look of defiance. "It wasn't an anniversary," she said, "it was a birthday. *His* birthday. And as a surprise I bought him the bowling ball he's been wanting. I had to lug his old one into the store so they'd know the size of the finger holes, right? What a wife, huh?" Anita turned away, her hand first covering her mouth and then moving up to wipe her eyes. "I'm sorry," she said. Heaving a deep sigh, her shoulders rose then dropped like a scream ride at an amusement park. "When I lifted the old ball out of the bag, I discovered a little surprise inside, hiding at the bottom." A bitter smile emerged on her face. "A pair of handcuffs."

Sean felt the plate loosen from his grip and whipped his other hand around to steady it from underneath.

"You look pretty shocked," she said. "But considering how Roger's asked me more than once to try that kinky shit before, I had a bad feeling about them. I mean, if he couldn't get his porn-star jollies from me, why'd he have them? And what were they doing at the bottom of his bowling bag? Wouldn't surprise me if one of the women you bowl with is Roger's new fling." Gazing down at her feet, she shook her head and laughed. "So when he came home from work and I asked him about it, he actually tried to convince me he was learning a magic trick with them. Can you believe that? So I asked him to show me what he'd learned so far. He just sat there and looked at me, not knowing what to do." She swallowed hard and stared into Sean's eyes. "When he couldn't even fake it, I knew. That's when I told him to leave. I'm not sure what time it was when he came back but it was late and I was already asleep."

Sean shook his head. "Sorry for what you're going through, Anita."

She reached out and grasped his shoulder. "I don't know why I'm telling you all this, Sean," she said. "It's my burden to bear. Good luck tonight, okay?"

Sean realized a missing piece of information needed an answer.

"What night was this?" he asked. "Was it this week?"

Anita stopped and looked at him, her head tilting slightly. "Why that matters to you I have no idea," she said. "But since you asked, yes, it was Tuesday."

He watched her walk toward the silent auction tables, his mind a brewing cauldron of speculation and suspicion. As he struggled to clear his thoughts for the moment about Roger, in addition to Adam and Stan, he realized he'd better concentrate on the matter at hand to make it through the show. Turning back to the buffet, he helped himself to some chicken wings before returning to the Michaels family.

∽∾∽

"You should have seen Amazing Stan the Magic Man!" Kayleigh exclaimed, wearing her Mid-Valley Youth and Family Directional Center cap. "Wow!"

"Yeah!" Randy shouted. "He did a trick where I picked a card and signed my name, and it wound up inside a sealed envelope!"

"And he turned a scarf into flowers!" Kayleigh said. "And he took Daddy's watch off and put it in his pocket, and Daddy didn't even know!"

Sean finished another mouthful of lasagna. "Sounds like you guys had a great time."

"Elliot was a very gracious host," Stephanie said. "He knew Kayleigh wasn't strong enough to walk everywhere so he let her use a computer in the office until we came back for the magic show. And now he has us sitting here center stage because he knows how much Kayleigh wants to see you up there."

Sean smiled and winked at his snow globe-headed little friend, a picture of beaming joy under her cap. "This isn't the Sean Hightower Band you're going to hear, Kayleigh," he explained. "Just a little background guitar for the kids who are going to sing." Observing how her smile hadn't waned, and concluding that nothing he'd say mattered, he resigned himself to her excitement. "But I'll try not to let you down."

"She loves her new guitar," Sean," Stephanie said, looking at her daughter. "I heard her practice today and she's really improving."

"Don't forget my lesson tomorrow, Mr. Music."

"Have you been working on those chords I showed you?"

Kayleigh nodded her head like a rapidly dribbled basketball.

The schedule called for the first of the three singers to perform at eight o'clock. When Sean saw Elliot walking toward the table he checked the time, verifying another fifteen minutes remained. More food remained on his plate and he intended to finish the rest.

"How's everybody doing over here," he asked, placing his hand on Kayleigh's shoulder.

"We're having a great time, Elliot, thank you," Jason answered.

"I hope these wind gusts aren't bothering any of you," he said. "I've had to use this to keep the silent auction papers from blowing away."

Sean had his head lowered, eating another chicken wing with one hand while reaching for his napkin with the other.

"Well that kind of tape will sure do it," Stephanie said.

The instant Sean looked up, Elliot captured his full attention.

"Let's hear it for our ever-handy miscellaneous supply box," he explained, chuckling. "From sponges to hammers to rope to tape, you never know what might come up. It'll take a hurricane to scatter them now."

Sean continued staring at the nondescript object in Elliot's hand, wondering if the item meant anything at all. After all, it was only duct tape. Common, store-bought duct tape.

Chapter 24

I'm in the parking lot."

"You're *what*?"

"I'm in the parking lot," Maldonado repeated. "I'm here to talk with Stan, full name Ulysses Stanley Claybourne."

"So that's what his initial ring stood for, huh?" Sean replied. "I assumed it meant the school."

"Ulysses Stanley Claybourne, forty-eight years of age, born and raised in Medford, Oregon. Attended the University of Oregon from 1978 to 1980 but didn't graduate. Eventually took up residence in Los Angeles in 1991. None of this tells us a damn thing, but I'm curious as to why somebody who worked with Miss Franklin and claimed a strong fondness for her didn't attend her funeral. There could be a perfectly reasonable explanation, but it's still a question worth asking."

Sean sat in the darkness of his car, holding the phone in his left hand while his right thumb rubbed circles along the inside portion of his fingers. From his vantage point, most of the parking spaces remained occupied, but he knew the reason for one of the vacant ones. Stan left the party an hour earlier at eight o'clock, and despite Sean's lack of true familiarity with Jenny, he liked her and felt a deepening fear for her safety.

"Stan's not here anymore," he said, his heart starting to race. "He went to pick up Jenny to take her to some party that hired him—or at least that's what he claimed." Sean lowered his head, clutching his forehead in worry. "Ray, I'm asking you to get over there *fast* if you think there's any chance he's the man you're looking for."

"Who's Jenny?"

Sean swallowed hard, his throat drying more by the second. "She's a woman I met recently. She told me she's gone out with the guy before so I don't know what to think."

"Do you know where she lives? An address?"

"Dammit, Ray, no!" he replied, fist pounding his thigh. "But it can't be too far. I heard him talking to her on the phone and he said it would take twenty to thirty minutes from here."

"Give me her last name. We could get addresses of all names that match and try it that way."

Sean stared through the windshield, dumbfounded at the sudden realization.

"I never asked her, Ray."

Silence.

"But her sister's here tonight. She may wonder why I'm asking but I could get the address from her."

"You'll either have to lie your way through some awkward bull- shit or tell her the truth and open up a whole can of panic we don't want. I don't like either choice."

Sean closed his eyes, trying to think of another way. "Wait!" he cried out. "Jenny told me that Elliot has the mailing addresses of everyone that donates stuff here and she's done it a few times. He'll have it in his records somewhere."

"That's better, but we'll obviously have to tell him this in pri- vate."

Sean opened his door. "Meet me at the entrance."

"No," he answered, "I shouldn't be seen. Bring him to my car so we can talk without people around. I'm in the southeast section of the lot. When I see you, I'll flash my lights. The one thing I'll do now is get Claybourne's car and license plate information to notify patrol units. Maybe we'll get lucky that way."

Sean hurried back through the entrance and stood by the silent auction table, scanning the grounds for Elliot. Seeing the Michaels family approaching, with Jason cradling Kayleigh against his chest, he felt trapped, knowing any time spent talking with them could literally be a life or death difference for Jenny.

"Kayleigh's hit the wall," Stephanie said. "But we had a great time, Sean, and she loved listening to you. Thanks."

Sean looked at Kayleigh, giving him a weak smile and wave.

"Good...good," he said. After a high-five slap with Randy, he approached Kayleigh and repeated the same motion, offering a soft hand-to-hand touch instead. "I've got to go talk to Elliot, but I'll see you tomorrow for your lesson, okay?"

With a single nod of acknowledgment, Kayleigh's eyes fluttered, struggling to remain open.

"She hasn't skipped a day of practice since you gave her that guitar," Stephanie told him.

First turning his right thumb upward, Sean waved goodbye and started walking away before stopping, wheeling around, and hurrying back. "Hey, Stephanie," he called out, catching up to them, "did Jenny tell you we saw each other here this week? She brought in some things to donate and I spotted her in the parking lot."

"I haven't talked to her since sometime last week," she answered. "Between a new work project she's taken on and moving into a new apartment, I know she's been pretty busy."

"Yeah, she told me she's moving," he replied. "Have you seen the place?"

"No, not yet."

"Well, hopefully she's not moving too far. I know how fond Kayleigh is of her Aunt Jenny."

"Fortunately, it's not much of a move at all," Stephanie said. "It's just a few blocks from where she's been living."

"We've gotta go, Steph," Jason said.

As they walked away, Sean whispered a curse before voicing to himself what he should have asked: "*A few blocks from where she's been living? Where was that, Stephanie?*"

Elliot offered a last chance. Reentering the courtyard, he scanned the entire area. Some guests sat eating their desserts at various tables, others stood talking in groups, while several more milled around the silent auction tables. When he spotted Eleanor McBride, standing to the right of her husband and conversing with someone blocked from his view, he peered through the narrow space between their bodies and identified Elliot's distinguishable light gray suit. On his way there, he saw Elliot's boyfriend, Martin, walking toward them carrying a dessert plate. As Sean arrived, he detected an immediate look of displeasure on Eleanor's face.

"Well," she said, her face a narrow-eyed mask of indignation and conviction, "in John, chapter eight, verse seven, Jesus said, 'Let he who is without sin cast the first stone,' so who am I to call that man a liar. I just wish he wouldn't have doubted my husband's word. If Adam says he's sure all the cards were there, then he should believe him!"

"Stan can be a bit temperamental at times, Eleanor," Elliot said solemnly. "I'm sorry that he upset you."

Adam remained silent, reaching for Eleanor's hand while using an up-and-down calming gesture with the other.

"I've helped out here a few times, and believe me, Stan is a good man," Martin said. "But he's admitted to me that he gets a bit scatterbrained sometimes because he's always running through tricks in his head."

"Hello, Sean," Elliot said, turning away from Eleanor with an apparent smile of relief.

"Sorry if I'm interrupting," he said, "but I was in the parking lot saying goodbye to the Michaels family, and on my way back, I saw a woman walk outside in tears. I asked her if I could help, and she said she wanted to talk to you but was too upset to come back in here. She's waiting in her car now but I need to show you where she's parked."

Elliot's eyebrows furrowed in confusion and surprise. "I wonder what happened?" he replied, looking from Sean to Martin.

"Do you want me to come with you?" Martin asked.

"No, that's okay," he said, grasping Martin's shoulder and smiling before moving past the McBrides. "Whatever it's about, it's better that I talk with her alone."

Sean led Elliot toward the flashing lights. Maldonado exited his car and waited by the hood as the two of them approached.

Elliot slowed and looked at Sean in confusion. "What's this about?" he asked.

"This is Detective Ray Maldonado of the LAPD," Sean replied.

Holding a notepad in his left hand, Maldonado stepped forward and extended the other. "Now that you know who I am," he said, "I'll tell you why I'm here." Removing a pen from his pants pocket, he took a step back and continued. "A woman named Jenny donated items here this week, and I need to know if you can get me her address right now. Her life may be in danger, but we don't know where she lives."

"It's Stephanie Michaels's sister," Sean explained.

"Oh, my God, that sweetheart's life is in danger? I can't believe it!" He glanced at Sean, then at Maldonado. "How can I help?"

"Do you know her last name?" Maldonado asked.

"McCauley," he answered. "Jenny McCauley."

"Sean told me you might have her address on file. We need that address and we need it fast."

"All I know is that Jenny moved to a new apartment," Sean said, "and Stan told her it would take twenty to thirty minutes to get there."

"Stan?" Elliot replied, leaning his upper body back in surprise. "Does this have something to do with him?"

Sean looked at a glowering Maldonado.

"Right now he's just a suspect," Maldonado explained, maintaining his eye contact with Sean. "No matter what my assistant here may be inferring. Now would you please get us that address?"

They followed Elliot to the darkened store. Unlocking the door, he turned on the room light and told them to sit in the two chairs by the window while he searched the computer's records. Within a few minutes after disappearing through the curtained divider, the sound of a printing machine emanated throughout the quiet of the room.

Clutching a piece of white paper, Elliot rushed back in and handed Maldonado a copy of the invoice with Jenny's address.

❧❧❧

Sitting in the same clothes from the fund-raiser, unmoved from the same spot on the couch he'd taken when he arrived home, Sean answered Maldonado's call on the first guitar sound.

"Miss McCauley's fine and Stan's pissed off at you."

Muting the television, he said, "What happened?"

"When my men arrived, nobody answered the door. We got in touch with the management company who sent someone over with a set of keys to her place. Once we saw everything was okay in there, the officers waited in the street until they saw Stan's car pull up to the front. He got out with Miss McCauley and started walking with her. This is where we had a choice to make. Either we could watch it play out and see if he returned to his car, or follow them and question Stan before they went inside if that was his intention. At that point, we started to surmise Stan wasn't our guy. The Beatles' Song Murderer wouldn't have left his car in front and walked with Miss McCauley where he could be seen by anyone.

He probably just walked her to the door because he returned a few minutes later."

At that moment, Sean realized he felt more than just a sense of relief about Jenny's well-being. He also liked knowing Stan hadn't spent the night.

"But that doesn't necessarily tell you he isn't the killer," Sean said. "Maybe it would be the next time, or the time after that."

"And how many more people would be able to link him with her?" Maldonado asked. "Plenty, and that's not the clumsy way the Beatles' Song Murderer operates. The guy is shrewd and understands how to avoid detection."

Sean hung his head in the semi-darkened room, the light from the television offering a clear view of a sleeping Hendrix on the cushion to his right. He thought of Merissa, realizing for the first time how her image from the night of the murder seemed less defined.

"After he returned to his car, we did question him about where he was the night of Miss Franklin's murder," Maldonado told him. "He claimed he spent the night by himself at the Comedy Store until it closed. Our men asked him who performed that night and he named a couple of guys who were there. We can't prove he *didn't* go, so there's nothing more we can do with that one."

"Did you ask him why he didn't attend Merissa's funeral?"

"Hired to work a business convention at the Hilton near LAX. We always knew there could be a logical explanation but we verified it anyway."

"So maybe Adam or Roger is the one," Sean said. "Don't forget the things I told you earlier."

A loud sigh preceded a long pause.

"We've got handcuffs found in a bowling bag and a missing Jack of Hearts from a deck of cards; two miscellaneous items that are relevant to the case. Coincidence, maybe, but certainly worth remembering."

Staring into the darkened portion of the room, Sean gripped the phone, feeling overwhelmed by helplessness again.

"I want this guy found," he muttered. "For Merissa, and for all the others. But I feel we're back where we started."

Maldonado didn't respond for several moments.

"Listen to me, Sean," he said, his voice low and calm. "This case is a priority not just for you and me, but for the entire department. And we feel we're getting closer. But solving cases like this isn't a sprint—it's a step-by-step process, and nights like tonight leave us as disappointed as you, believe me."

Sean ran his hand along Hendrix's back before placing him on the floor. He sat up and with frustrated aggression rubbed his face with his hand.

"I understand," Sean replied.

"I've been in blind alley moments like this more times than I care to remember, and sometimes it's best to find a healthy distraction, something to take your mind off it for a while. You didn't ask, but as for me, I'm going to pour myself a scotch, listen to some Tito Puente, and remind myself what's good in life."

Sean nodded in quiet acknowledgment. "Looking at the positive, Stan's now a person you can cross off your list. That's good for something, I guess."

"What it does," Maldonado said, "is possibly eliminate one of the suspects off the list, leaving us closer."

"Assuming your hunch is right, and it's someone Merissa and I knew."

"Tragically, Sean, the past tense applies to Miss Franklin, but, yes, my hunch still tells me The Beatles' Song Murderer is someone you know."

Chapter 25

"Did you have a good time last night?" Sean asked, tuning the G string as he sat on his couch with Kayleigh.

"Yeah," she said, her head nodding like a bobble head doll. "You play guitar like a rock star!"

Sean chuckled. "Did you know any of the songs?"

Kayleigh squinted in concentration, showing the familiar expression observed before—where her left eye turned into a quarter moon, while the folds of her right cheek surrounded and sealed her closed eye like a slow motion camera shutter. "I don't remember."

Sean laughed. "That's okay," he said, handing her the guitar, "they're not worth remembering anyway."

His cell phone rang from the table near the kitchen where he left it.

"Start practicing your chords," he told her, rising from the couch.

He glanced at the ID screen, hesitating at first before answering the call.

"Hi, Elliot."

"I hope I'm not disturbing your Sunday, but I'm calling for a couple of reasons. Got a few minutes?"

"I'm just starting Kayleigh's guitar lesson," he replied. "Can it wait?"

"I'm sorry," Elliot said, "but just tell me if Jenny's all right. I was very upset after our meeting and had a hard time making it through the rest of the night. Have you heard anything? And what's going on with Stan?"

Sean glanced at Kayleigh and held up a finger to signify he wouldn't be much longer before turning his back. "She's fine, Elliot. Detective Maldonado had reason to believe she was in trouble and that Stan had something to do with it, but I guess he didn't and everything's okay now."

"That's great news!" Elliot said. "About her *and* Stan. What a relief."

"What's the other thing you called about?"

"Martin and I are going to a movie this afternoon. If you'd be home around four-thirty we'd stop off so you could show him those electrical problems you mentioned."

"On a Sunday?" Sean asked.

"Yeah, I know," he replied, "but with his workload and your job, it's hard for him to meet you during the week. He could send an assistant, but he's grateful for your help last night so he's insisting on seeing it for himself."

Sean thought back to the night before last when his power went out in his bedroom after turning on his hair blower—the second time in two weeks. Stubbing his toe walking toward the fuse box pissed him off even more.

"Sounds good, Elliot. Call me when you're on your way."

He sat down with Kayleigh and helped place her fingers properly for the G chord. "I listened to you play while I was on that phone call," he said, watching her strum. "I can tell you've been practicing, just like your mom told me."

"Is Elliot coming over?"

"Yep," he told her, "with Martin. But not until after your lesson."

"Okay," she said, offering a single nod of acceptance. "When Mama and Daddy and Randy walked around the school with Elliot, Martin stayed with me and let me go on the Internet."

"I forgot about you and computers. The first time I met you, you told me that your brother taught you how to use one."

Kayleigh smiled, her partially closed eye working hard to match the excited look from the other.

"Uh-huh! That's when I told you that Mr. Marine used to be Mr. Computer. And you became Mr. Music!"

"Uh-huh!" Sean replied, laughing. "Now let's get back to your lesson."

"Hey," she said, bouncing on the couch, "did you see the tickets on the wall?"

"Tickets on the wall?"

"Yeah," she said, "Martin showed them to me."

"You mean that framed board near the office?"

Kayleigh repeated more bobble-headed exuberance.

"That was so cool! And you know what's the most-coolest thing of all?"

"No," he replied, although he knew what her answer would be. "What's the most-coolest thing?"

"The Lakers tickets!" she shouted. "Martin's Lakers ticket is on there with Elliot's, and it's the same game Coby scored six points and the Lakers won one hundred-nineteen to eighty-two!"

"Lucky Martin, huh?" Sean replied, nodding and opening his eyes wide to feign excitement. "Coby was The Man that night."

"And he told me he could see Coby's face the whole time, even when he was sitting on the bench." Kayleigh took a quick breath as her frail shoulders sagged and her thin, colorless lips tightened into a dreamy, schoolgirl smile. "I wish I coulda been there."

Sean recalled the first time Kayleigh mentioned this game, explaining about her ability to remember numbers, and today that innocent boast proved true again with her recitation of the final score. But her reminder of the tickets elicited a flood of darkness within him. He planned to kill himself that day he met her, and although the conviction of suicide dissipated to a nonexistent idea relegated to the past, the pain of Merissa's unimaginable final night still lingered, buried alive within the confines of his heart. The conversation with Kayleigh about the Lakers tickets needed to stop before his unhealed emotions got the best of him.

Sean pointed to the guitar. "No more Lakers talk for now," he told her. "Play me that G chord again."

෴

Elliot and Martin weren't due to arrive for another half hour, so taking his dog for a fifteen-minute walk before they arrived seemed like a good idea. But returning home, Hendrix caught Sean by surprise, pulling the leash from his hand attempting to catch a squirrel running up a tree, resulting in a fur full of sticky leaves from whatever plants he ran into.

"Dammit, Hendrix!" he muttered, grabbing the loose end of the leash. "Now I have to hose you down, you crazy mutt!"

As he approached his house, gratified to see they hadn't arrived yet, Sean called Elliot.

"My stupid dog ran into some plants and now he's full of sticky shit," he explained. "I need to run a hose over him for a few minutes. How close are you?"

"Maybe another five or six minutes," he answered. "If you want, we can wait in the car until you're ready."

"You don't need to do that. Just come around the side of the house and open the gate to my backyard."

When Elliot and Martin entered the backyard, droplets of water flew from Hendrix's shaking body as Sean turned off the spigot and reached for a towel draped over a nearby chair. "Almost finished, guys," he said.

"No problem," Martin replied, observing the scene.

"Is that a store catalog?" Sean asked, pointing his chin toward the dark green booklet in Martin's hand.

"Yeah, but it's not a homework assignment so don't worry about the size. It describes all the services we offer, but pages twenty-six and twenty-seven are all you need to look at."

"I swear, the man doesn't know how to do anything half-way," Elliot remarked.

Martin grinned. "Are you complaining?"

Sean caught Martin's wink and smiled to himself as he squatted down to dry his dog. Placing the towel over Hendrix's body, he rubbed his hands vigorously back and forth, under and over, until he deemed him ready to reenter the house.

"Okay," he said, looking up, "now we're ready."

Elliot and Martin started walking toward the side gate but Sean called them back.

"We'll go inside from here," he said.

Leading them to a door on the far end of the yard, blocked from view by a large shrub in the corner planter, Sean reached under a small terra cotta pot containing an unhealthy, droopy green plant. Grasping the hidden key, he inserted it in the lock before returning it to its original location.

"Your agapanthus looks like it could use some TLC," Martin said.

"My what?" he asked. Turning back, he saw Martin pointing toward the plant in the pot. "Oh, that. Yeah, I know. I don't use this door much and I forget to water it."

"Before I met Elliot, I wouldn't have noticed, and for sure I wouldn't have known the name, but this dear man loves his garden and now I'm his horticulturist in training."

Placing his hand on the side of Martin's head, Elliot leaned over and kissed him on the cheek. "I think you finally learned your agapanthus from your anigozanthus."

After Martin inspected the meter and fuse box, and examined the wires running through his garage, they returned to the kitchen.

"Anybody else want a cup of coffee besides me?" Sean asked.

The two men looked at each other for a few moments before nodding simultaneously.

"Why don't you guys wait out there and relax," he told them, pointing toward the front room. "I'll brew the coffee."

As the machine started percolating, Sean called the dealership to inquire about some information on the current and incoming inventory. Waiting on hold to speak to Olivia in the order department, he overheard snippets of conversation from the two men and realized they must be looking at the framed photo on the corner table of Merissa and him. The words "beautiful" and "tragedy" drifted through, as well as parts of sentences such as "So sad," and "Still hard to believe."

He also heard a comment from one of them that surprised him—something about a resemblance to Lady Di. *Lady Di?* Sure, they both had that same brownish-blonde hair coloring, and slightly hawkish nose and big eyes on a small face, yet he still considered the observation a strange one. But after hearing another remark about her "smile lighting up the room," something he agreed with 100 percent, he started rubbing his eyes to avoid the advent of tears before looking around for a distraction. Spotting Hendrix sleeping with his back against the wall, Sean focused on his tiny furry belly moving ever so slightly in calm, canine bliss. The sound of Olivia's voice coming on the line offered a welcome penetration to his somber haze, and after several minutes, his conversation, and the brewing cycle, both ended.

When the two men returned to the kitchen, Sean asked them if they wanted any milk or sugar.

"A little of both," Martin answered.

"Sugar only," Elliot replied, holding up a hand. "This poor lactose-intolerant body of mine rebels against any invasion of milk."

Sitting on the couch next to Sean, Martin opened the pamphlet to page twenty-six, showing photos of the parts he recommended and explaining their benefits. Elliot sat in an adjacent chair, and as he peered across the table to peruse the photos, Hendrix trotted in and sat at Martin's feet.

"As I mentioned outside," Martin said, leaning down to scratch the dog's head, "I'm not telling you to go out and buy new appliances, but your refrigerator and dryer are on the old side and not energy efficient. So what's best for now is to expand your capacity for more power allowance."

"Sounds good, if I can afford it."

Giving Hendrix a final rub, Martin returned to an upward position, reached for his cup, and downed quick sip before continuing. "The good news is by the time we're done, you'll have an upgraded system that shouldn't cause you any more problems."

"Is there a bad news with the good news?" Sean asked.

Martin winced before offering a sheepish smile. "The bad news?" he echoed. "To adapt our products to the way your house is configured, I'll have to order a device from back east. Sometimes they're quick about it, other times you feel like you're waiting forever and it's frustrating as hell. But I won't know what you'll need yet until I finish here, and it will take too much time to finish checking everything today." Raising the cup to his lips, he smiled and stared at Elliot. "After all, Sunday's a day of rest, right?"

Elliot fingered the rim of his cup, smiling and holding Martin's gaze for an extended period of time. "And the day for serving that poached salmon dish I prepared," he added.

"Should I leave you the brochure?" Martin asked.

"Sure, why not? I'll look through it and see what today's modern world of electricity has to offer."

"Believe me," Elliot said, "if you're like me when I peruse those pages, you'll feel like a caveman entering a whole new world."

Sean noticed Martin looking at Elliot with a quizzical expression before nodding in apparent acknowledgment about something.

"One more thing before we go, Sean," Elliot said. "Your answer earlier today about Jennie and Stan seemed a bit vague, considering all that happened last night. I was worried sick, and I feel I'm owed more of an explanation. First I get brought out to the parking lot on false pretenses, then I get told that Jenny's life could be in danger and the police need her address because they need to talk to Stan. Not quite the end of the successful evening I anticipated."

"It wasn't easy for Elliot after that whole incident," Martin explained. Reaching out, he grabbed Elliot's shoulder and leaned forward to kiss his forehead before turning back toward Sean.

"Sorry, guys, but I've got nothing to add to what I said earlier. Jenny's fine and it turned out to be a complete misunderstanding with Stan."

Sean observed their skeptical expressions, suppressing a brief urge to reveal the truth; that he feared for Jenny's safety last night because of his belief that Stan might be The Beatles' Song Murderer. His mind raced while his demeanor struggled to remain calm, knowing that two other men from Elliot's invitation list appeared as suspects on a much different kind of list.

Chapter 26

The bell clanging realization dawned on him as he lay in bed staring into the darkness, the impact of the latest news about Kayleigh still fresh in his thoughts.

"Kayleigh's doctor wants to do another test," Stephanie told him, her voice sounding monotone and measured. "'Abnormality' is the word he used when he looked at her latest blood work." A noticeable exhale burrowed its way between her full answer. "Her neutrophils are still lower than we hoped for at this point in her recovery."

"I'm…I'm sorry, Stephanie, but I don't know what those are."

"Oh," she said, uttering a short, unhappy laugh, "I'm sorry, Sean. I guess at this point I've learned enough medical terms to make me a real doctor." Another pause. "Kayleigh has acute lymphocytic leukemia, which means it's a cancer of the bone marrow. The neutrophils are the good guys, the healthy white blood cells. Without those, her defense system won't hold up, and she'll be prone to infections."

Sean stared at the floor as he held the phone, his thoughts squeezed into a cold hard box of numbing sadness. "And this test will show if the good guys are winning?"

"Exactly," she replied. "Doctor Chan told us that it isn't necessarily a warning sign, but the sooner we see the bone marrow recover, the better her chance for success."

It was Stephanie's remark about another subject, however, that brought the clarity he required to make him understand how to help.

"We need to come up with another five thousand dollars to meet the deductible," she explained, her voice breaking. "Sorry, Sean, it's not right of me to share our difficulties with you. All you did was call to change the time of Kayleigh's next lesson, but it's hard to hold it in sometimes, you know? Jason's business got hit with another big insurance increase and now this."

ᥱᢙᥱᢙ

Receiving confirmation that David could take his call, Sean sat on the edge of the couch and watched Hendrix gnaw on a chew toy.

His brother's usual tone, part sarcasm, part abruptness, greeted him when he answered.

"It's another lovely day in paradise, Sean. What's up?"

Sean gripped the phone and prepared to speak the words he'd practiced before calling, but a sudden trepidation overtook him, exposing a naiveté he'd not realized until now. "I hope it's not too late," he said, "but if they still want it, Wally's Window Wipes can use my song."

Several seconds of silence followed.

"You're serious?"

"I didn't call for your bedazzling charm, David."

"Statute of limitations hasn't terminated, Sean," David replied, his tone taking on a sudden lighthearted tenor. "You're still good to go, bro. And congratulations for coming to your senses."

Sean took a sigh of relief, but one other issue still remained. "I have one stipulation, however. And this is a make or break request."

"Jesus," David muttered, "you sound like a fucking lawyer." An exaggerated breath followed before he asked, "What is it?"

"I want a five-thousand-dollar advance, and I need it as fast as possible."

"An advance? Shouldn't you be asking ASCAP for that?"

"If there wasn't an urgency to it, I suppose so," he said. "But that high-flying law firm of yours can arrange it easier and quicker than I could. Just add an addendum on the paperwork that the first five thousand received goes back to you guys."

"Forgive me if I go Led Zeppelin on you, Sean, but you've got me dazed and confused right now. You've gone from being vehemently opposed to using your song to doing a complete one-eighty on the idea. And to top it off, you're insisting on an advance 'as fast as possible.'"

"That's right," he replied. "Five thousand dollars as soon as you can."

"I know, I heard you the first time." Neither one spoke for several moments. "Are you in trouble of some kind?" David asked. "Is everything all right?"

Sean closed his eyes and rubbed his fingers back and forth across his forehead. "This isn't about me, okay?" The sudden echo of Kayleigh's nauseous cries pierced his consciousness. "Give me a few minutes to explain."

Sean detailed his relationship with Kayleigh, the Michaels family, and the purpose for the money. He ended with the details about donating anonymously, and why the advance needed to be expedited without delay.

"I'm proud of you, bro," David replied, "and highly impressed. You're doing something wonderful for that little girl and, at the same time, overcoming your past feelings about 'Looking Glass,' for the commercial. You'll also make enough money to help yourself down the line, no doubt about it."

Sean grimaced at David's pie-in-the-sky remark. "I appreciate what you said about Kayleigh," he said, "but let me clarify something. My feelings haven't changed one damn bit. 'Looking Glass,' will soon go from a respected, classy lady aging gracefully, to an old, toothless street whore. Every time that fucking jingle plays it will be another dagger in my heart."

"Jesus," David grumbled, "and I thought lawyers were overly dramatic."

"Give me a fucking break, David."

"A fucking break?" David shot back. "Just remember something, okay? Beyond that selfless cause your advance money will go toward, every time that *fucking jingle* plays, it means dollars you can use to record new material. Isn't that what you always wanted? To write another great song and leave the shadow of 'Looking Glass' behind?"

The change of subject left him tense and frustrated. "I don't want to talk about this anymore," Sean said. He reached out toward Hendrix and pulled him close, stroking the soft fur of his right ear as he stared out the window toward the front yard where he first met Kayleigh. "Let's just say I'm hoping to turn lemons into lemonade."

∽∾∽

A guard directed Sean to the end of the hallway of the Administration and Admissions building where he sat and waited in a foyer decorated with leafy plants and a stack of timeworn magazines. Unsure where to go when he first arrived at the hospital, he wound up walking through the children's wing of the cancer ward, thinking that's where he could talk to someone about Kayleigh. He passed rows of photos interspersing Disney characters and super heroes alongside those of smiling children, many of them bald or nearly so, just like her. Putting a happy face to young cancer victims seemed disingenuous to say the least, but he somehow felt better knowing these kids received support and possessed hope. Kayleigh had the support. Now Sean wanted to offer the hope.

Another couple, similar in age to Stephanie and Jason, looked up for a moment as he entered the waiting room. So did a bald man who appeared to be in his late twenties or early thirties, with a thick black beard and a head that seemed to be screwed on to his shoulders, bypassing any need for a neck. Sean signed his name on the sheet of paper at the front desk, handed it to the woman sitting behind the open sliding glass enclosure, and picked through the magazines scattered in a wicker basket before settling for an old National Geographic.

Glancing at the couple, he observed the difference in body language and wondered if it symbolized anything. The man leaned forward as he read an article from Time, his elbows-on-knees position contrasting with the woman on his right, his wife, he presumed, who blank-stared at the floor as her left leg pivoted back and forth over the right one in a rapid, nervous motion. He wondered what their story was, and that of the bald guy. Cancer didn't differentiate between rich or poor, young or old. Entire families got sucked into the whirlpool of despair and fear.

After flipping through a few pages, Sean put the magazine on the empty chair next to him, leaned forward, and dropped his head in his hands, reflecting on the scare he experienced when a black mark appeared on his X-rays. How would he have handled a cancer diagnosis? How much would his insurance have covered? How much would his deductible and other out-of-pocket expenses total? Unlike the Michaels, who apparently had no rich parent to help them, he could have, most likely would have, gone to his father for help if he faced the possibility of death.

But how many millions of people per year faced rejected claims and destroyed their financial stability to save the life of a loved one, or even themselves? What do they do then? Stephanie told him that young people with serious diseases had limits in their coverage, resulting in cutoffs of payments while they were still young. She also explained that attempting to get another insurer when you had a preexisting condition was like walking around with a flashing neon sign announcing, *BEWARE, YOU DON'T WANT ME!*

About thirty minutes after he arrived, an attractive middle-aged African-American woman in white hospital attire, with cropped black hair, dark rimmed glasses, and hazel-colored eyes, opened an adjoining door near the sitting area and approached Sean.

"Mr. Hightower?" she asked, extending her hand. "I'm Donna Fitzsimmons. Please come with me."

Sean grimaced at the arthritic jolt striking his hip as he stood to shake hands before following her inside. Approaching one of the two empty chairs situated on the visitor side of her desk, she waited for him to sit, opened her drawer, and started perusing a page from a school-sized yellow notepad before taking her seat. Leaning forward, Fitzsimmons looked at him for a few moments before speaking.

"What can I do for you, Mr. Hightower?"

Sean sat with his hands clasped on his lap, feeling at ease, but preparing to wade into the unchartered waters of hospital protocol. "There's a little girl I know with cancer in need of a certain test at this hospital. From what her mother tells me, the doctor is advising it because he's not sure if she's improving or not, and this test will give him a much better idea of where she stands." He paused a moment before continuing. "I'm here to help the family pay for the procedure, but I first want to confirm that the doctor is still recommending it."

The woman turned toward her computer screen and placed her fingers on the keypad. "What's the girl's name?" she asked.

"Kayleigh Michaels."

"You say you've spoken with the mother. Are you friends with the family?"

"Yes," he answered. "They live next door."

Fitzsimmons waited several moments in silence, continuing to stare at the screen.

"Here she is. Kayleigh Alison Michaels, age ten. Jason Michaels, father, Stephanie Michaels, mother." She brought her face closer to the screen as her eyes scanned the information. "Doctor Joseph Chan is her primary physician, and he's recommending bone marrow aspiration and biopsy."

"What is that, exactly?" Sean asked.

"The doctor removes a sample of the soft tissue, the bone marrow, to determine how the blood cells are responding. A pathologist will examine the cells under a microscope to see what's going on."

Sean narrowed his eyes, fearing the worst. "That sounds scary," he said. "I don't think the doctor would recommend it if her markers were improving."

Fitzsimmons nodded her head in small, slow motion movements. "Most of the time you could say that's true," she explained. "If there's a possible indicator of an abnormality in the patient's blood work, it's best to find out for sure what's going on. But if a problem is found early enough, it can often be monitored and controlled. Let's hope this is the situation with Kayleigh."

Sean sat in silence for several moments, feeling his heart beating from fear for his little friend's life. "Kayleigh's mother told me they need five thousand dollars to meet the deductible for this procedure," he said. "I know they're living on a tight budget, so it's going to hurt them. But they'll pay it, of course, no matter what." Sean leaned forward, placing his arms on the desk. Staring into her eyes, he continued. "I want to help them, but I know they're too proud to agree to my offer. It's not as if I'm a family member, I'm just a friend, their neighbor. But a donation can be made anonymously, right? That's how I'd like to do it."

Fitzsimmons nodded. "Whatever amount you'd like to contribute can be made without a name attached, so, yes, we can accommodate your request."

"Good," he said, his head nodding in relief. "Can I pay it now?"

"There's a form you'll need to complete," she told him, "but other than that, your donation can be made whenever you'd like."

"How soon will Kayleigh's parents be told about the donation?" he asked. "We need that test done fast, so the sooner the better."

"If you pay it today, I'll make sure they find out today. Once the hospital informs the parents, I assume they'll be talking with Doctor Chan very soon to set up a date for the procedure."

Sean clapped his hands twice. "Great!"

Fitzsimmons leaned back in her chair. Removing her glasses, she stared at Sean as a small smile appeared on her face. "Mr. Hightower," she said, her voice taking on a less formal tone, "I've worked here for over twenty years, and one thing I've gained is a true appreciation for how much goodness so many people have in their hearts when it comes to helping others. Any donation is a blessing, of course, but it's the ones who want to remain anonymous that give me the biggest reason to pause and reflect on what that person is doing. You're paying a great deal of money, yet obviously not for any recognition or future favor. It's such a wonderful act of selflessness, and because nobody in her family will ever have the chance to express their gratitude, please allow me to express my mine."

Sean smiled before forcing a cough into his hand to clear the catch in his throat. "Thank you, Donna," he replied, his voice rendered weak. He paused, reflecting on that fateful day they met. "Without going into specifics, let's just say that little girl is living proof about good things coming in small packages. And I'm going to do whatever I can to make sure she keeps living."

Chapter 27

After three consecutive months of below-average sales, August's robust results generated a healthy turnaround that seemed to lift everyone's spirits, matching the warm and breezy, blue-skied Santa Monica weather of the last Friday of the month. A rejuvenated Tom Claiborne, walking the floor and joking with various employees, reminded Sean of a bear's reemergence from hibernation, representing an all-around, elevated mood that hadn't appeared for a while. The notable exception, contrasted by his usual inclination to laugh at even at the most inappropriate of times, was Roger. From the moment he'd arrived that morning, his somber disposition and weight-of-the-world body language implied something bothersome beyond the boundaries of work. The answer didn't take long to understand.

Shortly before eleven, Roger approached Sean asking for a lunch together that day. "I want to tell you something that's happened," he explained, "and a decision that I've made." After agreeing on a time, Sean started walking away but Roger grasped his arm. "I have a confession to make about Merissa because it's something you should know. But now's not the time." As the sunshine streamed through the store windows, Sean found himself in a sudden fog.

The park up the street provided an inviting location on this temperate afternoon, so after getting burritos, chips, and a soda from the local lunch truck, they walked the two blocks in what appeared to be, at least in Sean's perspective, Roger's avoidance of anything pertinent. Small talk about bowling and sales projections for the month ahead neither minimized his unease nor the tension he sensed in Roger.

After spotting an open bench on the grass between a children's playground and the tennis courts, they sat on opposite ends, each angled toward each other with space between them to place their cardboard lunch boxes.

"So what's going on, Roger?" Sean asked, his eyes narrowing in anticipation of something of which he had no idea, but wasn't necessarily prepared to hear. "What's this *confession* you want to make?"

Roger opened the box and clutched his burrito. Pointing to Sean's unopened box, he gestured for him to do the same before wiping a hand across his face and staring in silence for several moments. "The first thing I'll tell you is that Anita's filed for divorce."

Sean swallowed and reached for a chip, hearing something as unexpected as a child's shout from a playground slide. He didn't particularly care, and if nothing else, felt good for Anita.

"I don't blame her, either," Roger admitted, his voice quiet yet firm. "I've been a shitty, philandering husband, and she's a class act who never signed on for this."

"Sorry to hear that, Roger," Sean replied, hearing the echo of his clichéd response. "But it wasn't that long ago you claimed to be a new man, remember? You told me your cheating days were behind you."

"I wanted to believe it myself," he answered, food still in his mouth. Waiting until he swallowed, he continued. "But I'm too damn weak when it comes to women. I see them, and I want them."

"I'm sure a lot of married men will tell you the same thing," Sean said. "But most of them draw the line between what's in their heads and actually doing something about it."

In silent affirmation, Roger adjusted his sunglasses and nodded

"So that marriage counselor thing obviously didn't work," Sean remarked.

Roger closed his eyes and shook his head, uttering an airy nostril fueled laugh. "That marriage counselor turned out to be my first foray back into the cheating business."

Sean's eyes widened, genuinely surprised this time at the man's admission.

Roger took another bite and placed the half-eaten burrito back in the box. He leaned back, clasped his hands on top of his head, and gazed in the direction of the playground where a couple of women chatted while children played around them. "I also wanted to tell you this is my last day at work. Tom's known about it, but I asked him to keep it a secret." After letting that comment linger for several moments, he looked back at Sean.

"Why?" Sean asked, adjusting his sunglasses. "Because of the divorce?"

"Yep. I'm packing up and leaving town on Sunday"

"Where you going?"

"I'm keeping that to myself, buddy," he answered, a coy smile placing a visual period to the sentence. "I've hired a lawyer to take care of the paperwork and place whatever's mine in storage, so it shouldn't be a big deal. We don't have kids and the house is leased, so all that's left for me to do is hit the road, Jack, and not look back."

Sean placed the remaining scraps of his burrito back inside the box and took another sip of his orange soda. "I never had kids either, but my divorces busted my ass—especially the first one. She took half my money. You're lucky that yours won't have the stormy shit I went through."

Roger whistled softly. "You can say that again, brother." His eyes looked downward toward the grass, tightening into a squint. "Maybe in the back of my mind, I somehow knew to hold back on my commitment to Anita." He brought his gaze upward, looking at Sean again. "We certainly talked about kids, and her mother made no secret of her unhappiness without grandchildren, but I even think Anita wasn't sure about a future with me. Same thing with the house. We talked about buying a place one day, but that's all it amounted to."

Sean pushed himself into a straight-backed position and took a quick, deep breath. "Okay, Roger," he said, "what the hell is this confession you have about Merissa?"

Roger bit his upper lip and held his mouth in place, nodding slowly up and down several times. Sliding his hand down his chin, his expression turned solemn, perhaps, as Sean observed, even pensive. The breeze brushed across their faces as the trees rustled like a sleep-inducing soundtrack, creating a leafy audio buildup to whatever Roger intended to say. "You probably won't be seeing me again after today," he said. "So I've decided that I may as well clear the air and come clean as to my real whereabouts the night Merissa was killed. I feel I owe it you."

Remaining silent, Sean gripped the bench and nodded for Roger to continue.

"I've lied to you twice about where I was that night," he said. "The first time you asked me, I told you I was out drinking with some fraternity brothers. Do you remember?"

"Yes."

"Well, the second answer I gave you wasn't true either." Roger held his gaze, each succeeding second of silence seeming much longer to Sean. "I told you I screwed my dental hygienist but was home at eleven. I *did* screw her, but that was another time."

Despite the comforting ocean breeze continuing to blow through the park, Sean felt a surge of heat in the back of his neck. He didn't know where Roger was going with this, but the increase of his heartbeat preceded the trickle of sweat forming at the edge of his forehead. He swallowed and felt the sandpaper in his throat as he prepared to ask the question.

"So where were you that night?"

Roger looked down at his shoes, moving them back and forth in a small line along the ground. His finger slid across the bottom of his nose as he sniffed and stared back at Sean. "I'm not proud of my actions," he said, "but I was in a motel on Pico Boulevard with a prostitute named Lucy Sweets. And that wasn't the first time either. As long as the money's there, that woman always did whatever I wanted to keep me happy."

Sean rested his elbow on the top of the bench and his chin on the back of his fist, staring at Roger with partial relief over not hearing a murderer's confession, but also contempt for the scumbag husband continually betraying Anita. "If you weren't married to someone I know and like, I wouldn't give a shit where you stick your dick, Roger. But for Anita's sake, that's fucked up. *Really* fucked up."

Roger stared down at his shoes again, holding that pose. "I know," he mumbled. A long silence ensued between them.

"You also lied about the time you got home, didn't you? You told me eleven but Anita said it was more like two."

Roger's eyes darted back at Sean. "When did this conversation come up?" he asked, his voice rising. "You two talking about me in secret?"

Sean grasped the rail of the bench and squeezed it as his eyes narrowed in anger. "Oh, I see," he snarled, "suddenly you have a right to the truth about something concerning your wife? Who the hell are you kidding, man? You cashed in your 'right to know' card a long time ago."

Roger shot up from the bench and glared at Sean. "You're a fucking asshole!" he spat, looking down from lightning bolt eyes. "I'm glad I won't be seeing you after today, you sanctimonious piece of shit."

Sean's anger caused his will to strengthen as his thoughts deviated from Anita to Detective Maldonado. "If the police needed to question this *Lucy Sweets* to verify your story," he said, muttering the name through clenched teeth, "could you locate her for them?"

Roger's mouth opened but he didn't say a word, only staring in apparent surprise, even shock. He gaped at Sean as if he'd been asked if he had a vagina. Sean kept a cool, steady focus on Roger, making it understood that he meant what he said.

"What the fuck are you implying, Sean?" Roger's brows furrowed as pronounced lines of anger appeared on his forehead. "That—that *I* killed Merissa? Jesus Christ!" He rushed to lean down over Sean, glowering within a few inches of his face. "Fuck you, asshole!" he shouted, spittle emerging from his mouth. "How dare you think something like that? How *dare* you!"

He straightened up, yanked on the sides of his shirt, and stormed off. Sean continued to stare at him as he walked farther away, knowing he needed to inform Maldonado about all of this before Roger's Sunday departure for whereabouts unknown. After all, he never answered the question about this alleged prostitute named Lucy Sweets.

He sat back and looked at the two women by the playground who commanded Roger's attention earlier, wondering what dark deeds he may have been contemplating, what horrific act he may have been imagining. But after another few moments of contemplation, he closed his eyes and shook his head, still hesitant to believe a man he befriended and worked side by side with could be The Beatles' Song Murderer. Reaching into his pocket, Sean removed his phone and dialed the familiar number for a name he'd come to accept, but for a reason he never would.

✑✑✑

"Juicy Lucy Sweets?" Maldonado replied. Sean heard a humorless chuckle. "Oh yeah, she's real."

"So I guess Roger wasn't lying."

"Well, based on what you've told me about him, you're probably right. Lucy Sweets has been in and out of here a few times, but other than a possible STD or two, she's basically harmless and looking out for herself."

"An STD or two?" Sean thought of Anita and shook his head. "Good ol' Roger, spreading the love."

"Juicy Lucy is what she calls herself, by the way," Maldonado said, "and I have to admit, she's quite a character. She'll talk about everything from politics to penis size and is pretty damn funny about it." Maldonado chuckled again.

"I assume we scratch Roger off the list then?"

"Until we know for sure, I'm not ready to scratch anybody off the list, but it certainly makes him look like less of a candidate for the moment."

Sean flicked a spider off his pant leg, recognizing the appropriateness of Roger as the topic of conversation.

"We ever gonna find this guy, Ray?"

"Eventually, yeah," he answered, "and I really believe we're getting closer. Process of elimination is part of the course of things, but it takes time. Look at Roger, for example. I'm not ready to give him a pass just yet, but we'll find Lucy, show the photo, and see if she identifies him. Lucy probably won't remember if she was with him the night of Miss Franklin's murder, but if Roger told you the truth about being with her on multiple occasions, she'll recognize his face, and it'll prove he wasn't just throwing out a name he heard."

"He's an asshole."

"As is much of the world population, so it's fortunate that's not the sole criteria for finding this piece of shit. Process of elimination on that scale would take way too long."

⌘⌘⌘

The lunchtime conversation with Roger dominated his thoughts for the remainder of the day like a relentless rain, yet the soft, summer breeze caressing his senses as he approached his car to go home inspired him to first drive west along Santa Monica Boulevard toward Ocean Boulevard. Gazing at the enticing blue water in the distance as the sun continued to loiter, he decided the isolating windshield view from above wasn't fulfilling enough, so he drove to California Street and eased his way down the ramp to head north along Pacific Coast Highway. Like revisiting a former friend who meant so much despite a previous altercation, Sean sought a complete reconciliation. Tomorrow, an off day, he'd make his first return visit to the beach, spending the hours in the same blue skied, salt-air locale where the sirens of suicide beckoned several months before.

Chapter 28

As he drove west toward the beach along Colorado Boulevard, on a Saturday morning intended to feel as intoxicating as the summer zephyr blowing through his hair, Sean attempted to ignore those dissonant thoughts of another poorly timed phone call from his mother less than an hour before. With an apparent belief in her razor-sharp ability to resolve his needs, Sean evaluated her opinions in a different manner; an unparalleled capacity to irritate him.

This morning's nails-on-the-chalkboard conversation pertained to a friend of hers who had a niece, "a lovely, intelligent girl," transferring to the Los Angeles branch of her advertising company.

"You know, dear, I don't expect you to ever get over what happened completely, but you need to move on. You've got such a bright future in your father's business, and any woman in her right mind would be able to see what a kind, sensitive man you are, and…"

With the one-way conversation still reverberating like a brick thrown through glass, Sean turned off his cell phone and placed it in the glove compartment, dedicating the day to nothing but oceanic serenity without disturbances of any kind. Pulling into a public parking lot, he inhaled the invigorating salt air and hurried from his car to a prime spot on the sand, leaving his towel and folding chair in place before discarding his flip-flops to walk toward the shore.

Although the view seemed appealing again, the past sense of wonderment and motivation eluded him, leaving the mast of his thoughts unable to catch hold of a friendly breeze. Once his feet touched the water, however, the comforting sound and smell of the ocean offered a therapeutic shot of the Southern California lifestyle he always treasured, and stooping to examine a multi-colored seashell curled within itself like a cresting wave, he started to regain a connection to his surroundings. But as he proceeded northward, invisible fingers of wind caressing him and inciting his senses with each succeeding step, a sudden, stupefying sight brought his body and thoughts to an immediate halt.

Gaping open-mouthed, in transfixed confusion, he saw Merissa jogging toward him.

Sean stared in wonderment, immobilized by this clone nearing him as she ran, and he felt determined to observe everything about the woman as a tribute to Merissa's memory. She possessed the same high forehead with the shoulder length dark-blonde hair tied back in the ponytail style she often favored. She had those round, sensuous eyes, highlighted by the accent of long, angular eyebrows. The unique similarity also included the defined cheekbones, bookmarking the slightly downward dipping nose that created a visual pronouncement to those insecure moments of Merissa's over reactionary self-consciousness.

As the space between Sean and the woman lessened, he also acknowledged her similar height, with a matching body described in the line from "Devil with the Blue Dress" about being neither too skinny nor too fat. With unabashed focus, he admired and remembered the sizable breasts, so round and memorable, moving up and down in the subtle, arousing allowance from the sports bra beneath the sleeveless shirt. Nothing escaped his attention, including the perturbed expression she threw his way as she passed, causing the hypnotic spell he'd been under to dissolve slowly, like the watery white foam on the shore.

Sean continued staring at the woman as her figure diminished with the increasing distance. Still close enough for further observations, however, he reflected on the similar hips and ass, and those muscular calves and shoulders Merissa developed through her affinity for working out. When the final blurring details of the woman's body faded away, lost among other beachgoers walking to and from the shore, Sean returned to his towel and sat, shaken by the unexpected, surreal experience.

He thought of the jogger's flapping ponytail, reminding him of Merissa's secret decision to cut her hair and leave the ponytail days behind. Without informing him, she started saving pictures from magazines to show Dino, and as he explained to him after her death,

Merissa looked forward to witnessing his surprised expression that night—the night of her murder.

℘℘℘

"Welcome back, Dino," Sean said, settling into his chair.

Dino finished tying the smock and caressed Sean's cheek. "Thank you," he said, his eyes misting. Offering a smile, Dino ran his fingers through Sean's long, wet hair. "Oh my God, honey," he scolded, "your hair looks like you got the caveman special!"

"Haven't given much thought to my appearance lately," Sean replied, agreeing with the assessment as he looked in the mirror. "But now that you're here again, it's time."

"You're not the first man I've rescued from himself," Dino remarked with a wink.

Chuckling, Sean clutched his wrist. "I'm glad you're back."

Dino placed his scissors on the counter and turned back in silence, resting his hand on Sean's shoulder. Leaning close, he swiped a tear away. "I've thought about you a lot, Sean—how you're doing, what you must be thinking, if you're going to be all right." He pressed his lips together and gazed into his eyes. "I want to tell you something. I loved Merissa, she was such a sweet human being, and knowing I was probably the last friend she was with, well…it made me lose my mind for a while. I just needed to get away from here, from the reminders. This mirror that showed her reflection, this chair that held her body, it was all too much for me."

Sean nodded in small, almost undetectable movements. "I understand," he replied in a soft voice. "Are you okay?"

Dino's eyes widened as he tilted his head in apparent puzzlement. "Oh my God, Sean," he exclaimed, "you're asking if *I'm* okay?" His eyes narrowed as he proffered a hint of a smile. "No matter what I went through, I should be asking *you* that question, don't you think?" His eyes watered again as he clutched the back of Sean's neck and kissed his forehead. "But thanks for asking," he said. "It's just that every time I think about Merissa, I can't stop wondering why I wound up being one of the last people to ever see her, and talk with her." His voice caught as he choked back a sob. "Merissa called me on a whim that morning and told me what she wanted to do. We looked through magazine photos she saved, and the wonderful world of Dino took it from there." Looking down in silence as if reliving the moment, he lifted his head and broke into a broad, teary-eyed smile. "She looked awesome, baby. Sexy as hell. I don't know if she was more excited or nervous about what you'd think. She just wanted to go home, have a glass of wine, and wait it out until you got back."

೧೧೧

Sean remained at the beach until late afternoon, spending most of the time gazing at the horizon as memories of Merissa inhabited his thoughts. Four months had passed since that night, and although he'd overcome the struggle to endure whatever life now presented, emotional barriers frustrated, and, at times, dominated his waking hours. As long as The Beatles' Song Murderer continued to walk the streets, Sean's soul remained confined behind the iron bars of that reality. He yearned for that elusive role reversal, where his release occurred in synchronicity with the killer's imprisonment, and the ongoing nightmare dissipated into a new light of day.

Chapter 29

Entering his garage, Sean turned off the motor before reaching in the glove compartment for his cell phone. Staring at the device in his hand, he reflected on the days of yore before Apple and Blackberry descended upon the world like a technological heroin, engulfing us in their role as indispensable pusher to ours as their dependent junkie. Cell phones offered so many services nowadays that it seemed as much a human appendage as the hand itself, but outside the workplace, Sean rarely used his phone to call anybody anymore, comfortable in his continuing hibernation from much of society following Merissa's death.

He still appreciated the occasional phone conversation with his sister, Rebecca, and catching up on her stories from New York, but when the topic of conversation reverted to him, her tendency to traverse into a tone of pity and cautiousness turned good intentions into awkwardness and despondency. His brother, David, approached the omnipresent cloud of Merissa's death by avoiding any talk of it at all, preferring to remain in his comfort zone of business and family matters. His father never called him, but on those times when Sean phoned their house, his father asked the same two questions each time, first wanting to know how things were at work before the obligatory "How are you doing?" question. He meant well, but it seemed that his lack of outward emotion represented most of his male, World War II generation.

And then there was his mother, who believed she knew him better than anybody, understood what was best for him, and often left him wondering if he'd ever desire to talk with her again. Her obsessive desire to find his future wife had become tiresome to the point of resentment, and his gratitude for the invention of caller ID multiplied exponentially whenever she called and the phone went unanswered.

As for friends, the lack of names in his list of contacts reflected his reclusive personality and lack of desire to change. Merissa had reached inside of him, helping to open that sealed box of a persona and expose him to the sunlight of interaction. Joining the bowling team exemplified her influence, but after her death, without her prodding, he eventually reverted to his comfort zone of privacy, even with the occasional league match appearance.

Of the few names in his contact list, however, one called that afternoon, so when he turned the power on, and listened to the voice mail message from Detective Maldonado asking him to return the call, it reminded him that his cell phone still played a necessary part in his life.

"Sean, it's Ray Maldonado. We made a discovery about Adam McBride that you should know. Call me."

After rushing through his greeting of a bouncing Hendrix and feeding him dinner, Sean turned on the table lamp by the couch and called Maldonado. The final stubborn vestiges of sunlight lingered in a late summer, want-to-stay-up-here-a-little-longer defiance as he stared out his window and waited for Ray to answer. This time, however, Sean left a message, and when Hendrix scurried over to jump onto his lap, tongue dangling in goofy contentment, the curiosity about Maldonado's phone call vanished for the moment.

As one hand scratched his dog's head, now flattened against his chest, Sean held his phone with the other, viewing the upcoming week's agenda on his calendar—another recognized convenience from the gods of Silicon Valley. He had Mrs. Saginowski scheduled to return with her husband on Monday at ten o'clock to discuss the financing options for the Esquire she desired. Carl Stephenson wanted to take the Mustang for another test drive during his lunch hour at twelve-thirty, and a Mr. Kevin Nguyen made a four o'clock appointment to look at possible purchase for his son.

On Tuesday, other than a seven-thirty breakfast meeting at the I-Hop across the street, the rest of the workday remained blank. At five o'clock, however, having received permission to leave work early, he scheduled a meeting at his house with Martin. The electrical part he ordered several weeks ago finally arrived.

On Wednesday at ten o'clock, Sean had Jamaal Jackson scheduled to return with his wife. Unlike the previous Fords he owned, the man voiced complaints about his current one, but like congressmen whose low approval ratings don't seem to prevent successful reelections, the man's loyalty to the brand remained steadfast. At two o'clock, he made an appointment with Dayla Cunningham, a feisty elderly woman who impressed him with her knowledge of cars and engines during their brief conversation at the dealership. Scrolling to Thursday, he'd stopped reading when his phone rang.

"Hello, Ray."

"Are you still in touch with Adam McBride?" he asked, bypassing any greeting.

Sean lifted Hendrix off his chest and placed him on the floor. "Not much anymore," he said. Rising to his feet, he walked to the window and stared past a streetlamp at a girl, seemingly high school aged, getting out of the back seat of a car with a boy about the same age. The recollection of his past sped through his mind, when grand possibilities and optimism reigned, and sex dominated his thoughts. Closing the curtain, he asked, "Why? What's going on?"

"Do you remember me telling you about the last Beatles' Song Murderer victim, the woman from Simi Valley?"

Returning to the couch, Sean ignored the rush of hip pain as he sat on the edge of the cushion, his right leg jiggling up and down.

"Yes, of course."

"Her name was Jacquelyn Hastings, and about two months before she was raped and killed on July twenty-second, she purchased a new car, a Ford Fusion, from your father's Van Nuys dealership."

Sean closed his eyes as he tried to settle his breathing. His heart raced in sudden awareness of the reason for the call. In a slow, hesitant manner, he finished the sentence for Maldonado.

"And Adam sold her the car."

"On Sunday, May eighteenth. It was an oversight on our part, something we should have caught sooner."

Sean didn't respond, listening to Maldonado's muted cough before continuing where he left off. "Some people wait months before they put the license plates on their new car, and some people are like Jacquelyn Hastings. It usually takes about six weeks to get the registration, right? She wasted no time getting those plates back on, and that disguised how new the car was. It took a while, but the link was made, and now I wanted to talk to you about it. You told me he'd been transferred for a sexual harassment claim. Do you know if he's still working there?"

"Yeah," he answered, before realizing his knee-jerk response couldn't be verified at that moment. "I mean, I haven't heard anything, so I think so."

"You said you're not in touch with him, but what about that bowling thing you guys are in? You still doing that?"

Staring at the floor, Sean leaned forward, both his legs frozen in place. "I still am," he said. "We took September off and we started up again this month, but he was a no show both times." Sean rubbed his hand across his face, staring at the reflection of the streetlamp through the curtain. While part of him didn't want to believe in Adam's guilt, he wanted justice for Merissa more than anything, and if that meant marching that religious wacko away in his goddamn handcuffs, then let him rot in hell. "What do you think, Ray?" he asked, his tired voice leaking through an exhale. "Is it Adam? Is he the one?"

"It's certainly possible," Maldonado answered. "As far as we know, he's the first suspect that has ties to Miss Franklin *and* Jacquelyn Hastings, so that means something. I also find it interesting that he lied to you when he said he was home that night. According to my notes, you told me his wife said he didn't come home until after midnight, that he got some food and just sat in his car. Is that a lie, too? Maybe he's deceiving his wife. Maybe he's deceiving you."

"Can't you bring him in for questioning?" Sean asked. "I mean, if he's the one, why not make sure you capture him before he rapes and kills again?"

"Suspicion without hard evidence doesn't do us a damn bit of good," Maldonado answered. "The last thing I want is for this guy to slip through the cracks again knowing we're watching him. If he's the one, the web is closing in, and from this point on, we'll keep a very close watch on Mr. McBride. But you can also help."

Sean rubbed his hand down the back of his head, looking at the darkening shadows in the far corner of the room. "I don't know what I can do," he told him. "Like I said before, I'm out of touch with the guy."

"Well, get *back* in touch, okay?" Maldonado said, the level of his voice escalating for the first time. "See what he's been up to lately, if anything's changed. How's his marriage? Does he do activities with his kids? How's his job? Does he sell more cars to men or women? Whatever the answer, why does he think that is? What's he do after he leaves work? Does he go straight home? Any hobbies? Has he done any traveling? Anything you find out might be useful."

Sean tightened his lips, rolling them inward upon each other, and stared at the ground as he pondered the task ahead. "I'm not the kind of guy who goes around asking a lot of questions of people I know," he said. "What if I'm too obvious and he becomes suspicious? What if he asks me why I'm suddenly so interested in all these things? What do I say to him?"

"Tell him you're working on the new you, that your therapist is encouraging you to be more interactive with people you know."

Sean uttered a percussive one-beat laugh. "Shit, Ray," he said, a chuckle spilling forth. "That stupid therapist line is some clever bullshit. Where'd you come up with that one?"

A momentary silence followed.

"My therapist."

Chapter 30

The next morning, October twenty-seventh, per his usual ritual, Sean headed from his bed to the shower before heading for the kitchen to prepare coffee. Reminded by the yellow post-it note he placed on the refrigerator, he called Boyd's Electronics and left a message for Martin about a persistent garage light issue before selecting a jazz compilation CD to accompany his first cup.

As he started humming along to Wes Montgomery's classic "Bumpin' on Sunset," the doorbell rang. Annoyed at first by the interruption, he opened the door right away after looking through the peephole. With a slight, tight-lipped smile conveying concern rather than any kind of joy, Jenny stood facing him with her arm lowered around the slump-shouldered body of a teary-eyed Kayleigh, wearing the number fourteen Lakers jersey and wiping both eyes with the back of her hand.

"I hope we're not disturbing you, Sean," Jenny said, "but Kayleigh wanted to tell you something she just found out, and it seems it couldn't wait."

From the brief recognition of how good Jenny looked in her pair of tight-fitting jeans, and her soft brown hair sprawled over the shoulders of her caramel-colored cashmere sweater, his attention shifted toward his sad, little friend. Kayleigh stared with a distant look of distress, her eyes gazing straight ahead, level with Sean's thigh. Clutching the folds of his robe, he lowered himself to his knees and brought his face close to hers.

"What's the matter, Kayleigh?" he asked, reaching out to touch her shoulder. Glancing up at Jenny in confusion, he looked back at Kayleigh and waited through the alternating moments of sniffles and silence. Her lips quivered and the watery eyes made him feel terrible, even though he remained clueless over her sorrow and the surprise visit.

"It's…it's Coby," she said, her voice low and weepy.

Sean tilted his head, conjecturing about the cause for such grief and the need to come see him. A sudden troubling thought struck him, tightening his stomach in fear over the possible devastating repercussions to Kayleigh's psyche if the man's cancer returned, or worse, if he died.

"What happened to him?"

Kayleigh took a deep breath before wiping her nose with her arm.

"He's not a Laker anymore," she muttered, seconds before the tears resumed.

"I guess they didn't sign him to play again this year," Jenny explained. "Kayleigh went on their website this morning and found out."

In a small, cracking voice she said, "I wanted you to know, Mr. Music." Glancing into his eyes for a moment, she lowered her gaze to the ground again.

Sean looked up at Jenny. "Did she tell her parents?"

"They're in Santa Barbara for their anniversary, so I doubt they know," she said, stroking Kayleigh's patchy tufts. "I'm staying with the kids. When I heard her crying, I rushed to her room, fearing something awful. But after she told me what it was, and my heartbeat returned to normal, she insisted on seeing you right away."

"It *is* awful!" Kayleigh cried.

Sean smiled at Kayleigh and gave her arm a gentle squeeze. "You know something?" he asked. "I once felt the same kind of sadness about another Laker who played before you were even born. And he was my favorite Laker *ever*."

"Really?" she replied. "What was his name?"

"Have you ever heard of Magic Johnson?"

Kayleigh squinted as she thought about it, and then nodded her head. "Yeah, I think so," she said. "That's a funny name for somebody."

Sean glanced up at Jenny, their smiles joining together.

"It's just a nickname," he told her. "His real name is Earvin, but he was like a magician with all the amazing things he did on the court. Just when you thought he couldn't do more stuff, he always seemed to have another trick up his sleeve. So when somebody started calling him Magic Johnson, that's how he got to be known to everybody."

"Why did he make you so sad?"

"Well, he got real sick and had to stop playing. And it didn't just make all of Los Angeles sad, but the whole country, and even lots of basketball fans around the world."

"Wow," she whispered.

"So when you tell me about Coby, and I tell you about Magic, you know what they say about two people being sad about the same thing?"

Kayleigh shook her head.

"They say it makes it easier to take because both of them know the same kind of hurt inside. So instead of feeling alone about it, you know you have somebody else who understands how you feel because they went through the same kind of thing. And when you share something together, even something that makes you cry, it's nice to know you have company, right?"

Kayleigh nodded.

"Hey," he said, "what are you going to be for Halloween?"

The corners of Kayleigh's mouth tightened into a thin-lipped smile and, in less time than it took for the final moments of a twenty-four second clock to expire, the tears formed and fell again. "Coby Karl!"

Sean looked up into Jenny's misty eyes before reaching out to embrace Kayleigh, her weak sobs now joined in sorrowful harmony with the subtle shaking of her frail body. When he pulled away, he held her arms and smiled. "Tell you what," he said, "when your parents come back, tell them that Sean wants to invite you over for some pizza. And make sure to bring your guitar, okay?"

"Okay," she whimpered, her voice a raspy whisper.

Rising to his feet, he caught Jenny smiling at him while a tear broke loose and descended her cheek. He wished more time remained to talk with her, but work beckoned.

He hoped to find that time.

Chapter 31

Slogging through a molasses morning of mental fog and ineffective cups of coffee, Sean stared into the nothingness of his round, glass covered kitchen table, feeling drained from a restless night of regret and expectations of challenge for what awaited him today—Merissa's forty-third birthday.

Almost eight years older, he used to joke with her about respecting her elders, but Merissa's intelligence far exceeded his. A college graduate, unlike him, an avid reader, also unlike him, and an activist for helping women and children in abusive relationships, his admiration ran deep. The eternal, unanswerable question of why bad things happened to good people stuck to his thoughts like a shadow, but never to the degree as what this day, October thirtieth, represented, and what he planned to do about it.

Arranging a switch of workdays with another employee three weeks before, Sean recognized the importance of the upcoming day, but couldn't predict his reaction. Now, as he drove away in radio-free silence toward his destination, statue-faced and misty eyed, he felt the push and pull of emotions—relief for fulfilling the promise to himself and fear of regret for revisiting the scene of the nightmare.

Exiting the 101 freeway in Studio City, Sean arrived several minutes later at the tree lined cul-de-sac location of Parkway Condominiums. From her years of hard work in various jobs, Merissa saved enough money to move there, eventually bringing her pride and enthusiasm as one of the board members of the association. Although he disliked those time consuming, nighttime phone calls discussing projects, financial issues, or prospective vendors she'd been assigned to hire, he understood how much her participation in

Parkway's affairs meant to her. So today, on her birthday, he just wanted to walk the grounds and feel her spirit again.

An immediate aftereffect from that night confronted him as he approached the entrance and spotted something new—a guardhouse with a mechanized lowering bar to prevent automatic access into the condominiums. Easing forward to the window about a foot above his own, he eyed an earnest-looking dark-haired man appearing to be in his mid-thirties with a large head and thick neck protruding from his shirt collar. He displayed a clean-shaven face but the promise of dark stubble seemed evident from the approaching shadow on his cheeks and chin. Behind him, Sean spotted a bank of small television monitors revealing areas of the complex now possessing security cameras.

Maldonado mentioned a couple of old cameras that existed before, one for the garage and the other for the pool, and as Sean gazed at this too-little-too-late protective system, a spasm of resentment shook his composure and left him temporarily speechless. Sean acknowledged the guard with a nod of his head.

After a slight lean forward, the man addressed him. "Hello, sir."

A period of silence followed, and Sean realized the guard expected him to identify himself and his reason for visiting. The awkwardness of the situation sent a tremble through his fragile, fault line psyche, making him question his actions. Unsure what to do or say, he decided to simply tell the truth. "My name's Sean Hightower," he told him, "and I'm not here to see anybody. But that guardhouse you're in," he said, pointing, "and the security bar in front of me," then redirecting his finger toward the front of his car, "was no doubt a reaction to what happened to my girlfriend, Merissa Franklin, six and a half months ago." His voice broke, but he suppressed the pain to finish his reply. "She was murdered here on April eleventh."

The guard's head and shoulders retreated several inches in apparent surprise.

"I haven't been back here since I collected her clothes a few days later, but today would have been her birthday." A small, tight smile appeared on his face. "I just wanted to come here for a few minutes and walk around."

The guard responded with a small shake of his head.

"I'm very sorry, sir."

Sean's shoulders sagged in disappointment. His intolerance toward unbending, compassionless rule followers like this caused his heart to pound in frustration. How could this man turn him away?

"I don't know what I would do if that ever happened to my wife," he said in a soft tone. "I can't even think about it."

Sean looked up and saw the guard reach for his phone.

"Just let me make a call," he said. "I'm sure it won't be a problem, but I have instructions I need to follow."

After the bar rose to allow his entrance, Sean veered left and headed for the garage. His eyes darted in a direct line toward Merissa's old spot, occupied now by the black Mercedes reminder of the new reality. The vacant guest area to the left, the same one Sean used on numerous occasions, seemed smaller now. Quashing the urge to park there, he drove toward the back corner where the half-dozen visitor spaces allowed people like him temporary access.

He walked in a slow, deliberate manner through the garage, observing the bank of long, bright tubular lighting extending north to south and east to west along the entire overhead structure. Unlike the dim, tambourine-colored floodlights hanging from the ceiling before, these new ones offered a sleek and modern ambiance, providing a definite all-around upgrade.

Sean detected other changes as well. Bracketed along the upper walls on each side of the garage, silver hued surveillance cameras stood guard, keeping an electric eye on everyone's parking lot behavior. He reflected on Merissa's continual frustration over the roadblocks she often faced with the ownership group because of their reluctance to spend money on anything. But this time, after what happened to her, Sean felt sure the decision makers didn't hesitate in giving the go-ahead for a top of the line security system.

Walking up the one flight of steps from the garage to the first floor, Sean stood staring at the closed door of the second unit—Merissa's place. His legs grew heavy, and he leaned against the wall for support. The comfortable eighty-degree temperature of the moment couldn't prevent the hair on his arms from standing on end from the sudden chill spreading through his body. He spotted the camera at the end of the hallway, and looking up, saw a second one overhead.

As long deep breaths chronicled his solitude, he directed his attention toward Merissa's door again, picturing her in his sweats, opening the door, maybe smiling, and letting someone she trusted inside. But *who*? Over a half year later, The Beatles' Song Murderer remained nothing but a shadowy figure in his head, elusive and ridiculing. No matter how hard he tried, how intensely he gazed at that door and repeated the scene in his mind, the image of the person walking in that night remained a mystery—a mocking, faceless shape representing a stark contrast to the clarity of those surveillance cameras now locking him in their sights.

Chapter 32

Sean offered a cursory wave to the guard and accelerated away, sensing he'd seen the last of Parkway Condominiums, and anxious to create a rapid separation in miles *and* emotion. Until the moment he entered his driveway and reached for the remote to open his garage door, his hands maintained the same grip on the steering wheel and his body remained motionless. After a fleeting acknowledgment that three of his four garage lights flashed on and off again in harmonious malfunction, he turned off the engine and closed his eyes, focusing on the sound of his breathing. The tranquility soothed him, easing his way toward the enticing allure of entering the womb of his home for welcome seclusion.

A sudden tapping on his back window startled him. Glancing at his rear view mirror, the sight of an obviously female torso from the shoulders down to the waist captured his attention, but the face remained unseen. Placing his cell phone in his pocket, he opened the door, looked to his left, and felt an immediate boost to his spirits when he gazed up at Jenny.

"Hi, Sean," she said, smiling. "Hope I didn't scare you."

She wore an unbuttoned black sweater over a full-length blue and green cotton dress that allowed a bit of cleavage to show and accentuated a shapely figure previously unnoticed. Her dark brown eyes seemed softer and more welcoming, offering a magnetism that drew him in. At that moment, Sean recognized something he'd overlooked—Jenny offered more than just kindness. He found himself staring at a lovely, sexy woman.

"Well, I admit I was in my own little world," he replied, looking up at her from his seat. "How are you, Jenny?"

"Fine, thanks," she said, approaching him. "Work's taking up a lot of time, but that's a good thing, so no complaints. You and I drove up the street together, so when I saw you pull in I wanted to say hello before you went inside. How are things with you?"

Sean exited his car. Standing close, he felt relaxed and sensed a mutual sensation with her. He leaned back against the side of his hood and tendered his own smile. "Well, today hasn't been the best, but it's better now."

Jenny reared her head back in apparent surprise, and for the brief silence that followed, Sean wondered about the appropriateness of his reply. Maybe she disliked the appearance of his flirtatious answer. "That's the nicest thing that anyone's said to me in a long time. Thank you, Sean."

"Perhaps I should be the one thanking you," he responded.

This time they eyed each other in a longer period of silence, each maintaining their smile.

"I better go now," she said. "I'm helping Kayleigh with her homework."

"Would you mind accompanying me to my mailbox before you leave? I might have bills waiting to be caressed by these grateful hands."

"Well," she said, grasping his arm, "it's a little out of my way, but I'll manage."

As they walked down his driveway, Jenny stopped in mid-stride and brushed his shoulder with her fingers. "I had lunch again with Adam this week," she said. Shaking her head, she rolled her eyes and chuckled. "And he still insists on keeping it a secret from you."

Adam's name caused Sean's stomach to knot, and he forced himself to avoid volcanic thoughts of a Merissa repeat. He hadn't yet spoken with him as Maldonado requested, but another "secret" lunch with Jenny concerned him. Maybe she could provide some insight.

"I forgot why he doesn't want me to know."

"It's so silly," she said, giggling. "He's afraid you'd think he's being unfaithful to his wife."

Sean took a long, slow breath. "First of all, why should he care what I think? And, secondly, I wouldn't think that anyway."

Jenny held her hands out and shrugged.

"I remember you said you went to high school with him, so what do you talk about? Is it one of those 'Glory Days' Bruce Springsteen conversations, reliving past accomplishments of your youth?"

"Oh, please!" Jenny shot back, making a face. "Just shoot me if I ever get like that."

Sean's body tightened at the response.

"You look upset," she remarked.

"I'm sorry," he replied, forcing a smile. "It's just…it's just that Adam can be such a fool."

"In that sense, yeah, he's weird," she answered. "I've tried to understand his secrecy, but all I'm left to think is that he's a sweet, timid man, married to a dominating wife, and he's scared to make waves in any way."

"So, my unfortunate Springsteen reference aside, what do you talk about?"

For several moments Jenny didn't answer him, but the fullness of her subtly painted lips formed a tight smile. "Wrong of me to divulge this, but most of the talks have centered on Eleanor and his marriage. On the one hand, he seems to idolize the woman, but then he'll also talk about how frustrated he gets with her sometimes. He uses the word 'handcuffed' a lot."

"Handcuffed?" Sean repeated, his muscles tightening again.

"Yeah, but then he goes back and talks about God and the holy matrimony idea, and his kids, and how blessed he is to have all of that. 'Blessed' is another word he uses a lot. But, you know, that's Adam."

"What I don't understand is if he cares so much about keeping your lunches a secret, why even take the chance getting together with you? What if somebody he knows sees him?"

"I see your point," she said, "but this was only the second time I've had lunch with the guy, and both times it was at a Chinese restaurant miles from his neighborhood, so we didn't expect any surprises."

"Think you'll have another marriage counseling session with him?"

Jenny smiled. "I don't know. Maybe. I feel sorry for the guy because I can relate to that kind of emotional abuse. My ex was a real jerk, and it took me a while to overcome those scars." Her eyes narrowed as she looked down at the ground in a moment of apparent contemplation. Biting her upper lip, she looked up again and chin-nodded toward the mailbox. "I think those bills have waited long enough for some TLC."

Sean stared at Jenny, admiring her kind face and vulnerable honesty. "Thanks for saying hello, Jenny. I was having a rough day until you came along."

Jenny reached out for his arm and offered a gentle squeeze. "You just made my day, Sean Hightower."

"Are you still dating Stan?"

The question surged forth in a quick and unexpected way; a lightning bolt that leaves an undeniable reaction after the initial impact. She stared at him, her expression a blank canvas devoid of clues. Sean felt a sudden acceleration of his heartbeat, wondering if he'd overstepped his bounds.

"No," she answered, shaking her head.

Sean noticed how her soft brown hair fell across her cheekbones as she nodded back and forth.

"I like having a good time as much as any girl, but dating a married man isn't worth the trouble."

"I hope you don't mind that I asked a personal question."

Jenny looked at him and smiled, the tiny crinkles from the corners of her eyes exposed and endearing when she started to laugh. "No, that's all right," she said. "The relationship wasn't going anywhere, anyway. Even a magician can't make certain realities disappear, like a wife and kid at home."

They smiled in silence again.

"Something else I should tell you," Jennie said, "but don't kill the messenger, okay? Adam's coming over on Saturday."

Sean's eyes narrowed as he tilted his head in an uncomfortable curiosity, waiting to hear the rest.

Jenny waved her hand in the air, brushing off any concern. "Oh, it's no big deal," she told him. "He's going to set up my sound system to play in different rooms. I moved into my condo over three months ago and still use my laptop to listen to music."

Sean raised his eyebrows in surprise. "Your sound system, huh? Looks like there's more to Adam than just God and selling cars."

Jenny chuckled. "He told me he worked in the entertainment section at a Best Buy store before becoming a car dealer. He's got some parts he's going to bring over, so if he's offering, I won't say no." She looked into his eyes and smiled. "Why'd you want to know about Stan?"

The sudden sound of Sean's ringtone interrupted the moment, and when he read Maldonado's name, he held up his hand for her to wait there.

"Hi, Ray, can you give me a minute? I'm just saying goodbye to someone."

"Yeah, go ahead," Maldonado replied.

Looking at Jenny, Sean rubbed his hand across the back of his neck, feeling his skin tingle as a sudden schoolboy nervousness overtook him. "I have to take this, and I know Kayleigh's waiting for you, but…would you like to go out sometime?"

With a single definitive nod, she brushed his cheek with her hand. The warmth of her touch and the radiance of her smile almost made him drop his phone. "I would love to." Reaching into her purse, she removed a business card. "I'll talk to you soon, Sean."

Watching her turn and walk away, Sean smiled as he glanced at her card before placing it in his pocket. "Sorry, Ray," he said, grasping the envelopes, "what's up?"

"I've been thinking about that first meeting we had at the station," Maldonado said, his voice softer than usual. "When I told you The Beatles' Song Murderer could be someone Miss Franklin knew. And you, as well."

Sean closed the lid and stood still, staring up at the darkening late afternoon sky in anticipation of Maldonado's admission of error, validating his fear that all the months of speculation and suspicion meant nothing. "All I know is that it's been a long six and a half months and a lot of sleepless nights wondering who the fuck it is."

Maldonado uttered a laugh, brief and sarcastic sounding. "Sleepless nights, huh? Like the one I had last night after a phone call I got at two in the morning? I've been up ever since and I have a feeling tonight won't be any different."

Sean tightened his grip and closed his eyes in the expectation of another rape and murder report. "Did it happen again?" he asked.

Several moments passed before Maldonado replied.

"Maybe, but not the same way."

"I don't understand. Wouldn't you know by—"

Maldonado cut Sean's question off in midsentence.

"And if it is him," he said, "because I did something I shouldn't have done, I feel largely responsible for the homicide that took place last night."

Sean realized he hadn't moved, remaining in the street by his mailbox. Hurrying back toward the garage, he headed for his car seat.

"What happened, Ray? And why are you calling *me* about this?"

"I've been thinking about that first meeting we had when I showed you the photos of the suspects," he said. "In addition to Ulysses Stanley Claiborne, who wasn't in any of them, it seems that over the last few months we've kept a more watchful eye on two others: Roger Peterson and Adam McBride. You with me so far?"

Sean stared at the murky nothingness through his windshield, his lone functioning overhead light's five-minute duration now expired, transforming the near blackness of his surroundings into something ominous. Looking behind him, he gazed down his driveway toward an ineffectual street lamp across the street before reaching up to push the remote button, triggering the one overhead light as the other three repeated their on-and-off problematic behavior.

"I'm confused, Ray," he said. "And to be honest, you've got me on edge without knowing why."

"Listen, Sean," he said, his voice sounding tired, "you'll know as much as I do by the time I'm done, all right?"

"Sure, go ahead."

"Remember Lucy Sweets, the woman Roger said he was with the night Ms. Franklin was killed?"

"Yes, of course. Juicy Lucy. You were going to show her a photo of Roger to confirm she knew him."

"We found her around eight p.m. last night drinking a martini in the bar of the Ritz-Carlton downtown. My men asked her to ID Roger from the three photos we had of him from the memorial service but Lucy was adamant about wanting us to leave because she was expecting 'a friend' as she put it, and didn't want to be seen talking to us."

"Isn't prostitution illegal, Ray?"

"Yeah, it still is," he replied, "but drinking a martini at a bar with a friend is as legal as eating popsicles in a park. Now, are you going to let me finish?"

"Sorry."

"I wanted Lucy to see all three photos because each of them together added a greater chance of identifying him for certain. So she
put them in her purse and said to meet her in front of the Bonaven-
ture at midnight. She wound up approaching one of our street pa-
trols about eleven thirty with a message that she had a change of
plans and wouldn't be going there. But she was sure about Roger.
In fact, she even had a nickname for him: Handcuff Honey."

A meteoric shiver struck Sean and his muscles grew tense.

"You told me handcuffs are what The Beatles' Song Murderer
used on Merissa!"

"Yes, and maybe there's a clue there, no doubt about it. But that
kind of sexual shit goes on all the time, right?"

"Of course, but still—"

"Just to let you know, we've been trailing Roger with the help
of the San Jose PD ever since he moved there. He's currently living
with his twin brother, Anthony. I guess charm runs in the family 'cause Anthony was arrested on a rape charge last March."

Eyes widening, Sean stared in short-lived silence. "Are you
fucking kidding me?"

"You want jokes, go to the Comedy Store. The case was
dropped for insufficient evidence. So far, nothing out of the ordi-
nary, but we'll continue to keep a watch."

Sean nibbled his upper lip, thinking about that final blowout in
the park. Rising through the discomfort of stiffness in his hip, he
realized he better turn on the manual light switch before the overhead light timer expired, enveloping him in darkness again. "So
Roger was telling the truth about knowing Lucy," he said, getting
to his feet. "But April eleventh must be too long ago for her to remember if she was with him that night."

"That's true, and like I just said, we've got eyes on him. But
let's remember there's other suspects here in town that we can't
ignore." Maldonado coughed, and then continued, his voice sounding raspier by the minute. "Lucy told the patrolman something else,
Sean." He paused, and when he continued, his voice seemed tighter,
making it harder to hear. "Something we weren't expecting."

As Sean flipped the switch, a sudden popping sound followed
by a spark inside the panel box caused the sudden blackening of the
garage.

"*Shit!*"

"What happened? You all right?"

Flipping the lever down again, Sean reached through the dark for the doorknob and entered his lightless kitchen while Hendrix bounced at his feet. "I'm fine," he told him, "but hold on a minute." Feeling for the indoor light switch, Sean turned it on before returning his hand to the panel box, checking to ensure the area remained cool and safe. Making a mental note to call Martin again, he leaned back against the sink to resume his conversation. "So what did Lucy say that you weren't expecting?"

"She recognized another man from the photos."

"*What?*" Sean felt his mind spinning in confusion as he closed his eyes and envisioned the men who attended the service. Maybe Roger turned one of those guys on to the woman. It wouldn't surprise him if that philandering asshole added to his memorable legacy a prick *and* a pimp. "So who was it, Ray?"

"We don't know. Lucy didn't have the photos with her, and given the fact we only gave her three of them, there's more men than you might think; Adam McBride, Elliot Hayden, Martin Boyd, Hank Sendowski, Dino Esposito, Leander Karras, and Carlos Carrillo."

"Can't you ask her again with the photos this time?"

"No," he said, "we can't. We can't do that..." His tone seemed more subdued, more distant, his voice trailing off into an odd silence hanging heavy in the air and pinpricking Sean into a sudden clarity. He held his breath and stared through the open door of his darkened garage, anticipating the name of the homicide victim.

A long, noticeable sigh preceded the answer. "Lucy Sweets was murdered last night."

Sean gripped the counter and lowered his head, feeling sadness for a woman he never met. Then a sudden thought occurred to him. "Do you feel her murder is linked to those photos, or am I overthinking this?"

"You're not overthinking it at all," Maldonado answered, "because there are connections to the previous murders that can't be overlooked. Whoever the killer was employed the same bullet type that the Beatles' Song Murderer consistently uses. And my guess is the same gun type, too. Judging by the force and trauma it caused, probably a Glock. And the *way* Lucy was shot, in the same area of the forehead just above the right eye, that also matches the way all the other victims were killed. And the fact that she was in possession of those photos leaves me pretty damn certain her murder wasn't just a coincidence."

Sean stared at one particular square of his beige-tiled floor, eyes narrowed in thought as he sifted through Maldonado's information. He wondered if the man who'd killed Lucy, the Beatles' Song Murderer it now seemed, somehow discovered her intention to identify him as someone she knew. "Explain something to me," he said. "Apparently one of those guys in the photos had been with Lucy enough times that she recognized him, just like Roger, but that doesn't necessarily incriminate him, right? He might be nothing more than another paying customer."

"Yeah, there's always that possibility," Maldonado replied, "but right now I have another murder case to solve by starting at square one and asking how the most street-savvy prostitute I've dealt with in my entire career gets caught up in a situation where she's shot and killed the same way as all the other victims of The Beatles' Song Murderer."

"Any ideas?" Sean asked.

Maldonado cleared his throat. "Right now I'm looking at two general possibilities—either he's a deranged asshole who kills hookers, of which there have been several like that in my experience, or he's a deranged asshole whose identity needs protecting for some reason, and who Lucy trusted beforehand, just like Ms. Franklin."

Chapter 33

The final match of the season between McDougal's Ford Marauders and Tolbert's Chevy Terrors guaranteed a well-attended night at the lanes. Although an unlikely lopsided score in favor of the Marauders provided the lone avenue for overtaking the Terrors for the year's bragging rights, there remained plenty of vocal bravado from several of Sean's teammates when they spotted him strolling through the doors.

Approaching the steps leading down to the lanes, Sean halted in surprise when he noticed Eleanor McBride sitting in one of the upper level chairs overlooking the section where the two teams congregated. For a Bible-toting conservative woman like her, a cuss filled, beer-drinking event seemed an out-of-place venue, but there she was, leaning forward with her hands on her knees, staring with the same attentiveness as if listening to a church sermon. Or maybe her eyes centered on Adam, sitting and conversing with two female teammates, Shayla and Margaret.

"Hi, Eleanor."

Eyes widening in recognition, she beckoned him with a wave of her hand. "I've been wondering how you are, Sean, but Adam says he doesn't see you anymore except at these bowling matches."

"Yeah, I know," Sean replied. "We miss him at work. He was the one gentleman among the rest of us cavemen." Tilting his head, he smiled in curious amusement. "I'm surprised to see you here. Is this your first time?"

She turned her head and glanced in Adam's direction before looking back. Her thin smile seemed sorrowful, and her eyes continued narrowing until they closed for a moment. She took a deep breath and shook her head, reminding Sean how much of the drama queen gene this woman possessed, even from a simple question.

"Yes," she said, "it's my first time, and as the Lord is my witness, I've already heard enough bad language that I pray we all don't get struck down any minute." Crossing herself, her expression turned grim as she continued. "If you think *you're* surprised, you should have seen the look on my husband's face."

Sean spotted Adam staring at them. Acknowledging each other, they both smiled and waved.

"I better get my shoes and ball and go down there," Sean said. "Try not to fall asleep watching all the excitement, okay?"

Eleanor's solemn demeanor remained unchanged, offering no reaction at all to Sean's light-hearted remark. "I'm not about to do that," she told him. "I'm a loyal, God-fearing wife, and I want to make sure my husband remembers the eyes of the Lord are upon him, too."

Sean gave a quick nod and hurried away, not understanding what the hell she meant, but knowing his opinion of this religious nut-job had walked through the valley of validation once again.

After a few minutes of small talk, back slaps, handshakes, and hugs, he found the ball he liked and returned to put on his shoes. No more than a few moments later, Adam sat next to him and leaned forward with his elbows on his knees as Sean tied one of his laces.

"I can't believe my wife showed up," he said.

Sean raised his eyes for a moment before resuming tying his shoes. "All I can tell you is the Eleanor McBride I know doesn't like to be around people who drink or swear, so she may not stick around for long."

Adam hung his head and nodded, thin red strands of hair dabbing his forehead. "I know," he replied. "And Eleanor's not so forgiving, so she'll probably give me a hard time at home."

Finishing with his other shoe, Sean sat up and looked at Adam. "It's not like you invited her here, man. And besides, you can't be held accountable for anything the rest of us beer-drinking, foul-mouthed, going-to-Hell heathens do, right?"

Adam offered a tight-lipped smile. "Sometimes Eleanor seems to forget that the Lord decides everyone's fate in the end. It's not up to us to judge."

Sean winked. "Well, I hope the Lord understands that it's a chance for hard-working people to unwind and have a little fun."

Rising from the bench, he turned toward a waitress taking drink requests and ordered a beer. "You want something, Adam?"

"Diet Coke, please," he answered, reaching in his pocket for his ringing cell phone.

Soon after answering the call, Adam's expression changed, reflecting a man who now appeared quite troubled. He glanced at Eleanor, turned away, looked back, then turned away again, speaking in a voice too low for Sean to hear from a few feet away. His sudden furtive mannerisms—steeped in a kind of animated Nixonian cautiousness of furrowed brows, darting eyes, and hunched shoulders—created a strange transformation from gentle to jittery, leaving Sean puzzled, yet also reminding him that he left his own cell phone in the car.

From the time he gave Jenny his number, their increasing correspondence changed his previous blasé attitude about keeping his phone nearby, so with a few minutes remaining before the first frame, he headed for the parking lot, opened his door, and retrieved the phone from the cup holder. A slight sense of disappointment from the blank screen commanded his attention until he spotted Adam walking out from the building to stop, stare, and wave at the back of a black SUV exiting the driveway. Within moments, the car accelerated into the street, leaving Sean with a glimpse of the last two letters of the license plate—RH.

Perhaps the familiarity of those two letters as the initials of his sister, Rebecca, brought them to the forefront of attention, but the need to remain hidden from sight mattered most to him at that moment. He observed Adam remove a note from his windshield, read the contents, stuff the paper inside his pocket, and then move to the back of the car. Dropping to his knees, he disappeared for several seconds before returning to his feet. He appeared to hold a hand-sized packet of some kind, but the second-rate parking lot lights prevented Sean from deciphering more than that.

Approaching the bowling center entrance about a minute or two after Adam had returned, Sean lurched to the side to prevent the door from hitting him as an obviously distraught Eleanor, head bowed, charged through the door like a lineman blocking for his running back.

"Oh!" Eleanor cried out, her moist eyes glistening from the overhead lights. "I'm sorry, Sean. I didn't see you."

"That's all right, Eleanor."

"I'm just so...hurt!" She took a deep breath and crossed herself, her mouth tightening into a grimace as her chin quivered. "Forgive me, Lord, if I speak an untruth, but I think my husband is having an affair." Tears streamed down her cheeks when she looked at Sean before tilting her head toward the sky.

Placing his hand on the door, he opened it part way, keeping his eyes on Eleanor. "That doesn't seem like the Adam I know," he said. He reached out and tapped her arm. "Maybe it's all a big misunderstanding."

Already several steps inside, Sean turned back when Eleanor called his name. Her body remained outside but her upper half leaned in. Her face seemed calm again, with no sign of the distraught emotion from a minute before

"I just want to clarify something you said," she told him, her eyes locking on his. "The Adam you *think* you know isn't the Adam you know."

"What does that mean?" he asked.

"The night Merissa was killed? When we had an argument and he didn't come home until one o'clock? He's been doing that sort of thing for years. Just kind of...disappearing, you know? Now I wonder if he was really alone."

℘℘℘

After the drubbing suffered by the Marauders against the Terrors, aided by Sean's worst personal score of the season, he walked toward the parking lot with Adam, hearing about the banal events occurring with his daughter's college applications and his son's accomplishments in the church basketball league. Sean's mind teetered between distraction and disinterest, preferring to focus on Eleanor's final comment and the note left on her husband's windshield—presumably from the person driving that black SUV.

Although the link between Adam and the last two victims seemed peculiar, with Sean leaning toward the probability of a tragic coincidence, the lingering uncertainty from these two mysteries created an underlying suspicion he wanted resolved. Devising an approach to gain a greater understanding of the man's true sensibilities, Sean waited until they reached Adam's car.

"There's something I should let you know," he said, placing a hand on the roof and a hip against the door. "The detective who's working on finding Merissa's killer told me about another rape and murder that occurred in July, and, crazy as it seems, your name came up."

Having opened the back door to retrieve his jacket, Adam stopped in mid-motion, his empty left coat sleeve dangling in armless anticipation. "*Me?*"

Sean studied his reaction—a look of genuine shock. "It's a terrible coincidence, Adam, but apparently you sold the woman a car not long before she was killed. And based on the evidence, her killer is the same person who killed Merissa."

"*What?*" His eyes grew wide as his mouth opened, remaining in a circular paralysis for several seconds. "I don't believe it!" Shaking his head, he gazed into the distance behind Sean. "The same killer?" He hurried to finish slipping on his jacket before moving closer. "I remember the woman, Sean."

"You do?" Sean asked, eyebrows raising. "Judging by your reaction, I wouldn't have thought so."

Adam stared at Sean with an intensity that appeared as if he was looking through him. "Oh, I know what happened," he said, his voice subdued and somber. "Her name was Jacquelyn Hastings. She was an attractive brunette about my size, with an easy laugh and great sense of humor. But my Lord, that woman was also a tough negotiator, believe me." Pausing, he presented a faint smile that evolved into a quick chuckle. "She wound up getting close to three thousand off sticker." Turning toward the car, he leaned back against the side of the trunk. "It was big news at work. I thought maybe you guys might have heard about it over there. But—I just can't believe it was the *same guy*." He stared at Sean, several seconds of silence between them. "Are you sure?"

Sean nodded. "I only know what the detective tells me, and that's what he said."

Rolling his tongue along the inside of his mouth, Adam looked into the distance toward the street before snapping his head back with a sudden scowl that startled Sean, his eyes half-closed but zeroed in. "Wait a minute," he spat, pushing away from the trunk. "Are you inferring what I think you are?" He continued glaring at Sean, advancing toward him in what appeared to be threatening steps. His upper body leaned forward with his arms jutting in a rigid downward angle across the side of his legs.

Glancing at his hands, Sean noticed the stiff, immovable fingers extended for possible attack. "Easy, Adam, *easy*," he said, motioning up and down with his hands in front of his chest, hoping to lower the tension. "It's just Detective Maldonado doing his due diligence and finding people and places that connect. Nothing more than that."

Adam approached the door, his eyes continuing to burn a hole through Sean. "We're all sinners," he said, yanking on the handle. "Some of us more than others."

Several seconds later, the engine started and Sean stood alone, watching and wondering as Adam drove away.

Chapter 34

A dam's final comment lingered in Sean's thoughts like an unfading echo. "We're all sinners," he said. "Some of us more than others." What did that mean? Was it just an overreaction Christian thing, like not returning change overpaid by a cashier? Driving above the posted speed limit? Laughing at a dirty joke? Or did he infer something dark and insidious?

Staring, almost unblinking at the road ahead, his eyes stung, unable to prevent the shifting of his thoughts from curiosity to concern. Maybe the remark about sinners served as a clue to dangle and deceive? Perhaps those previous thoughts of commonplace transgressions like speeding, or cheating a cashier, missed the mark. Squeezing the wheel, blood surging toward his fingertips, Sean contemplated the validity of a sudden new fear. Was Jenny safe?

✑✑✑

On a drizzly Saturday afternoon, three days after his talk in the parking lot with Adam, Sean sat in a booth at an Italian restaurant waiting for Jenny to arrive. The moment he spotted her walking into the restaurant, smiling at him as he waved, any melancholy feelings related to the weather or his questions about Adam melted away like an ice cube on a summer sidewalk.

Clutching her folded umbrella as she approached, Jenny swayed gracefully in a knee length, fully buttoned tan raincoat that exposed black jeans and boots. Standing to greet her, he watched as she unbuttoned and removed the wet garment before sitting, her lavender cashmere sweater and navy-blue floral blouse offering a welcome contrast to the dreary gray lighting seeping through from outside.

"Happy to see you, Jenny," he said. "You look great."

Jenny reached out and squeezed his upper arm. "What a lovely thing for a woman to hear," she replied. "Especially when that woman is *me!*"

Sean placed his hand on top of her arm, still resting on his. "I mean it," he replied, "but I haven't been on a date in a long time, so hopefully I won't blow it." They smiled and simultaneously leaned back when the waitress greeted them before asking if they'd like anything to drink.

For the next couple of hours, they filled each other in on aspects of their lives. Sean listened with interest to Jenny's reputation in grade school as that of a brainy and nerdy girl no boy looked at twice until Mother Nature reached out, waved her magical pubescent wand, and turned her into a high school prom queen runner-up and the quarterback's girlfriend. She attended San Diego State, partied hard, but worked hard, and graduated with a business degree. She met her ex-husband at an outdoor Vivaldi concert in Chicago, and, asshole that he turned out to be, still got credit for introducing her to fine wine, Scuba diving, and an affinity for professional boxing.

He told her about his upbringing, disinterest in school, and eventual foray into the music business where, as she already knew, he achieved success with "Looking Glass."

"Did you ever write anything else I may know?" she asked.

A wistful smile appeared, imprinted by the resignation of longing and disappointment. "I wrote plenty of other songs, but nothing you ever heard."

"Were you ever married?" Winking, she added, "Or were there too many groupies to deal with?"

Sean placed his elbows on the table, resting his chin on his clasped hands as his eyes narrowed in kaleidoscopic recollection. "I've been married twice," he answered. Pausing to observe her brief expression of apparent surprise, he continued. "I wrote a song about my first marriage called 'Between Forever and Goodbye.' All you need to know about that one is in the opening two lines: 'Feel like a stone, skipping on the water. We started strong and fast, now we're losing all our power.'"

Jenny nodded. "That about says it all for a lot of people. Kind of like my marriage, too."

Sean stroked his chin a couple of times, admiring the disheveled way her hair fell across her forehead. "Maybe so," he said, "but since you referred to your ex a few minutes ago as an asshole, there's another song I wrote that better describes what it's like when things go south in a bad way. I know it sure does for what I went through. 'You're a sharp piece of metal hiding in the sand. An unforeseen slice beneath the grains. I take a step, extend my hand, just a matter of time before the pain.'"

Jenny looked away, nibbling on her upper lip. "Yep," she said, her voice small and reflective. "Things seemed fine and dandy until that first cut." A sad, despondent expression appeared on her face, her cheeks flattening in a muscular resignation of regret. Reaching for her glass of wine, she drank several slow, meditative sips. "So tell me, Sean," she said, looking into his eyes with a sudden intensity, "do you think that metal we stepped on means we'll never want to walk on the beach again?"

Sean returned her stare, riveted by the subtle green and soft brown color of her eyes. He hadn't mentioned Merissa, and had no intention of divulging that secret anytime soon, but the unrelenting soul storm tormenting his emotions seemed much less intensified during this moment. As he looked at Jenny, hearing her voice and her story, and feeling her therapeutic sensitivity spread throughout his entire being, he realized that the previous "Do Not Disturb" sign hanging around his heart now read, "Help Wanted."

"This is what I think," he said, a controlled calm overtaking him. "Maybe you keep your shoes on for a while as you venture forth on that sand. At least that way, you can still enjoy the beauty of everything the beach has to offer. And then, hopefully, eventually, you might realize how much better, how much truer that walk could be, feeling the sand on your feet again."

Jenny smiled in silence and reached for her drink, placing her left elbow on the table and dropping her chin on her open hand. She took a sip, letting the liquid linger for a while before swallowing. Sitting up, she offered a quick nod of her head. "I like that little analogy of yours, Sean." Reaching for his hand, she gave a gentle squeeze and let it remain there. "I miss those barefoot walks on the beach."

Sean felt his skin temperature increase and his heartbeat quicken. But as he moved his other hand on top of hers, looking at her pretty, smiling face, a sudden trepidation barged into his thoughts—spurred on, he knew, by the beach references. He visualized that day when he saw a woman with an uncanny resemblance to Merissa jogging toward him as he walked along the shore. An undeniable fact linking Merissa with Jenny frayed his nerves, a static electric realization jolting his senses—*They both befriended Adam McBride.*

Removing her hands from his, Jenny pulled away as her expression changed in an instant from affection, to surprise, to embarrassment. "I'm sorry," she said, looking down, "I guess I shouldn't have said that."

Sean shook his head free from thoughts of Adam. "No, no, I'm really happy you said it!" He smiled and nodded, staring into her eyes. "You only said what I've been thinking myself, Jenny."

"But the look on your face seemed so...I don't know...*troubled.* Like you weren't happy with what I said."

"I'm sorry. I didn't mean to let my mind wander, especially when you had something so nice to say. But it did, and I guess it showed."

Jenny sat in silence, pursing her lips in apparent bewilderment.

"Tell you what," Sean said, removing his credit card, "I'll take care of the bill, and then I'll walk you to your car. I want to talk to you about our friend, Adam. To use your word, he's the one I looked 'troubled' about."

Jenny leaned back in surprise, a smirk of disbelief on her face. "*Adam?*" she said, chuckling. "*Really?*" Shrugging her shoulders, she giggled some more. "I never would have guessed."

Fluffy lime green camphor trees, posing in their grooved bark swagger, lined the street they strolled upon as they clasped hands and swung their arms in slow, joyful movements.

"So, Detective Hightower," Jenny said, her tone ominous yet playful, "are you telling me I should beware of the evil intentions of one Adam McBride?"

Sean nodded at Jenny. "Maybe I am," he answered. "There's just something about the guy that bugs me. It's as if there's something more there, something that he's hiding. I just have a feeling he's not as prim and proper as you think he is."

"Okay," Jenny said, "so we agree that Adam is a bit...odd, but I also know he's completely harmless. I just think I offer him a chance to talk to another woman instead of the overbearing wife he has now. And the fact that we went to school together probably makes it more comfortable for him."

Without any knowledge of the background behind his suspicions, Sean understood Jenny's skepticism about Adam's intentions, deciding to move on and enjoy the moment. Squeezing her hand, he reveled in the mutual blossoming affection, inhaling the energetic aroma of the surrounding earthy dampness. "You're right," he told her. "Case closed for Detective Hightower."

"Good, and just in time," she said, pointing straight ahead. "There's my car."

In an instant, Sean's walk slowed into an immediate old man's shuffle, staring wide-eyed at Jenny's black SUV and the last two letters of her license plate: "RH."

"Something wrong?" she asked.

"Were you at Roscoe Avenue Bowl on Wednesday night?"

"Wow!" she replied, rearing her head in surprise. "I was only in the parking lot for a few minutes. I didn't even know you were there."

"I was in my car when I saw Adam waving at someone in a black SUV. When you pulled into the street, I caught the last two letters of your license plate and they stuck with me because they're the same initials as my sister, Rebecca. That's the only reason I remembered them."

"It's kind of stupid what happened," she told him. "Adam came to my condo last week to set up my sound system. Zone one, zone two, zone three, it's great. But before he did that, he insisted on showing me some magic tricks."

"Things he learned from Stan, I guess."

Jenny laughed. "Yep. He takes lessons from him."

"Still doing that, huh? Stan told me about it the night of Elliot's fundraiser."

"Did Stan tell you that Elliot's also part of the class? He mentioned a third guy, too. He works with Adam, so maybe you know him."

Remembering his conversation with Stan before the fundraiser, Sean recognized Jenny's unnamed reference to Roger as that third person. But now that he and his handcuffs resided in San Jose, Sean figured Roger was no longer learning tricks, just looking for women turning tricks.

"So what's this got to do with you being in the parking lot?"

"Adam called me after he left and was upset because he forgot his 'special' deck of cards and was too far away to come back. He told me where he'd be Wednesday night and would stop by before going home. It made sense, right? I only live about ten minutes away. But I was tired and wanted to go to bed early, so I called him from the parking lot."

Sean nodded. "Well, that explains it. I saw him get something from under the back of his car and put it in his pocket. Now I know what it was."

"I had no choice but to leave it under his car," she explained. "I wanted to come inside to give it to him, or have him come outside, but when I called he got all panicky because Eleanor was there, so his paranoia flag was flying high and whipping in the wind."

Sean uttered a small laugh. "It's funny how I went to my car during those few minutes you were there. I never would have known."

Jenny smiled, looking prettier than ever. "Guess there's no hiding from you, Detective Hightower." Grabbing his hand, she looked at him, her eyes locked on his. "But maybe that's not such a bad thing."

Standing by her door, as the first kiss lingered under the cover of umbrellas and the encircling music of a gentle rhythmic drizzle, any worries about Adam disappeared.

Like a card from a magician's deck.

Chapter 35

The opened cardboard box lay angled on the table, the first two slices already consumed from the aromatic pepperoni and mushroom pizza Sean ordered for the televised Lakers-Piston game. With seven straight wins to start the season, the men in purple and gold remained unbeaten and still number one in Kayleigh's heart, despite the absence of Coby Karl.

"This is the best pizza I *ever* had!" she said, attempting to talk and place more in her mouth at the same time. Her elbows pushed against the sides of her body as her thin, pale, arms jutted upward from her baggy jersey, vertical irrigation pipes with hands, cradling the diminishing slice of her favorite food.

Sean smiled. "You say that every time."

Kayleigh covered her mouth with a napkin as she zeroed in on the action. Her high expectations for the favored, unbeaten home team remained unrealized, and with one quarter in the books the tight score persisted. The Lakers broadcasters complained about the team's lethargic play, while Detroit looked like the more disciplined and determined of the two.

"What's wrong with the Lakers, Mr. Music?" she asked, her wispy eyebrows furrowing in concern. "They should be *killing* these guys! They've already lost two games and the Lakers haven't lost any!"

"Six and two is still pretty good, Kayleigh."

"Not as good as seven and zero! Could I have another piece, please?"

When the first half ended, the Pistons led fifty-three to forty-four, and a noticeably concerned Kayleigh helped clear the table while she followed Sean into the kitchen.

"I don't want the Lakers to lose all year!" she said, a girlish defiance punctuating her voice. "That will be the best birthday present *ever!*"

Sean looked at her, angling his head and nodding with a slight grin. "Since your birthday's tomorrow, why don't we first see if they can win tonight's game for you, okay?"

Kayleigh tightened her thin lips, almost causing them to disappear.

"You don't really think they can go unbeaten, do you?" Sean asked.

"Yep. The Lakers are the best!"

"Well, for one thing," he said, depositing the dirty napkin into the trashcan, "it's never happened before."

"So?"

"I don't know as much about basketball as I do music, but I know that one of Michael Jordan's teams only lost twelve games all year sometime back in the nineties, and that's the record for fewest losses."

Kayleigh scrunched her round, tiny face, new wrinkles surrounding her naturally half-lidded expression. "Who's Michael Jordan?"

"Probably the best basketball player to ever play."

"Well, I don't think so," she said, her head moving left to right, then left to right again. "Coby's the best."

Sean gazed downward, chuckling to himself

"My daddy told me he's playing for a team in Spain now."

"I didn't know that, good for him."

"Mr. Music, do you remember when you told me that Coby was sending a message to people with cancer?"

Sean turned back from the sink and smiled. "Of course I remember. By playing for the Lakers he showed everybody what can happen if you keep fighting and never give up hope."

"Do you think he's sending a message in Spain, too?"

Sean nodded. "I think he's sending a message to everyone, no matter where they live."

"Can I have some ice cream?"

"Mint chocolate chip?" he asked, flashing her a wink.

Kayleigh's left eye widened in excitement, while her right one fluttered in its failed attempt to do the same.

"Promise?"

"Promise," he answered. "Why don't you go back to the couch and listen to what the announcers have to say? Then you can tell me if we need to be worried."

Exiting the kitchen holding two dessert bowls, Sean observed Kayleigh gazing at the framed photo of Merissa and him on the small, ovular table near the front door. In her hand she held a thin, unrecognizable magazine-sized booklet.

"I thought you wanted to listen to the halftime report."

Kayleigh shrugged her shoulders. "They talk about stuff I don't understand."

"Ready for your ice cream?"

Ignoring his question, she pointed toward the photo. "I forgot who that lady is in the picture with you."

Sean inhaled and held his breath for a prolonged moment before following with an extended exhale. For these many sad, complicated and often lonely months since her murder, he often gazed at the photo of the two of them smiling and holding their wine glasses as they celebrated his birthday in Paso Robles. This time, however, staring in unison with Kayleigh, he realized the new reality of Jenny occupying the largest room in his thoughts. Having made plans to cook dinner for her on Friday, he made a mental note to remove the picture and place it somewhere unseen by guests.

"I already told you who she was the last time you were here," he said. "So I'll answer you one more time. Her name is Merissa, and she's a friend of mine."

"The last time I was here, did I also ask you where she lives?" Kayleigh turned toward Sean, looked down at her shoes, then back up again with a sheepish expression. "Because I don't remember that either."

Sean provided the same explanation as before, that Merissa moved back home to England because she missed her family.

Kayleigh stared at the photo again.

"Merissa looks really nice. I bet I woulda liked her."

A sudden incursion of uninvited moisture prepared to penetrate past the "No Exit" sign inside his eyes as he whirled around and headed back toward the couch, each hand holding a bowl.

"C'mon," he said, his voice subdued, "it's ice cream time and the second half's starting."

Kayleigh returned to the couch and placed the booklet on the side of her lap. Sean looked over and identified Martin Boyd's business card attached to the Boyd's Electronics store catalogue. From the time Martin first showed him a choice of options to resolve his electrical issues, the pamphlet not only remained unopened but forgotten. Seeing it now, he realized Kayleigh must have spotted it on the round glass table by the light switch where he gathered reading material he planned to peruse...eventually. Somewhere among the clutter of a *Mother Jones* magazine, a *Westways AAA* magazine, a *Sports Illustrated* magazine, an envelope with copies of home insurance papers, a calendar still turned to the previous month of October, a neighborhood store discount catalog, a multi-colored lined notepad, and a plastic tray holding a couple of dealership inscribed pens, Kayleigh discovered Martin's brochure—quite a coincidence, considering his pending appointment with him tomorrow to discuss track lighting and ceiling fan installations.

"I'm surprised you found that," he said, nodding his chin toward the booklet.

"I saw Martin's name on the card," she explained. "It was sticking out and...sorry, Sean, I guess I shoulda asked first, huh?"

"No big deal, Kayleigh. I forgot it was there."

She reached over, grabbed the pamphlet, and turned the cover page. They both glanced at the full-sized photo of Martin with three men and two women standing and smiling between a wall display in back and a table in front, showcasing various products they sold. Kayleigh continued to turn a few more pages before placing the booklet on the cushion and leaning forward to plunge the tip of her spoon into the bright green scoop. Sliding the utensil into her mouth, she paused for a moment of flavorful appreciation. Her circular face took on a more triangular form whenever she flashed a full smile, the rounded tips of her puffy cheeks extending in an elongated manner while accentuating her bony, fulcrum-like chin.

"This is the best ice cream I *ever* had!"

After the Pistons called for a time out with a little under five minutes remaining in the third quarter, the phone rang. Sean looked at the screen and turned to Kayleigh before answering. "It's your dad. Hi, Jason...Yeah, it's a close one. Detroit looks like they came to play tonight...Of course," he replied, chuckling. "She's a nervous wreck, just like you'd expect...Okay, I'll tell her...Oh, yeah? That's great. I'm surprised she didn't tell me...You got it, we'll see you soon." Hanging up, he turned back toward Kayleigh. "I didn't know your brother's coming into town for your birthday. You must be excited."

Bouncing on the sofa like a basketball, she answered in a sing-song voice. "I'm gonna see my brother, I'm gonna see Mr. Mari-ine!"

"Your dad will come get you after the quarter's over. Where'd you put your sweatshirt?"

"Ummm." Bringing her delicate finger to her lips, she squinted in contemplation, her narrow eyes turning into slits. "I think I left it on the table by the bathroom."

As Sean approached the crumpled pink sweatshirt, its tiny sleeve hanging down from the corner edge as if reaching for something on the faraway floor, he heard Hendrix's muted cries from the adjacent room and pivoted toward the door in concern.

"Hey, Kayleigh," he called out, laughing. "Come here. I want to show you something funny about your poor friend, Hendrix."

Kayleigh waddled toward him, smiling in anticipation. Sean stood at the doorway and pointed.

"He cracks me up when he does this. The dog has toys he forgets about until he rediscovers one he can't reach and then wines about it." As the dog continued nudging his nose and reaching his diminutive paw under the wooden dresser, the sad cries continued.

"*Help* him, Mr. Music, he wants his toy!"

The approximate two-inch area between the floor and the bottom of the desk prevented Sean from enough adequate space to reach underneath, so, rising to his feet, he secured the lamp with one hand and slid the table several feet to the left. The moment he looked down, his heartbeat accelerated into frenzied pumping as he lunged, wide-eyed, toward the object, just beating the dog's mouth to the prize.

Grasping the "toy" by its firm, flat edges, Sean's fingers trembled as he stared in disbelief at the Jack of Hearts.

 essess

After Kayleigh left, he wasted no time calling Detective Maldonado. "Should I put it in something for you?" he asked. "A Ziplock bag, maybe?"

"That would be one of the worst things you could do," Maldonado replied. "If condensation forms in there, you'd probably destroy what little chance we have of finding any trace of fingerprints. Put it in an envelope of some kind. Paper's a safe way to go."

"When can I get it to you?"

"Are you working this weekend?" Maldonado asked.

"Tomorrow, no, Sunday, yes."

"I've got a community affairs breakfast tomorrow with local veterans in the morning and meetings after that, but I can be there between five and five-thirty if that works for you."

"I'll be here, Ray."

"By the way," Maldonado said, "you saved me a phone call. We recently got some interesting information about Elliot Hayden." After a brief pause, he added, "Interesting *and* confusing."

Sean's eyes narrowed in curiosity. "What's up with Elliot?"

"Do you remember where Hayden told you he was the night of Ms. Franklin's murder? That he couldn't go with Martin to the Laker game because of a charity affair?"

"Now that you reminded me. What about it?"

"Yes, there was the event that night, that part of the story checked out. But what he didn't tell you is that he left before dinner, claiming he didn't feel well."

Sean stared into the nothingness of the blank beige wall across from him, trying to remember the details of his conversation with Elliot from months before. He didn't recall that part of the explanation. "It seems strange that he wouldn't mention that," he remarked. "Especially when most of the night wasn't even spent at the party."

"I agree," Maldonado said.

Sean closed his eyes and slid his hand down his face in disbelief. "We agree on it, Ray, but I know where you're sniffing with this, and you're on the wrong track. He's *gay!*"

An audible exhale followed. "How many times have you seen television reporters interviewing neighbors of some killer after he was shot dead or captured, and all they can say is what a nice, sweet person he seemed to be, how he always said hello, and they had no idea, et cetera, et cetera."

"Sorry, but I'm not convinced."

"All I'm saying is things aren't always as they appear."

"Well, you better send the patrol cars tomorrow," Sean said, a sudden weariness overtaking him, "because Elliot 'Serial Killer'

Hayden will be here with his boyfriend in the morning." A lengthy pause followed.

"Your sarcasm aside," Maldonado said, his tone brusque and resentful, "you need to find out where the *fuck* he went after he left the party that night. That's a valuable piece of information gone missing, don't you think?"

Sean remained silent, his mental fatigue ratcheting up too fast to reply.

"See you tomorrow, Sean."

Nursing his way through a second glass of Johnny Walker in the semidarkness of the room, Sean reflected on his conversation with Maldonado as the muted strains of Joe Bonamassa's blues guitar provided a comforting soundtrack to work through the muddled landscape of his confusion. The obvious conundrum of Elliot's involvement, a man whose homosexuality and love for another man seemed genuine, created a new, unexpected puzzle. By omitting the part about leaving the party early, did this really legitimize the possibility of his involvement? Or did the frustration and desperation of all these fruitless months make this seem a bigger deal than the situation warranted?

Sean stared into his glass, feeling heavy-lidded and light-headed from the booze. He snorted a gust of air, chuckling at the ridiculousness of his paranoia kicking into overdrive from his conversation with Maldonado. Closing his eyes, he leaned back and placed his elbow on the top of the cushion, pinching the bridge of his nose as exhaustion enveloped him. He thought of Jenny, and his wish to move on and make her a bigger part of his life. She'd been the inspiration behind his invitation to Martin and the desire to upgrade his dated home with modern lighting. Elliot asked if he could tag along, and until Maldonado's unsettling disclosure, the man's presence meant nothing more than the likelihood of preparing an extra cup of coffee. Now he hoped to get the chance to talk with him alone.

Still dubious at the idea of any culpability on Elliot's part, Sean's thoughts took a sharp turn, focusing on the irony of how things transpired with "Looking Glass," and his concession about the value of the Wally's Window Wipes earnings he'd received. Having already paid off his five-thousand-dollar debt to David's firm, allowing the anonymous donation for Kayleigh's procedure, his latest check provided the means to move ahead with the long-overdue home lighting upgrade.

Rising to his feet, he noticed the Boyd's Electronics booklet protruding from the split between the cushion and the armrest of the couch. Grasping the corner, he tossed it on the table before crossing over to Merissa's picture by the door. But it wasn't the photo captivating his unwavering Johnny Walker gaze—it was something he'd placed there before his first drink. Squinting through the lens of alcohol and mystery, he stared for a long while into the eyes of the Jack of Hearts, searching for clues, listening for whispers, waiting for answers.

He yawned, held his eyes closed for several seconds, and rubbed his face as if washing it with a small towel. Throwing one more dart glance at the Jack of Hearts, he turned away and yawned again, comforted in the knowledge that the nearness of sleep offered one sure escape from his growing assemblage of doubt and confusion. He reflected on what Maldonado mentioned about things not always appearing as they seem, shaking his head at the bitter irony that "Looking Glass," a song written almost twenty-four years earlier, echoed a similar sentiment. In a subdued tone, he sang the first two lines. "Can we ever trust our point of view, when what seemed real is far from true?"

Approaching the light switch, he gazed at the black screen of the television and thought of Kayleigh. For her, tonight offered another example, albeit different and innocent, of things not always appearing as they seem. With the Piston victory, there went her belief in the Lakers' chances for an undefeated season.

Chapter 36

A slight chill accompanied the gray slathered mid-morning sky as Sean opened the door for Elliot and Martin. Elliot's usual stylish attire exemplified the perfect LA chic pairing to his equally debonair boyfriend, Martin, dressed in charcoal gray slacks, black and silver designer sneakers, red and black plaid buttoned down shirt, black corduroy jacket, and red cashmere scarf hanging down the front of both shoulders. Although Sean's late autumn preference remained an old pair of jeans with broken-in sneakers and a flannel shirt, he acknowledged the appeal of a sharp-dressed man. Two gay guys weren't what ZZ Top had in mind with their classic tribute, but the corner of Elegant and Refined has always been located in a neighborhood welcoming all sexual preferences.

Closing the door as they entered the house, he nodded his head and extended his hands out with palms up.

"Eleven o'clock on a Saturday and you guys are dressed for a party in Beverly Hills," he said. "You take a wrong turn or something?"

Elliot laughed. "It's funny you say that," he replied. "For some reason I drew a blank and forgot where your house was. I had to call Marty for help and he met me down the street."

"You came in separate cars?" Sean asked.

"Elliot's meeting with some new family members at the Center, so with great difficulty, I'll pass on that excitement," Martin explained, rolling his eyes.

Shaking his head at Martin, Elliot blew into his hands as he looked back at Sean. "You almost got it right about going to Beverly Hills. We're invited to a birthday party in West Hollywood for a dear friend of mine, so you're just a few miles off."

"I wish we had a dog, Elliot," Martin said, giving Hendrix a final few head scratches before rising to his feet.

"We've talked about this Marty. It would be unfair to the poor thing if neither of us are home so much of the time."

"I know, I know," Martin said, nodding. "I'm just not a cat person as much as you are."

"Just don't let Princess hear you say that." Looking at Sean, Elliot explained, "Princess is our Abyssinian cat."

"Would you guys like some coffee?"

"That sounds divine," Elliot replied, rubbing his hands together.

"Your brochure's on that table over there, Martin. Let's get the coffee and talk some lighting."

As he turned and headed for the kitchen, he heard Martin say, "You're only fifty-one cards short, Sean."

Looking back over his shoulder, Sean stared in alarm as Martin flashed a silly grin, pointing toward the Jack of Hearts.

"Don't touch it!"

Martin lurched back with a startled expression, throwing both hands in the air as if the victim of a holdup. "Okay, okay."

Observing their confused looks, Sean scrambled for a plausible fabrication, intent on avoiding any discussion of Merissa's murder, in particular the personal, heartbreaking reason for the original discovery of the card. Speaking in a slow, deliberate manner, he formulated a story.

"Sorry for shouting at you, Martin, but someone broke into my house a few weeks ago, and I found that Jack of Hearts under my bed yesterday. I don't even own a deck of cards, so I figured I should call Detective Maldonado. He's coming to get it so they can check for fingerprints." Sean initially glanced at Martin as he answered, but studied Elliot's expression to gauge his reaction. A slight opening of the mouth and widening of his eyes seemed to suggest his belief in the manufactured story.

Returning from the kitchen with their coffee, Sean placed his cup on the table and glanced for the first time at the page left open by Kayleigh from the night before. Photos of various security cameras, their model numbers exhibited under each one, appeared on the page.

"Those are some of the best security cameras on the market," Martin said.

"Getting something for our library is long overdue, Marty," Elliot told him, leaning forward from Martin's other side. "We've been lucky so far, but that neighborhood has problems, especially at night."

Sean didn't look up, his eyes scanning the various devices resembling futuristic objects out of *Star Trek*—cameras similar to ones he saw at Parkview Condominiums. "And here I thought you only did basic home stuff," he remarked.

"We're a full-service company," Martin explained. "And security installations are the fastest growing part of our business. Not just homes, but schools, apartments, condominiums, office buildings, interior, exterior, you name it."

"It's good news and bad news as far as I'm concerned," Elliot said. "The good news is Marty's business is doing very well and all of his hard work is paying off. The bad news is he's so busy nowadays that I hardly see him."

Reaching over toward Elliot, Martin smiled and stroked his cheek. "Just a busy time right now," he said.

Elliot grabbed Martin's hand and held it to his face. "I just miss you, Marty."

Martin returned his attention to Sean. "The first time I came here I noticed your house wasn't protected. Maybe you'll consider doing something now that you've had that break-in."

Sean remained silent with his head down, his thoughts stuck in a muck of confused contemplation. *Should I ask him or not? Yes...No...Yes...No...Yes...Yes!*

"Did you install the security cameras at Parkway Condominiums?" he asked. Lifting his head from the pages, he looked at Martin. "I went there a couple of weeks ago on Merissa's birthday— October thirtieth. Just to walk around and remember her, you know? Reflect on the good times. I wasn't aware they have a new security system with a guard shack and cameras all over the place." Pointing toward a couple of them on the page, he added, "These two look like the ones I saw."

Martin glanced at Elliot before offering Sean a tight-lipped smile. Looking at Elliot again, he remained silent.

Elliot reached for Martin's hand and squeezed it before taking a sip of coffee and turning toward Sean. "I helped get that contract for Marty shortly before Merissa was killed," he said. "His work-load was getting to be too much for him and the deadline was looming. Two other companies had already submitted their bids, and Merissa was the one in charge." Elliot looked at Martin, nodded his head, and stared back at Sean. "Marty came to me for help because of my relationship with her. We turned the proposal in just in time and, through her efforts, the board awarded Boyd's Electronics the contract."

Sean lowered his eyes back toward the brochure. "Looks like you did a pretty thorough job over there, Martin."

Martin lowered his cup to his lap. "Look at me please, Sean."

Doing as requested, Sean looked up and observed a slight mist in Martin's eyes.

"I didn't expect to ever have this conversation," he said. "But now that it's out there, now that you know, I can tell you not a day went by where I didn't think about that terrible—" Martin swallowed hard and rubbed his hand back and forth across his forehead as he looked away. "And how I wished that our system, or something like it, had been in place before that night. We'll never know, but maybe it could have made the difference."

As Martin turned away, gazing at the floor and running his finger around the rim of his cup in slow, continuous circles, Sean allowed himself a chance to focus on the once cherished specifics of Merissa's fading memory; the soothing, feminine sound of her voice, the joy he derived from her laugh, the look and feel of her naked body, the escapist pleasure of her companionship—and it saddened him to think that life worked this way. As the passage of time diminishes memories, sometimes it's a blessing for one's sanity, other times, a sorrowful, regretful reality.

Silence between the three of them ensued for several long moments.

"Marty," Elliot said, grasping his hand again, "maybe it's best for the two of you to talk about your products another day." He looked at Sean. "Your call, Sean. After this conversation, if you don't feel up to it, it's understandable, okay?"

Sean took a deep breath, held it in as if it aided his judgment, and then exhaled in a hushed flow of decision-making. After this sad, what-could-have-been reminder of Merissa, he realized Elliot's suggestion made sense. The thought of discussing recessed lighting and ceiling fans took on a sudden disinterest, even more, a vicious irrelevancy. Reaching down to close the booklet, his hair dangling in partial blockage of his vision, he held the strands back with his other hand, making a quick mental note to call for a haircut appointment with Dino.

Hair...cut...Princess...Princess Diana...Lady Di.

Within moments, as if struck by a slap across the face, a sudden revelation occurred over the name of Elliot's cat, Princess, and recollection of a remark one of them made several months before as they looked at the photo of Merissa and him in the front room. Overhearing their discussion from the kitchen, he caught a reference to a comparison with Princess Diana, remembering how nonsensical that comment seemed because the oft-photographed Diana had short hair and Merissa's descended beyond her shoulders.

Until the day of her murder.

Perhaps his imagination overtook rationality, but why would anyone liken Merissa's looks, with her long, wavy locks, to someone whose neck-length hairstyle defined so much of her facial appearance?

Unless that person knew how Merissa looked with short hair.

Attempting to quell his nervousness, Sean devised a plan as he felt their eyes upon him. "I know I need new lighting in this house," he said, "but you're right, maybe another day is best." Glancing back and forth at them, his eyes settled on Martin. "Sorry if I screwed you up, but right now the thought of getting out of the house for a burger and beer down the street seems very appealing."

Martin nodded in several small, rapid motions. "I understand," he replied. "We'll just do it another time." Reaching for the booklet, he turned the pages to the lighting section. "These are the various light fixtures we offer," he said. "When you get a chance, look through them and see if there's something you like." He turned the brochure over and flipped back to the second to last page. "And here's the ceiling fans."

Sean feigned attention as his heartbeat accelerated, realizing the critical importance of remaining believable.

"Before you guys go, I want to ask a favor of you. It'll just take a few minutes of your time."

The two men glanced at each other before looking back. "Of course," Elliot told him. "Sure," Martin replied.

"Well...other than the music lessons I give Kayleigh, and that one fundraiser for you, Elliot, I haven't played my guitar since

Merissa died. My old band mate, Rocco, owns a place where I used to perform, and the other day he asked me if I'd like to start again. I'm thinking that the time may finally be right."

The two men both clapped, nodding in agreement.

"That's wonderful news," Elliot replied.

"Absolutely," Martin added. "But if you're asking us to be your backup singers, that's one favor I *refuse* to do."

Elliot laughed, offering a thumb up gesture as Sean smiled and rose from the couch.

"I'll be right back." Returning to the room with his guitar, he brought the chair from the corner table and placed it about ten feet away. Observing their curious smiles, he prepared himself to be alert for any sudden change in their expressions, knowing those initial seconds might make or break everything. No sold out performance ever matched the nervousness he felt facing these two men. "What better way to mark my return," he said, "then to play Merissa's favorite Beatles' song for two friends here in my home." Glancing at the two of them, the only noticeable change in their demeanor showed an elicitation of delightful surprise.

"Oh, my," Elliot remarked, smiling. "This is the favor? To hear you play a Beatles' song for *us*?"

Sean waited for his heart to slow, but the pounding continued. Realizing he couldn't delay any longer, he sang the opening words to "Hello, Goodbye," strumming the first chord as his eyes shifted back and forth.

Observing nothing more than two big smiles, he continued.

No change.

The next line.

No change.

The next two lines.

No change.

The next three lines.

Now both men nodded along, moving their lips to the words. They seemed as content as ever, and as Sean's disappointment mushroomed, making him feel like a complete fool, the torment of the song threatened to overwhelm him.

The performance ended in mid-strum, along with any hope for a breakthrough.

∽∾∽

When both men said their goodbyes and walked outside, Sean lifted Hendrix into his arms, staring in shame at the untouched Jack of Hearts before approaching the open doorway. He felt disgusted with himself for his overreaction, and as he watched the two men stroll toward their cars in a slow, affectionate manner, their arms around each other with heads tilted and touching, the scene playing out before his eyes exacerbated his embarrassment.

What the hell was I thinking? I may as well have been singing "Mary Had a God-damn Little Lamb," for all it mattered. They're gay and I'm an idiot.

Directing his attention toward Elliot, it occurred to him that he didn't get a chance to ask him about his whereabouts after leaving the party early that night. His obvious innocence aside, Sean still wanted to know why Elliot omitted that fact, making it seem that he spent the whole time at the event. Maldonado told him he claimed illness as the reason, so going home seemed the logical assumption. But why didn't he just say that? Sean decided he needed an answer *now*, even if Martin remained and heard the question.

After a brief kiss on the lips, the two men entered their respective cars. Increasing the pace and waving his arm, Sean battled to suppress his sudden nervousness as he drew near, realizing the delicate nature over how to best phrase the question. Standing by the open driver side window, he looked down at the inquisitive face of Elliot.

"What's up?" Elliot asked, stealing a glance at his watch.

"Do you need me for anything," Martin called out, grasping the top of his open door to support his half in-half-out position.

Still clutching Hendrix, Sean reflexively threw out his free hand as he shook his head back and forth. "No thanks, Martin," he answered, conscious of the rush to his reply. "I just want to ask Elliot something about…the Directional Center."

"Okay, see you later," Martin replied, nodding his head. Dropping into his car, he shut the door and started the engine. Sean re-situated Hendrix, moving him in a methodical manner from his right arm to his left until Martin drove away. Swiping his tongue across the inside of his mouth, Sean paused before speaking.

"I didn't tell him the truth," he admitted. "I don't want to talk about the Directional Center."

Elliot angled his head, his brows furrowing in sudden inquisitiveness.

"What, then?"

Sean took a breath, inhaled some courage, and proceeded.

"You're aware that Merissa's killer hasn't been caught yet, right?"

Elliot stared at Sean for a few silent moments before replying. "I always figured when that time came, you'd tell me," he answered. "Why do you ask?"

"To be honest, Elliot, in the eyes of the police, everyone who knew her is still a suspect. To them, it doesn't matter if you're straight or gay."

"*What*?" Elliot bellowed. His eyes widened into an incomprehensive look of shock before boomeranging back into narrow slits of what appeared to be outrage. "That's...that's *ridiculous*!" His jawbone tightened into a hardened visage. "What do *you* think, Sean?" he asked, anger coating his tone. "Is this *gay* man, who loved Merissa like a sister, also a suspect in *your* eyes?"

Sean stared at Elliot. "No," he answered, shaking his head for emphasis. "Personally, I don't think you should be a suspect in any way, shape, or form. But you need to own up to something that you brought entirely on yourself."

Elliot's expression softened, his facial lines dissolving into emotionless curiosity. "Please continue," he told him.

"When I asked you where you were the night Merissa was killed there's something you didn't tell me." His determination strengthened as his trepidation subsided. "You remember that day, don't you, Elliot? In the Von's parking lot? You said that you had Lakers tickets but couldn't go because of some party you had to attend?"

Elliot stared back at Sean, his eyes unwavering. "And that's where I was," he said. "At a party thrown by William Alexander, one of my biggest contributors." He leaned his head back. "You don't believe me?"

"I believe you," he said, offering a small nod of his head. "The police verified it anyway."

As Elliot's expression changed into a brazen look of satisfaction, Sean bristled at the obvious lack of forthrightness. Bringing his face closer to the window, his glare intensified. "But you didn't stay for the whole thing, did you? You told them you weren't feeling well and left early."

Elliot's eyes widened for a moment—something that didn't escape Sean's notice.

"So what I want to know, and what Detective Maldonado wants me to ask you, is why didn't you *fucking* tell me that?" Sean's eyes burrowed in on Elliot's. "If you had gone home that would have been the logical answer, but because you *didn't* tell me that, it makes me wonder why. And because you're still on Maldonado's suspect shit list, if you went somewhere else, he'll eventually find out." He leaned in and stared. "That'll just make things worse for you if you don't want anybody to know."

Elliot squinted and pursed his lips, as if the question somehow pained him. Turning his head to gaze through the windshield, he held that position for several moments before dropping his head. Bringing his hand to his forehead, he closed his eyes and moved his fingers back and forth across the closed lids. Sean held Hendrix in a firm grip, using him as a canine life preserver for his sudden anxiety. Feeling confused about everybody at this point, his ability to remain calm seemed impossible. Sean believed in Elliot's innocence, but no longer trusted his own judgment to believe anybody's story anymore. Elliot raised his head, advancing a slight smile before responding.

"I was having an affair," he said, his tone wistful. "It was mad and delicious, but not meant to last. A lusty, sports car kind of affair that went zero to seventy in a flash before crashing and burning." He shook his head, wiping his hand across his mouth. "All I can say is thank God Martin never found out." Elliot looked away, emitting a deep sigh as his shoulders raised then dropped. He looked into Sean's eyes and smiled again. "So now you know where I went that night and why I didn't tell you. It was a sinfully guilty pleasure for me, but for you, and Detective Maldonado, it's my proof of innocence."

Sean couldn't tell if he felt a greater sense of happiness or disappointment. Had he really wanted a confession from Elliot? Did he want to hear him say he raped and killed Merissa, putting an end to the search for The Beatles' Song Murderer? Or was it a relief to know that another of Merissa's friends didn't belong on Maldonado's list?

"I'll tell Detective Maldonado what you told me," he said. "For what it's worth, I believe you."

Elliot nodded one time. "I only ask that if the detective ever wants to confirm my story, I'll arrange a meeting with the man I was with, but Martin can't ever find out." Elliot reached out and grasped Sean's elbow, his large hands squeezing tight. "Please, Sean. Make sure Detective Maldonado understands that."

"I will," he answered.

As the engine started, Sean backed up a step and waited for the car to drive away, but Elliot shut the motor off. "Sorry, Sean, but I need to use your bathroom. I think I had something with milk in it and my stomach's acting up. I don't want to drive like this."

Waving him out of the car, Sean watched as Elliot rushed away and hurried toward the partially opened front door without waiting for him. Arriving at the doorway about fifteen seconds later, he released Hendrix and headed for the closet to change into a warmer jacket before taking his cell phone with him to the entrance area to wait. After reviewing his calendar for the upcoming week, he started reading a group email from Tom Claiborne when Elliot reappeared, looking embarrassed and shaking his head.

"What can I say?" he asked. "Mother Nature can be a naughty lady sometimes."

Sean shrugged. "We've all been there."

Elliot started heading outside but stopped.

"Hey, I almost forgot to tell you. Your old work buddy, Roger, came to the Center to say hello."

Sean's stomach tightened. "*Roger?*" he said, his voice rising in surprise. "I thought he left town."

"He did, but his divorce is getting messy and his lawyer needed him here."

"I didn't know you two were friends."

"More friendly than friends. But he's close with Stan, and he used to be part of our magic class that he teaches. Adam was there, too, just like always."

Sean leaned against the side of the door and watched Elliot enter his car, start the engine, and drive away. As the branding iron of his speculation burned the images of Roger, Stan, and Adam deeper into his consciousness, a realization he fought to deny continued to taunt him, leaving his spirit a shredded mess. A suffocating galaxy of suspicion now engulfed his thoughts, filled with the poisonous atmosphere of each man who remained a suspect. From his initial meeting with Ray Maldonado, this was the mindset expected of him; but suspicion is a part of a detective's mentality, not regular guys like him.

Although the jacket kept his body warm, and one hand remained buried in his pocket, the exposed hand gripping the door felt like ice. Staring at the gray, spiritless sky above, he had a change of heart about leaving the house. Heating up a can of tomato soup, grilling a ham and cheese sandwich, and lying on the couch watching TV seemed like a more comforting idea. Needing to get one errand out of the way first, however, he retrieved his wallet and car keys from the kitchen table.

"Time for a quick ATM run, Hendrix," he said, looking down at his little friend. "I'll be right back."

Hendrix tilted his head and looked at him, his shiny, dark button eyes focused through the furry black forest of his face. His tail moved, but in a hesitant, unsure motion. Sean stared back, smiled, and scooped up his dog as he headed toward the garage. "You win," he told him. "Can't have you suffering through an uneventful fifteen minutes."

Chapter 37

Sean glanced at the car clock as he turned into his driveway. "Fifteen minutes exactly," he said, looking at Hendrix. "Just like I told you." As he entered the kitchen from the garage, the doorbell rang. Hendrix barked as he always did, and when Sean peered through the peephole without seeing another face, he glanced down and spotted the recognizable semi-bald head of Kayleigh, motionless as a boulder.

Opening the door, Sean squatted to her height, opened his arms wide, and shouted, "Ladies and gentlemen, it's the birthday girl!"

Kayleigh's zero-shaped face condensed into an immediate freeway system of fleshy wrinkles as she smiled and threw herself at Sean. Releasing her from his hug, he looked toward the walkway to see if anyone accompanied her—Jenny, perhaps—but discarding that quick moment of disappointment, invited her in and closed the door. Hendrix wasted no time dropping his body at her feet and rolling on his back for a belly rub. Kayleigh obliged in an instant, dropping on her knees to perform the task.

"Mommy wanted me to call first," she told him, still hunching over Hendrix, "but I *had* to show you what I got for my birthday!" Kayleigh looked up with her hands remaining on Hendrix's belly. "She hopes I'm not bothering you. Am I bothering you?"

"Of course not," he answered. "So what'd you get?"

Kayleigh pushed herself off the floor to stand, wobbling a bit as she straightened before shifting her weight back and forth from heel to toe as if standing on a rocking chair.

"Guess!" she shouted.

"A pony, and you're going to name him Coby?"

Kayleigh's eyes widened, the left one more than the right, as always. "*What?*" she exclaimed, giggling. "No, silly! Not a pony named Coby! Guess again."

"Mind if I take my jacket off first," he asked, winking as he hurried through the buttons. Turning toward the corner table near the door, he started draping it across the back of the chair but stopped and stared, bewildered by what he saw; or, more to the point, what he didn't see. No Jack of Hearts.

Sean looked on the floor behind the table, but seeing nothing there, stared at the empty space in a daze, replaying everything in his mind from the moment Martin asked him about it.

"Come on, Mr. Music, guess what I got for my birthday."

"Hold on, Kayleigh," he said, his back remaining turned. "I'm missing something important, and I don't know where it is."

Hendrix barked once from the other room. Then he barked again.

"Quiet, Hendrix!" Sean shouted.

He barked again. And again.

"What's the matter, Hendrix?" Kayleigh asked, marching toward the dog.

Sean spun to his left, heading in the same direction until stopped, midstride, by a revelation that left him light-headed. After all the long, cruel months of uncertainty over Merissa's killer, the answer appeared like a flashing neon light, revealing the identity of The Beatles' Song Murderer. Maldonado had been right all along: *Things aren't always as they appear.* Elliot only pretended to need the bathroom, emphasizing the supposed urgency by rushing in ahead of Sean to steal the card. The sudden awareness also validated his hunch about the Lady Diana comment, and offered a prime example of Elliot's devious ability to lie straight faced, manufacturing an alibi about an affair a mere few seconds after Sean confronted him.

Knowing the importance of Maldonado identifying the caller ID, Sean used his cell phone rather than his unlisted home phone, but the sound of the Detective's recorded voice forced him to leave a message.

"Ray, you need to call me right away! Elliot did it! Elliot!" Cognizant of Kayleigh's proximity, he walked farther away, bringing the phone closer to his lips and speaking in a lowered but forceful tone. "*Elliot killed Merissa!*"

After hanging up, his refocused awareness of chatterbox Kayleigh's silence puzzled him, but the unfamiliar sound of something else wrapped itself around his senses, converting his thoughts to immediate concern. Hendrix wasn't just barking, he was *growling*.

"Kayleigh?" he called out, his steps tentative as he moved toward the room. "Kayleigh?" Rounding the corner, Sean's cell phone dropped at his feet as a tidal wave of terror enveloped him. With a large hand held firmly against Kayleigh's mouth, and a gun pointing at her forehead, the unmasked face of a monster stared at him through the hostile, vigilant eyes of a serial killer.

Sean forced himself to speak, his paralyzing fear suppressed by his overwhelming need to save Kayleigh.

"Please!" he exclaimed, his arms extending outward. "Don't hurt her. She's just a little girl." Looking into Kayleigh's wet, frightened eyes, he added, "A very *brave* little girl."

Hendrix continued to growl and bark.

"Open that door and put the dog outside, or I'll put a bullet through his head."

In an instant, Sean grabbed Hendrix with one hand and followed the order before returning to the same spot.

"Now pick the phone up off the floor and call Maldonado back. Even if you have to leave a message again, tell him you made a big mistake. You thought the card was stolen, but you found it and everything is fine. Nothing's changed." In a lowered, more ominous voice, he added, "You got that?"

Sean nodded and struggled to control his shaking hand as he waited for Maldonado to answer or to hear his recording again. His heartbeat thumped noticeably while attempting to quell his nervousness, but when Maldonado answered, his fervency evident, Sean almost crumpled from the sudden weakness in his legs. He swallowed hard before speaking, never taking his eyes off of Kayleigh while the gun remained pressed against her head.

"Ray...I'm...I'm really sorry, but...I made a big mistake."

"*What?*" Maldonado shouted. "What the hell gives, Sean? *Jesus!*" After a few moments of silence, he continued in a subdued tone. "You just called me a minute ago and suddenly you're changing your story?"

Sean forced a small laugh. "I'm—I'm sorry, I thought Elliot stole that Jack of Hearts card. He knew you were coming over to check it for fingerprints, so—you know—what else was I to think but he was the killer. You know what you've told me—that things aren't always as they appear, right? I guess—I guess I got carried away. But I found the card, okay?" He looked up into the evil blue eyes glaring at him. "Everything's fine, nothing's changed."

When the conversation ended, Martin leaned down, placing his mouth near Kayleigh's ear, and spoke in a soft voice. "I'm not going to hurt you, sweetie," he said, and then shifted his eyes toward Sean. "As long as your friend, here, does what I tell him to." He returned his attention to Kayleigh. "When I take my hand away, you better not scream, because that would make me mad. You don't want to make me mad, do you?"

Kayleigh didn't move her head for several seconds. Then, in small, rapid motions, she shook it back and forth.

"Now this is also very important," he told her. "I want you to go over to Sean and stay there, okay? Because if you try to run away, I'll have to kill him."

Sean closed his eyes and fought against the mushrooming fear threatening to overwhelm him. When he reopened them, he stared in pain as her tears poured forth again.

"Do you understand, Kayleigh?"

This time she responded quickly, slamming her eyes shut and nodding her head in an animated up and down manner.

"Good girl!" Martin said. Releasing her from his grip, Kayleigh rushed into Sean's arms, crying uncontrollably. Sean dropped to his knees and wrapped his arms around her, holding the rag-doll body close to his.

"Shhh, shhh," he repeated. "Everything will be all right, Kayleigh. Be brave. You're the Fourteenth Laker, remember? You're tough. Coby tough."

Martin took a few steps closer, his gun now held to his side. "You weren't supposed to be home yet, Sean. I just came for the card, nothing more. I figured I'd be out of here in a minute. Then a short walk around the corner where my car's parked and that would be that." He shook his head. "Now things have gotten complicated." He walked toward the side door, peering out the window on the right side. "By the way, your agapanthus plant looks a lot worse." He turned back and smiled, reaching into his pocket to remove the object he now held up for Sean to see. "But at least you still have your key under the pot." Martin looked up at the different corners of the ceiling. "You could have used an alarm system in here." He chuckled, causing a shiver to course through Sean's body. "That's why you had that unfortunate break-in you told us about."

As he continued to hold Kayleigh, Sean didn't respond, his mind a jumbled mesh of disconnected wires unable to formulate more than one thought; protecting his young friend.

"You know, Sean," Martin said, "it took a lot of effort for me to keep smiling through your *performance* today and not give anything away. Once you started singing the song, well...I read your message loud and clear. You obviously suspected something." Sean kept his eyes fixed on the gun as he held Kayleigh. "That's when I knew I had to get that card back. If my fingerprints were still on it, the police could match them to my coffee cup."

Martin took a deep breath, glaring at them in ominous silence while rubbing his hand several times across his mouth.

"We've gotta leave," he said. "Get up!"

Kayleigh burrowed her way back into the sanctuary of Sean's arms. He held her head against his chest and looked up at Martin, hoping for some compassion, but the sight of the gun pointing at them eviscerated that notion.

"Now!" Martin shouted.

Clutching Kayleigh's shoulders, Sean rose from the floor, lifting her simultaneously. Keeping his arm around her, he asked, "Where are you taking us?"

Martin strolled toward them and placed his hand on Kayleigh's shoulder.

"She'll wait here while you get your keys."

Sean stared in contemplation for several moments, wondering what came next. Retrieving the keys from his jacket pocket, he returned to place his arm in a protective gesture around Kayleigh again.

"The first thing we're going to do is get in your car," Martin explained. "And in case you try something stupid, I'll sit in back with the Glock in my hand, the girl on my side, and the back of your head in splattering range." He spoke in a calm manner, yet the words he uttered shouted the directive and rattled Sean to the core. "You'll drive us to my car a few minutes away, park yours, and then we'll all take the same positions in mine. We're going to drive a long way, Sean, but somewhere along the line, if Kayleigh's a good girl, we'll find a safe spot to drop her off."

"Drop her off?" Sean asked. "Where?"

"'Where' isn't the question that concerns me right now," Martin replied. "*When* is what's important." Approaching Kayleigh, Martin stroked the uneven hairs on the back of her scalp. "You just might be my ticket to freedom, sweetie."

"What do you mean by that?" Sean asked, his voice rising in anger.

"You ever play poker, Sean? She's my wild card. I've been dealt a bad hand here, but she could keep me in the game."

Sean turned Kayleigh away from Martin and hugged her. "You're not going anywhere without me."

Martin stood in front of Sean, his gun held steady. "Now here comes the tricky part," he said. "You're going to make one more call. Get on the phone and call Kayleigh's house. Tell them you're on your way to the pet store, and you'll be back in a half hour. That's all the time we'll need for now."

"No, I won't do that," Sean answered.

Martin took a step back and extended his arm toward him, the small, black, circular hole of death at the gun barrel's tip waiting like an obedient soldier for the kill.

"This baby staring at you is a Glock Nineteen, Sean. It's made with a special striker fired mechanism that allows me to keep firing away for up to fifteen rounds. Even the military uses it, that's how dependable it is. It only took one shot to kill Merissa and I was just a few feet closer to her than I am to you. So I'm going to tell you again, one more time. *Call them!*"

He placed his hand over Kayleigh's mouth and pulled her away, her cries muffled yet piercing Sean to the bone. Pointing the gun at her head, Martin observed and listened to the phone call.

"No, she didn't tell me yet, wants me to keep guessing...yeah, she's funny...Okay, I'll have her back in time...right, it shouldn't take long. Bye, Stephanie."

"Very well done, Sean. Now drop your phone on the floor and leave it there."

Martin released Kayleigh, but instead of hurrying over to Sean, she started holding her stomach, grimacing and moaning.

"I have to go potty real bad," she said, crying. "Please? It hurts!"

Martin studied Kayleigh with an angry expression before relenting. "Listen to me, little girl," he told her. "Let me show you where Sean will be while you're in there." With the ever-present gun in his hand, he pointed his chin toward an area of the floor. "Lie face down and don't move until she comes out." Sean hurried to the spot, diving forward through the stiffness in his hip and remaining still as she moved in the direction of the bathroom.

"Wait!"

Kayleigh looked at Martin, clenching her teeth and shifting her weight from her left foot to her right as she continued to clutch her stomach. "Just remember," he said, "if you lock yourself in there and don't come out, your friend will be killed. *Understand?*"

"But I always lock the door when I go to the bathroom!" she cried. "I swear I'll come out. I swear! I swear!"

Martin placed a foot on Sean's lower back, his gun pointing toward his head. "Okay, lock it, but remember what I said."

Before shutting the door, Kayleigh blurted something to Sean about "doing what Coby did," causing him to tear up over this remarkable little girl's attempt to instill him with courage—the same courage she revealed at that moment.

"Let her go, Martin," Sean pleaded, his bottom lip brushing the floor. "She's just a little girl! A sweet, little girl, fighting goddamn *cancer!*"

"You ever think if she dies young, she'll be the lucky one, Sean?"

Sean's body stiffened in fear. "What—what's that supposed to mean?"

"The pain's coming," he answered. "I don't mean the physical pain, not the cancer, but the life pain."

Sean listened, uncomprehending, but sensing the words of a madman.

"I was once a happy kid in a happy home," Martin said. "Had a loving mother and father. A younger brother, too." He emitted an audible sigh, then continued. "My dad was a great man. We used to play ball, camp, fish, you know—all the good things that a father and son do. He worked long hours running a small electric store. Taught me how to fix things from an early age. Now I've got a pretty successful business and it all started with him."

Sean wondered why Martin felt the need to discuss his past. He didn't need to wait long for the answer.

"But everything changed the day my dad and brother were killed in a hit and run. It was a drunk driver, a kid." Several seconds of silence followed before he continued. "Now it was just my mother and me. My mother. My *mother*." Sean heard the heavy nasal breathing of quiet, unhappy reflection. "The way I see it, there were two paths for her to choose. She could have realized I was all she had left and done the right thing by raising me the way my father would have wanted. Or...do what she did, thinking only of herself and her own, depraved needs. Over time, different men started showing up. A couple of them tried to be nice, but they weren't my father. The others were assholes that didn't give a shit about me. But the one who was the worst of all, you'd never know it. His name was Freddie, a large boyish faced man with red fleshy cheeks and a perpetual smile. My mother thought he was such a sweet guy, such a 'kind and loving man,' that she could trust him to be alone with me when she worked late."

Sean remained quiet, feeling helpless as he listened to the backstory of a rapist/killer.

"Freddy didn't have any body hair," he said, "skin as smooth as the day he was born. I don't think I need to tell you how I know that, do I? I also remember those extraordinarily long fingers — long, hot, swarming fingers wrapped around my stomach and chest every time he took me from behind."

Sean listened, the unavoidable image of a boy's rape pulsating like a gaping wound.

"He told me he'd cut me into pieces if I ever said anything, or if I stayed away when he came around, but by the time my mother found out the truth—about what he did to me—all those times— what he did to me, that happy kid was dead. Now payback is my aphrodisiac, Sean. Anger's my erection. I can get it up for anybody, man or woman, because life's taught me you better be the one doing the fucking or guaranteed you'll be the one getting fucked. And pretending I'm gay, with a boyfriend who shares everything with me like sweet, naive Elliot, is the perfect camouflage for my...*proclivities*. In fact, Sean," he said, a whispered evil coating his tone, "Elliot taught me the card trick I showed Merissa that night." Martin chuckled. "But after that, it was time for the 'Hello, Goodbye' finale."

Sean pounded the floor in anger as tears of rage filled his vision. "You're a sick, fucking asshole!"

"With a gun pointing at your head."

Through clenched teeth, Sean spoke, forcing himself to stay as calm as possible. "Plenty of others went through the shit you did. They didn't turn out like you."

Martin raised his shoe and brought it down hard on Sean's back, causing him to cry out in pain. "*They're not me!*" Martin screamed. He leaned closer, hovering over Sean's head. "All of my mother's 'men friends' just wanted the one thing, and she was all too happy to give it to them. And do you know why? Because they brought out her inner whore, and all women have that inner whore inside of them, don't you know that? Merissa was no different. She used her body to tempt me, to mock me, make me feel weak. So after I had my way with her, after I exposed her for the whore she was, I rid the world of another impure, cock-sucking woman. A woman just like my *mother*."

'You're insane!" Sean shouted, tears burning his eyes into watery blindness. "And so fucking clever with your Beatles' song sign-offs, you piece of shit!"

"You got it all wrong, Sean," he said, his voice a maddening calm, "I don't do it to be clever. I do it because my mother loved The Beatles, sang their songs all the time. But after that horrible day, I never heard her sing a Beatles' song again—never heard her sing *anything* again." Martin applied more pressure with his foot to Sean's back, leaning down farther before he resumed speaking. "Those songs take me back to a happy time and place. Now do you understand? When I do to women what I did to Merissa, when I expose them for the whores they really are and kill them for their deceptions like they deserve, they're all my mother. And at that final moment, when the name of a Beatles' song is written for the world to see, I'm happy again." After a momentary pause, Martin had one more thing to say. "Every Beatles' song I choose isn't *my* calling card, it's *hers*."

With the sound of the flushing toilet, Martin removed his foot from Sean and stepped back. "Get up!"

When Sean rose to his feet, Martin looked at him and smiled. "I'm not the insane one," he said. "It's men like you who are fools. The only women I respect are the prostitutes who don't hide from themselves, the whores who follow their true calling."

"Like Lucy?" Sean muttered. "If you *respected* her so much, why'd you kill her? It's you who killed her, right?"

Martin nodded his head and shrugged. "Such a shame it had to come to that," he said, "but how lucky for me I was with her that night. Imagine my surprise when she showed me the photos from the service and asked me how I knew Roger. What else was I supposed to do, Sean? And the rest, as they say, is history."

Kayleigh opened the door, standing with her head down and hands gripped around the sides of her coat collar, holding them closed around her neck.

"I bet you never even went to that Lakers game and saw Coby," she said. Looking up, her lips tightened into a disappearing act as the half-mast of her right eye struggled to match the left one in their angry glare. "You're a big liar! And a bad man!"

Martin sneered. "That's a bet you would win, little girl. Now quit wasting more of my time." Shifting his attention to Sean, he took a step closer and aimed his gun toward his chest. "Let's go."

A minute later, with the gun now pointed at his back, Sean lifted Kayleigh and carried her toward the garage.

Chapter 38

The gloomy day produced a dull, lethargic light idling in from the bottom of the garage door, and, as Sean stood there, waiting for instructions, he held Kayleigh close. His thoughts sped at a feverish but failed pace, fostering unreasonable ideas without a viable plan or commonsense conclusion. One thing seemed abundantly clear, however, no matter what Martin said about letting Kayleigh go, logic dictated that he couldn't afford that gesture. Her existence prevented his secrecy. As did Sean's.

Kayleigh wept as she tilted her forehead against the side of his face. At that moment, feeling the unique, course texture of the hairs from her globular scalp, Sean empathized, more than ever, with the lifelong struggle this courageous child warrior endured. He also reflected on the day they met, remembering how her friendship offered him a life preserver from the inevitability of a planned suicide. She took him to a happy place, with conversations about music and basketball, and innocent comments that made him laugh. She also reminded him life was worth fighting for. Without her, he'd be dead—another clichéd rock 'n roll story, discovered on the couch with a suicide note and a body full of pills. Through an act of fate, she'd saved his life, and now, by any means necessary, the time had come to return the favor.

"As soon as the door opens," Martin said, "get in the car first. I trust you're not stupid enough to run away without her."

Kayleigh wrapped her arms around Sean's neck, squeezing hard. "*I want my daddy!*"

Sean turned toward Martin. "You're right," he said, his voice rising to be heard over her cries. "I'm not going anywhere without her, so can I at least put Kayleigh in the backseat and buckle her up myself? I'll talk to her and calm her down. Or do you want a sick, screaming kid bringing attention to us when we get in your car?"

Martin glared at Sean, shifted his focus to Kayleigh, and then back to Sean, holding his gaze for several long moments. "All right, go ahead. But do it from the driver side of the car where I can watch you."

"Thank you."

"Just remember," he said, his eyes piercing with peril, "I learned to shoot as a kid, so don't test me."

Moving forward, Sean lowered his foot on the garage step and pushed the button to raise the door. As had been the case since the day a spark inside his panel box cut any remaining overhead lights, the garage remained dark with the only visibility provided by the early afternoon grayness. Sean experienced a brief moment of gratitude that the problem still existed.

The passing seconds as he watched and waited for the door to fully open seemed endless, a repetitious battering ram reminder that his plan could be the last one he'd ever have. Dead men weren't known for new ideas. Sean steeled himself in preparation for the precious few seconds awaiting the execution of his scheme. If he hesitated at all, they'd be killed.

Before taking his first two steps, Sean consoled a weeping Kayleigh as he stood close to Martin, speaking at a level just loud enough for him to hear. But as he carried her toward the car, moving at an unsuspicious, deliberate pace until reaching a distance he judged out of Martin's earshot, he spoke in an urgent whisper, relaying rapid instructions he needed her to hear and understand immediately.

There wouldn't be a chance to repeat them.

"Kayleigh, listen to me. The garage door's open, and we need to escape. I'm going to put you down and tell you to get in the car. But you'll refuse and in a loud voice, say, 'No.' Then I want you to reach up to hug me again, and when I lift you up, hold me as tight as you can and stay perfectly still. Don't move!" Sean leaned his head back a few inches to look at her. "Nod your head if you understand me."

Kayleigh stared in apparent incomprehension for several moments. Then she nodded.

Sean lowered her to the ground facing the car door and opened it.

"Get in, Kayleigh," he said, raising his voice again.

Kayleigh stared into the car, shook her head in a violent motion, and yelled, "*No*," before spinning around to grab Sean.

"Come on, Kayleigh, do as Martin says."

As he prepared to lift her, the pounding of his heart accelerated into a mad drum solo when Martin stepped from the doorway into the garage.

"Get her in the car!"

In an air horn instant, Sean charged from the garage in a protective posture with Kayleigh braced against his body, ensuring that nothing remained exposed. And, for a moment of freedom, escape seemed possible until a crippling explosion of pain in his lower back caused him to stumble forward and collapse—but not before managing to twist to his left to shield Kayleigh from the fall. As his hands clawed at the ground, feeling as if someone took a torch to his tissues, he wondered if this is how it felt to die.

Lifting his face from the concrete, he struggled to look around, hoping Kayleigh fled. What he saw and heard however, through the haze of suffering and semi-consciousness, seemed like a dream.

A blurry streak of green crossed Sean's vision as a woman's scream, reverberating in an up and down voluminous pitch, echoed near him. A man's voice, angry, loud, and powerful, penetrated his awareness before morphing into sounds of gunshots and manic shouts. He didn't understand why he visualized a war scene. Where was he? Did he hear sirens? Everything seemed smaller, as if the world shrunk into a noisy box of light and dark, shadows hovering around him, coming and going. Somewhere in time, lacking any perception of how much, an indistinguishable figure knelt before him, holding his hand.

He heard a voice, unintelligible sounds floating in and out of his fading attentiveness, and as he struggled to speak before the encroaching blackness enveloped him, he uttered one thing. "Kayleigh."

He didn't hear the reply.

"She's safe."

Chapter 39

When the Michaels family visited him in the hospital, Sean learned how much he didn't know, starting from the time Kayleigh acted as if she needed to use the bathroom. "Here's my birthday present," she said, holding her cell phone. "It was in my jacket the whole entire time."

Sean stared as if looking at a guitar made on Mars.

"I didn't really have a tummy ache, but I pretended so I could text my brother, Mr. Marine. He was the only number I had 'cause he put it there for me."

"I can't believe it," Sean replied, speaking in a weakened voice from his bed. "You're an amazing girl. And a great actress."

"I tried to let you know in secret when I told you I was going to do what Coby did," she explained. "Remember what you said to me about Coby sending a message to people with cancer?"

As his head lay on the pillow, Sean smiled, a combination of affection and curiosity. "Yeah, I remember."

Beaming with pride, she exclaimed, "Well I sent a *text* message!"

Sean failed to fight back tears as Stephanie handed him a tissue to his free hand, the one opposite from the side with the intravenous tube. Then she took one for herself before describing the rest of the story.

"I was so scared," she said. "When Anthony showed me Kayleigh's text, I called nine-one-one immediately, but my son refused to wait for them. He's a marine now, and he was going to save his sister, no matter if it cost him his life." Stephanie dabbed at her eyes again. "Just like you, Sean. You could have died. We can never repay you."

In a simultaneous motion the three adults wiped their eyes as Kayleigh and Randy watched.

A sudden recollection filtered through Sean's memory from that murky period of time just after being shot.

"Was Anthony wearing military gear?" he asked. "Green military gear?"

"Yes," Jason answered. "He arrived earlier that morning still wearing his uniform. And even though that guy had a gun, Anthony charged at him like a wild bull. He got off one shot before our son was all over him. He beat that guy up so bad, it took two policemen to pull him away." He shook his head, his eyes closing for a moment. "We're so proud of him. For what that *bastard* could have done to my little girl—and to you—" Tearing up again, Jason lowered his head and walked to the window, staring out in silence.

Kayleigh shuffled closer to the bed. "Mr. Music," she said, "when you're all better, I want you to see my new poster of another place I want to go to. It's a big garden in Canada called the Bu...Bu..."

"Butchart Gardens," Stephanie said.

"Yeah, that's it!" Kayleigh shouted. "The most biggest, most beautiful garden I've *ever* seen. I can't wait to go there."

At that moment, navigating its way through the gelatinous haze of painkillers and fatigue, from a long abandoned part of his soul, an idea for a song hatched in his thoughts.

"I like the gift my sister brought you," Stephanie said, holding the stuffed animals in her hand. "Two bears sharing an umbrella. It's cute."

"Our first date was on a rainy day, so there's a little meaning there. Same with the card that comes with it."

Stephanie read the words aloud. "'When things go bad, and the rain starts to fall, call me at one-eight-hundred PARASOL.'"

Sean smiled to himself, remembering Jenny's parting words when he lay immobile in bed, weakness permeating his body and a tube dripping medicine through his arm. Feeling the wetness from her eyes as she leaned down to kiss his forehead, cheeks, and mouth, she lingered in that position for several long moments before brushing her lips against his ear, whispering a healing remedy of her own. "There's a lot more where that came from, Mister Hightower."

A short time after the Michaels family left, Sean looked toward the door in surprise when Stephanie poked her head back in.

"I didn't know if you'd be sleeping," she said. "There's something I want to tell you."

Walking to the bed, she looked down at him and stared, teary eyed, without saying anything for several moments. Sean offered a tentative smile, confused and questioning.

"What is it, Stephanie?"

Nodding her head, she started with a question. "Do you remember a few months ago when you called to change Kayleigh's time for her guitar lesson, and I told you about another test she had to have? And how worried I was because we needed to come up with a five-thousand-dollar deductible?"

Sean looked at her in silence, wondering where this was going. "Yes."

"I never told you this, but through a *miraculous* coincidence, somebody made an anonymous contribution for that exact amount. And thanks to the results from that test, Kayleigh's medicine was changed and her markers have improved."

Sean turned his thumb upward. "That's great news, Stephanie."

She stared in silence again, placing her hand on his face. "My mother used to always say, 'Things happen for a reason,' but I didn't believe that stuff." Stephanie chuckled. "Now, I'm not so sure anymore. The way things have gone this last year, I'm wondering, maybe, just maybe it's true sometimes, you know? Maybe we moved next door to Sean Hightower for a reason."

As tears formed and fell, she leaned down to kiss him on the forehead before turning away to leave.

Chapter 40

The morning after returning home from the hospital, bored and incapable of doing much while still recuperating, Sean stared at his closed guitar case in the corner of the bedroom, recalling the idea for a song arising from Kayleigh's enthusiasm over her Butchart Gardens poster. Hesitant to turn his thoughts into action, he waited until the afternoon before removing the guitar to start playing. Within an hour, before winter's early sunset arrived, a new song sprang forth, and Sean couldn't remember a time when the marriage of music and lyrics united as quickly. Reflecting on that, he realized that for the first time ever, a hit record wasn't the intention he desired nor the reward he sought. Somehow that goal didn't seem as high and mighty as before. And over the past sixty minutes he rediscovered his roots—writing for the pure, unpolluted pleasure of the music.

⁰⁄ɔ⁰⁄ɔ

He sat in a beach chair with a guitar on his lap and a walking cane within reach to his right, listening to the rhythmic beat of the beautiful, blue Pacific. Sean felt at peace as he enjoyed the final day of free time before starting a full-time job as a car salesman at his father's dealership. With Jenny in his life now, all the previous chaos and uncertainty about his place in this world didn't seem relevant anymore. For the first time in many years, the balance from his priorities seemed right again. He almost died—an occurrence to instill perspective like no other. If he didn't gain enough of an appreciation after his cancer scare, he garnered a full-blown awareness from a bullet. And he could laugh at his arthritis now. What was a little hip pain once in a while when he came frighteningly close to living life on Wheelchair Way?

When he listened to "You Can't Always Get What You Want" on his car radio, the billionth time he heard it, the two chorus lines affected him in a unique way, and he recognized their relevancy to his life.

Listening to Jagger sing about not always getting what you want, he felt that truer words had never been spoken. In a perfect world, he wanted to make it big again in the music business, but only in the rarified air of the very few were situations in life seemingly perfect. Perhaps for Mick and Keith it turned out that way, but not in the lower stratosphere he occupied.

That second line, however, about sometimes getting what you need, defined his life today. The dream of what he *wanted* proved an elusive fantasy he couldn't get.

But the reality of what he *needed*, Jenny's love...well, nothing equaled the importance of that.

It was time to say goodbye to the past.

Testing the sound of his new chord change, Sean strummed his guitar, preparing to sing the opening verse to "Imagination Airlines," a song dedicated to the little girl who retrieved his soul by reminding him that life was more than just a one-sided coin of negativity, and that the value of life was equal to what you put into it, even if only through your imagination.

As he looked up, watching several seagulls glide in majestic configurations, he started to sing.

> "No limit to my starry sky
> No desire too extreme
> There's so much to believe in
> 'Cause I dare to have a dream
> No place is much too far away
> No matter where it lies
> On Imagination Airlines
> I just have to close my eyes."

Sean smiled, envisioning Kayleigh's delight when she heard a song written for her. He felt good about himself, and, as he watched the waves pound and engulf the shore, offering a timeless, soul-enriching music comparable to no other, his gaze danced across the water, reveling at the open paradise of new possibilities from that horizon beckoning him once again.

THE END

Author's Note

Coby Karl played in seventeen games for the Los Angeles Lakers in the 2007-2008 season, averaging 4.2 minutes and 1.8 points per game.

9 781644 371992